THE EAST END GIRL
IN BLUE

Fenella J. Miller

An Aria Book

This edition first published in the United Kingdom in 2021 by Aria,
an imprint of Head of Zeus Ltd

A CIP catalogue record for this book is available
from the British Library.

ISBN eBook: 9781838933487
ISBN Paperback: 9781800246133

Cover design © Lisa Brewster

Typeset by Siliconchips Services Ltd UK

Aria
c/o Head of Zeus
First Floor East
5–8 Hardwick Street
London EC1R 4RG

www.ariafiction.com

For my son Lincoln. He won't read this
book but he is still the best son in the world.

I

'LACW 1377 reporting for duty, ma'am,' Nancy Evans said to the NCO with a smart salute.

The salute was returned. 'There's no need for all that. You don't salute an NCO or call her ma'am. I'm Deirdre Brown. What's your name?'

'I'm Nancy Evans. Cor, this is a turn-up for the books. Ever so posh in here, ain't it? I never thought to be working in the Officers' Mess.' She gestured to the splendid lawn and flower beds and the big cars parked outside the windows. 'I never came in through the front door, but it's like one of them grand homes you see in books. White pillars and all that and steps to come up.'

'The officers are lucky here. This is a proper building made of bricks and jolly smart.' Deirdre led the way from a small office where they'd met, into the wide passageway with a public phone on the wall.

'You come highly recommended, Nancy. I know you're new to catering but I'm certain you'll get the hang of it.'

'Don't seem nothing to it, really. I'm quick on me feet, know how to cook, and when I'm serving them officers I'll mind me Ps and Qs, don't you worry.' Nancy had attended the cook and butcher's course at Melksham and already had her LACW – leading aircraftwoman – tape sewn on her sleeve.

'You've got two stripes, which puts you above most of the girls in here. Once you know the ropes you'll be in charge when I'm off duty.'

'Blimey – what me giving orders like? I don't reckon I'll be much good at that, but I'll give it a go.'

She was more used to a caf serving a nice fried breakfast than the things officers would be eating. The bar, where they were now, was spotless. There were half a dozen tables with plain wooden chairs all around – none too smart and none what matched – up one end. There was a dartboard and shove-halfpenny board and that was all apart from a battered piano.

'Will I have to serve drinks and that?'

'No, they have barmen doing that. We just have to keep the place clean, empty the ashtrays, collect the dirty glasses and so on. The men often sit outside with their drinks so you'll have to go out there as well to find the glasses. It isn't waitress service; they come into the bar to order for themselves.'

'Righty ho – that ain't too hard.'

The dining room had five long tables, which would each seat a dozen or more. They were laid up nice and proper with white cloths and everything. 'Is it like this every night?'

'No, there's a bigwig here tonight so we're doing something special. You'll have to work as a waitress for dinner when there's a formal meal. Normally, it's self-service and no tablecloths.'

'What about cooking and that? I ain't clear if I'm helping in the kitchen or just doing the clearing up.'

'We cook and serve the breakfasts and lunches, make sandwiches and so on, but the RAF catering corps supply the chefs for dinner. You'll have two different shifts – one is cleaning and you'll work from 8 a.m. to 6 p.m. and on alternate days you will have the cooking shift, which starts at 5 a.m. and finishes about 2 p.m.'

Her last words were drowned out as a squadron of Spitfires roared overhead, closely followed by a flight of Defiants. Them poor blokes, the pilots, were on constant alert and some were living in tents at dispersal. They was protecting the poor buggers in the Merchant Navy who were being bombed something rotten by the Germans. They never got a decent meal at the moment. She was grateful her Tommy was safe working in a hangar. She was used to that racket, as she'd spent the last year on RAF bases.

'The squadrons are all over the shop – do I have to go to Manston or Rochford?'

'No, the NAAFI vans take the food there. You just have to go to the dispersal points on this airfield. Okay, I think you've seen everything now. Do you drive?'

This would have been a bloomin' stupid question before the war but now lots of girls in the WAAF – the Women's Auxiliary Air Force – had been trained to drive. She was one of them, as delivering the larger items, ordered by the mechanics for the aeroplanes, when she was still working in the stores was impossible on a bicycle.

'I can – learned a few months ago.'

'Good, then today you can take the sandwiches and thermos flasks to those waiting to be scrambled. Those nearest get half an hour to dash across to the mess hall and grab something to eat. Then the next squadron comes and so on. Only those with their kites parked on the far perimeters have food delivered.'

The kitchen was a hive of activity. Half a dozen girls, wearing white overalls and with white squares tied like turbans on their heads, was busy preparing the midday meal. The girls cleaning wore navy blue button-through overalls and clogs. Nancy had already been issued with hers and she'd turned them up and they were neatly stored in a locker waiting for her to change.

'Do I change to deliver the grub?'

'Yes, put on your white overalls. You're going to be making the sandwiches and filling the flasks. You have to take them in a couple of hours so you'd better get a move on.'

She recognised some of the girls as they shared a dormitory. The women's hostel was up Sutton Lane, off the camp completely, nowhere near the blokes. The barracks for the men was a mile away. The other girls were a cheerful bunch and were happy to tell her where everything was kept. Just before twelve o'clock the sandwiches were ready, neatly wrapped in greaseproof paper and carefully labelled with the contents. The thermos flasks were full. Four had sugar in and two didn't. It was lucky that those two had red tops so she'd know the difference.

Everything was piled into large wicker trays. Being short made it difficult for her to grip the basket handles properly but she staggered out with the first one and shoved it in the back of the van. On her return with the second a couple of officers saw her struggling.

'Allow us to assist you, fair maiden. It wouldn't do for you to drop the sustenance meant for our comrades,' the tallest of them said with a lovely smile as he removed the sarnies and that from her arms.

'Ta ever so. I nearly dropped the bleedin' lot last time.'

They walked away laughing and she wished she could talk proper like them and not swear all the time. Her best friend, Jane, were always telling her off for using bad language. Nancy scrambled onto the driver's seat. The seat wouldn't budge and her legs was too short to reach the pedals properly.

She reckoned she'd manage if she sat right on the edge and never met nothing and didn't have to brake hard.

Tommy Smith hadn't needed to go on any training courses when he'd transferred from maintaining a bomber to Hornchurch, where he now had a Spit allocated to him. His pilot, Sergeant Pilot Harry Jones, was a good bloke and an excellent flyer. It was a pleasure to keep his kite in working order. He'd been fortunate to be allocated a Spitfire and not a Defiant. The Spits were everybody's favourite kite.

'Oi, Tommy, isn't that your fiancée driving that van?' Ronnie Atkins poked him with a spanner and gestured towards the van heading for the tented dispersal points at the far side of the airfield.

'You're right, it's Nancy. I didn't know she was back from her course – this must be her first day on duty.' He scrambled down from the wing of the Spit and stepped out from the hangar so she could see him.

She waved but didn't stop. He'd catch up with her when they were both off tonight. Sometimes he and Ronnie had to work all night to do maintenance and repairs and have the kite ready for when their pilot was on duty again. Harry's Spit was in tip-top condition, unlike some of the others that had returned from the last sortie full of holes. Today was just routine maintenance. This was essential and had to be carried out whenever the flyer was off duty.

'She's delivering char and wads,' Ronnie said. 'Do you think she'll have any over for us? My belly thinks my throat's been cut.'

'Doubt it – the blighters will be as starving as us. If we crack on then we'll get this finished in a couple of hours and we can go to the mess and get something to eat.'

He was in the cockpit a bit later when Nancy's lovely face appeared beside him – she was standing on the wing. 'I got me stripe, passed with flying colours, I did. Here, I saved you and Ronnie a couple of sarnies. They ain't got no labels on so I ain't sure what's in them. I made them meself so I know they'll be tasty.'

He pushed himself upright and leaned over and kissed her. She responded enthusiastically and there was a series of catcalls and whistles from the other buggers in the hangar.

'What time do you finish tonight, Nancy love?'

'I'm not sure as I ain't been put on a roster yet. Them what wear these white overalls finish at two o'clock, but I never started when they did so I reckon I'll be working until six at least.'

'We've got to get spares when we're done here, but then,

unless we're needed somewhere else, I'm knocking off from teatime until Harry's on duty. Pity you're not working in our mess hall, then I'd know when you'd finished.'

She jumped nimbly from the wing despite being no more than five feet tall. Her lack of height hadn't held her back.

'She's a bit of all right, your girl, Tommy. You set a date yet?'

A flight of Spits thundered overhead. He hoped the poor buggers had had time to eat their sandwiches. The bloody Germans meant business. He reckoned that Hitler intended to bomb them into surrender and it was up to the RAF to stop them.

He watched them vanish over the rooftops on the hunt for incoming bombers and Messerschmitt 109s, the fighters that accompanied them. Since Dunkirk there'd been a lull for a few weeks, which had given them time to repair and recoup. The offensive had begun at the beginning of the month and he was proud that the first German ME109 to be shot down on British soil had been by Harry on the 8th of July.

Everyone knew this was the start of the Battle of Britain and there wouldn't be much free time for anyone. Tomorrow some bigwigs from the East India Fund were going to present eight spanking new Spits to No 65 Squadron. There was going to be a bit of a shindig and he prayed there'd be no enemy attacks to spoil it.

The lucky buggers who'd be taking care of the new kites had to be in their best blues and on parade for the ceremony. He and Ronnie would be in their overalls as usual doing whatever was needed. Every time Harry took off, he wondered if he'd come back in one piece. The three of them had only been together for a few weeks but were now firm friends.

He'd wanted to be a pilot but an accident when he was a lad had damaged one ear, making it impossible for him to fly because of the pressure involved. At least he was a valued member of a team and doing his bit for the war effort.

When they could hear themselves speak, he answered his friend. 'September – nothing grand – we've only got a twenty-four-hour pass. The padre's agreed to do the ceremony in the chapel here. Can't wait – I don't want any other bloke pinching her from me. She's surrounded by officers and they've always got an eye out for a pretty girl.'

'She's not interested in the Brylcreem boys, Tommy – don't worry about that. I'll be your best man if you want.'

'You can be a witness; we're not having any fuss. Hopefully, we'll be able to go in the NAAFI and have a bit of a knees-up afterwards.'

'Lucky sod. How old are you? Bit young to be tying the knot, aren't you?'

'I'm twenty-one on the first of September, which is why we're waiting till then. Nancy had to get permission from her folks as she's a few months younger than me. Come on – you lazy devil – we can eat and then get this finished. Don't forget we've got to be back on duty to see Harry off safely tonight.'

'Let's hope it's quiet. At least we get a few hours' kip when it's dark as they don't fly then.'

They wolfed down the sandwiches but had to do with water as there'd been no tea left in the flasks. A second flight of kites tore down the grass strip and into the air. There was a big flap on somewhere. How many of the blokes would come back?

The only good thing about being ground crew was that he'd see this conflict out unharmed and could look forward to a long life with his sweetheart. The blokes had spent weeks making protected spaces for the Spitfires with piled-up sandbags. He sat in the cockpit and Ronnie guided him out of the hangar. This was the closest he got to being a flyer.

Tommy nipped back to his billet, joined the queue for a shower, then, all spruced up, he headed for the mess hall. Harry's kite had been returned to the perimeter, was refuelled and rearmed, and was ready to be scrambled when that dreaded telephone call came through to dispersal.

The bowsers would be waiting with the fuel and the blokes who rearmed the kites would also be ready. Things were hotting up now and the last couple of nights Harry's flight had been scrambled twice. So far this month no one had been killed or seriously injured – but one pilot had written off his plane and another had ditched in the sea and been picked up by the Royal Navy.

Just as he arrived at the mess hall Nancy called his name. He turned and held out his arms; she raced into them. As there were officers about, he only gave her a brief hug and then, with his arm casually about her shoulders, they headed to the far end of the buildings to the NAAFI – the canteen run by the Navy, Army and Air Force Institutes.

It would be quieter there as you had to pay for your scoff and it was part of the deal in the mess hall.

'What do you think, love? Are you going to like being in catering instead of working in the stores?'

'It's okay, but I liked me other trade better. Mind you, I ain't complaining as I changed so I could be with you.'

'I know, and I really appreciate it. I've not had anything to eat today apart from your sandwich. Do they feed you in the kitchens at the Officers' Mess?'

'Ain't time to eat but I reckon when they have one of them posh dos we might get the leftovers.'

'Find a table. Do you want your usual?'

'Yeah, anything fried with chips – don't care what it is.'

The food might not be free but it was better than what you got in the mess hall. He was happy to pay so he could sit and talk to Nancy in relative privacy.

'Cor, that's grand, Tommy love. Just the ticket. Put it down and let's tuck in.'

There wasn't much talking as they ate. He loved a girl with a healthy appetite. Although, to be honest, he didn't know where she put it all – she must have hollow legs because there wasn't an ounce of fat on her anywhere.

'That were smashing – ta ever so. I don't suppose they've got any afters? I could do with a nice bit of spotted dick or roly-poly with custard.'

'As this is my treat, I'll go and look. Can you get rid of the dirty plates?'

They didn't have either of her choices but they had bread pudding and she was just as happy with that. When they'd finished she fetched the tea.

'It's a lot noisier here. Them blooming Spitfires and other planes are taking off and landing every five minutes. I can't see that I'll get a wink of sleep tonight if it goes on.'

'We don't fly in the dark at the moment so from ten o'clock until dawn it's quiet. You get used to it, anyway. Those bleeding great bombers make far more noise.'

'They do, but they only take off once and come back once and ain't backwards and forwards like bluebottles.'

As they sipped their tea he studied her, wondering how he'd been the fortunate bloke to capture this gorgeous girl. She might be small but she was rounded in all the right places, had a lovely face and sparkling blue eyes.

'Do you like what you see?'

'No, I love it. You have to be the most beautiful girl on the base. I'm the luckiest bloke here to be marrying you in a couple of weeks.'

'September can't come fast enough for me. I'm the lucky one, Tommy love. I reckon I couldn't do no better anywhere.'

'Are you quite sure you don't want more of a do? Just us and a couple of witnesses, no wedding breakfast or anything?'

'I'd have loved to have a wedding like what Jane and Oscar had, in a church and all that. But we ain't like them – we ain't got the money for a start. No, as long as we can be married then I don't care how it's done.'

'I've asked Ronnie to be my witness. Do you have anyone in mind for yourself?'

'Jane's coming if she can get a pass. I don't know no one here yet but I reckon by then there'll be someone who'd be willing to stand in at the last minute, like, if necessary.'

'I've pushed the boat up and booked us a night in that hotel you told me about, the one in Westminster where you and your friends stay when you go to London. We'll have dinner there as well.'

'The Sanctuary? They do good grub. If we get time, I'd like to introduce you to my family. It ain't that far to Poplar on the underground.'

He was hoping they'd spend every available minute in bed together but he didn't like to say so. At nine o'clock he walked her back to her billet, kissed her a couple of times, and then had to race off to change into his overalls and be ready for action.

2

Nancy didn't see Tommy for the next few days. Her fiancé wasn't getting any time off. The poor blighters weren't even getting time to return to their billets for a bit of kip and a wash. Night and day duty were abandoned and they flew sortie after sortie and grabbed some shut-eye wherever they could.

She'd been like a blue-arsed fly delivering sandwiches, cooking and cleaning. It would be easier if you did the same thing for a week or more but duties changed every other day. She was grateful she wasn't asked to wait on the officers and bigwigs when they had the posh do last week. Catering were a bleedin' sight harder than working in the stores, that's for sure.

She was getting used to the constant noise of the fighters landing and taking off at all hours. Tommy had been right to say she'd be so knackered she'd sleep through anything. Some of them bloomin' planes flew in with bits falling off and holes in the sides – fuselage, Tommy said it were called. God knows how the pilots got home safely in them.

It was only two weeks to her wedding and she'd had a letter from Jane saying she couldn't come but Deirdre was a mate now and she'd agreed to be the other witness. Her monthlies were due on her wedding day. The thought that after all the waiting they wouldn't be able to do it was a real worry. A lot of the girls had already been with men and was proud of it. She was glad she hadn't and that Tommy would be her first.

She finished at two o'clock today and she was heading for the mess hall when Tommy skidded to a halt beside her on his battered bicycle. 'Harry's kite has a hole in it we can't fix. It's got to go back to the MU for repair. He hasn't got another Spit so I'm free until midday tomorrow.' He grinned and she fell into his arms and they kissed. 'That's the good news, love, but the bad is that I'm going to be at Rochford, the forward base, from now on. I won't see you at all until our wedding.'

This made her decision so much simpler. 'Shall we get off the base? Go to Romford and make a night of it?' Her heart was thudding as she thought what else they might do. He was a bit shy, a real gent, so wouldn't suggest they slept together. 'We'll be married in two weeks – let's not wait any longer.'

His eyes lit up. 'Are you sure? I thought you didn't want to make love until after the ceremony.'

In for a penny in for a pound. 'I'll have me monthlies on our wedding night. This might be the only opportunity for weeks, maybe months. I don't want to be your wife in name only.'

'In which case, we'd better get a pass double quick. If we're going to stay in a B&B then you'll need your wedding ring. I'll bring it with me.'

She was supposed to be on duty at eight o'clock next morning, which meant getting back from Romford in time might be tricky. She'd walk the couple of miles if necessary, as long as she got to spend even part of the night with Tommy.

The NCO in the office was a friend of Deirdre's and listened sympathetically. 'What rotten luck, to have the curse on your wedding day. You've not had any leave since you got here and you've certainly made a good impression. You can have until midday tomorrow.'

'Cor, ta ever so. Much appreciated.'

Nancy raced back to her billet, hastily shoved her toilet bag and change of underwear into a small bag and was ready. Heat travelled from her toes to the top of her head at the thought of what was going to happen tonight. She didn't bother to put in a nightie – she wouldn't be needing it.

There was a local bus pulling up outside the gates and hand in hand they raced towards it. The conductor saw them coming and held it for them. The journey was less than three miles and they scrambled out in Romford High Street ten minutes later.

'Here, let me put this on your finger before we go looking for somewhere to stay.'

She quickly removed her engagement ring and then held out her hand and he pushed the gold band over her knuckle. It fitted perfectly.

'As far as I'm concerned, I'm Mrs Tommy Smith now. Anyone can see this ain't a brass curtain ring.'

'We'll say we just got married and have got a one-night honeymoon. It's almost true, isn't it?'

They found the perfect place in a quiet side street. The house was modern, very smart, and had a printed shingle hanging outside – not a piece of cardboard in the window.

'Rose Briar House – I love the name and there's a vacancy sign,' she said, her hand clenching in his at the thought of what they were going to be doing later on today.

'Leave the talking to me, love. I know how to charm a landlady.'

There was no need to charm anyone as an elderly lady opened the door with a broad smile. 'Come in, my dears. I'm Mrs Reed. I've got the perfect room for you. I saw you admiring your new ring. Have you just got married?'

'This morning – just a couple of witnesses. We've only got until tomorrow,' Tommy said with a smile.

The room had a massive double bed, pink candlewick bedspread and darker pink curtains. There was also a matching wardrobe, chest of drawers and dressing table. Ever so smart – just what she'd want herself one day.

'The bathroom and WC are adjacent to your room. Breakfast is from seven o'clock until nine. I can't run to egg and bacon but I make my own bread, and can do boiled eggs and soldiers for you as a special treat.'

'That would be splendid, ma'am. My wife and I would like to find somewhere to eat tonight. Is there a café or restaurant nearby you can recommend?'

'I don't think you'll get anything at this time of day apart from fish and chips. There's a lovely place right next to a pub and the landlord is happy for you to eat them in his garden if you buy a drink.'

'Thank you, Mrs Reed, we'll take your advice,' Tommy said.

Nancy eyed the bed but he shook his head and laughed.

'We've waited this long, love, what's a few more hours? I reckon Mrs Reed would be shocked rigid if we went to bed now, honeymoon or not.'

It was impossible to forget what was going on as flights of Spitfires and Hurricanes were constantly roaring overhead. Whilst they were eating their delicious fish supper they watched a dogfight overhead.

They both cheered when the two Spits scored a direct hit and the German fighter plummeted to the ground a few miles away trailing smoke and flames.

'It ain't right that we cheered, Tommy. That poor bleeder might be German, but we just watched him die. I hate this war.' She didn't fancy any more chips and was about to roll up the newspaper parcel and throw it away.

'Don't waste good food, love. There's a war on...'

'I ain't blind, Tommy, I know there's a bleedin' war on. You eat them – I ain't going to. I've lost me appetite.'

He shook his head and took a long swallow of his beer before answering. 'Nancy love, why do you swear like a trooper? It's not ladylike.'

'That's all right then because I ain't no lady. I'm an East End girl – take me or leave me.'

'Eat your chips before they get cold. You're going to need all your energy for tonight.' He winked at her and her irritation vanished.

'Give them here, then, don't want to be nicked for wasting food. Sorry, I've not seen anyone die before. It shook me up something rotten. I'll try not to swear – but can't promise nothing.'

'Fair enough. I love you just how you are. I'm getting another pint. Do you want another gin and it?'

'Go on then, why not? But I don't want to be tiddly and neither do you.'

They got back to the B&B as the sun were setting behind the houses. Tommy had said nine o'clock were all right to go to bed without upsetting the landlady. The front door was unlocked and she could hear the distant sound of music from the kitchen. They crept up the stairs and into their bedroom, not wanting to disturb anybody.

Tommy closed the door and turned the key.

'Don't do that. I got to use the bog first and want a bit of a freshen up in the bathroom.' She grabbed her toilet bag. She didn't want a bath so stripped off and washed top to bottom. She regretted not bringing a nightie or dressing gown as now she had to put everything back on.

He rushed off as she walked in. Hastily, she stripped off, unpinned her hair, relieved she hadn't smothered it with lacquer today to hold it in place, and nipped into bed. She knew what was what when it came to sex. Most of her friends had already done it and been happy to share their knowledge with her, but it wasn't the same as first-hand experience.

He was back in no time and this time she didn't complain when he locked the door. He turned his back and undressed rapidly. She watched with interest. His shoulders were broad, his bum neat and round, his legs solid.

She wasn't sure about seeing him in his birthday suit from the front so slipped under the sheets before he turned. The bed dipped as he got in beside her.

'I love you, Nancy, and I wish we could have waited until we were actually married. What if you get pregnant?'

'You don't get in the family way the first time so we're all right. Anyway, it don't matter as we'll be married soon and any baby would come along in nine months like what it should.'

He hesitated. There was still a gap between them. Her heart was pounding; she just wanted to get it over with. The first time it could hurt but after that it got better – so she'd been told.

She reached out and touched his chest. His skin was rough, with a thin covering of hair. She could feel his muscles moving beneath her fingertips. This were the encouragement he needed. He pulled her closer. She expected to be kissed, fondled and loved before anything happened.

Instead, he rolled on top of her, pushed her legs apart with his knee and then plunged into her. It was over in minutes and she'd not enjoyed it at all. She waited for him to say something, ask if everything was all right, but he turned over and went to sleep.

This wasn't how she'd expected things to be. She was sore down there, had felt nothing but discomfort, and unexpected tears trickled down her cheeks.

Tommy woke in the darkness. He'd made a right mess of things. He was as innocent as Nancy and hadn't known quite what to do. His desire had overwhelmed him and he'd made love to her without any preliminaries and she must wish she hadn't come. She was lying as far away from him as she could and there was a gap of at least two feet between them.

Tentatively he reached out and ran his fingers down her back. Her skin was smooth, warm beneath his touch. She didn't react but she didn't tell him to stop either.

They'd fall off the edge of the bed if he went to her so he put both arms around her waist and moved her into the centre of the bed. She must be awake but she didn't speak and he couldn't see if her eyes were open.

'I love you, and I'm sorry for what happened earlier. I'm going to make it up to you now, if you'll let me.'

Still no response, but she was definitely awake. He kissed her softly, starting at her eyes and then travelling down her face, her throat, and pulled her nipple into his mouth. This time she gasped and her back arched.

Much later they lay entwined, both of them now satisfied and happy. 'Tommy love, I never knew anything could be so wonderful. The first time wasn't so great, but we've got the hang of it now.'

He nuzzled her cheek and she sighed and stretched like a contented cat beside him. 'It was a first for me too, love, and I'm glad I waited until the right girl came along.'

'Blimey, who'd have thought it? I can see why it's called lovemaking – don't reckon I'd enjoy it with someone I didn't love – bit too personal. Don't understand how some girls will do it with anyone they fancy.'

'I knew you weren't that kind of girl the moment I set eyes on you, Nancy love. I didn't wait for any moral reasons, you know, I just wanted my first lover to be my last.'

'Well, I ain't one to be breaking me wedding vows. When I say, "till death do us part", I'll bloomin' mean it.'

He kissed her again and then they spooned and fell asleep. Next time it was Nancy who started things going. They only just got down in time for breakfast and received several knowing smiles and winks from the other couples in the dining room.

As far as he was concerned Nancy was already his wife – she was wearing his ring – and saying their vows was just a formality. They devoured everything put in front of them and certainly got their money's worth.

He settled the account and they hurried off hand in hand to catch the next bus.

'We'll be back in good time to have a shower before we need to report for duty. I doubt that I'll see you for a while, love, but if I get a few hours off I'll come and find you.'

They showed their passes at the gate as squadrons of fighters and fighter-bombers screamed overhead. They paused to look at the sky, which was crisscrossed with vapour trails as the German fighters engaged with the Hurricanes and Spitfires overhead.

'Keep your wedding ring on, love. Doesn't seem right to take it off after what we've just done.'

She stretched up on tiptoes and kissed him in full view of the men guarding the gate. 'It's on for life, Tommy love. Take care of yourself and I'll see you on the fifth to make it legal.'

He was sorry to leave Hornchurch for the forward base of Rochford – here there were proper facilities, good accommodation, decent scoff and the brown jobs were positioned around the perimeter with their guns.

There wouldn't be anything like that where he was going.

He and Ronnie got Harry off okay and then, like everyone else who was moving, he piled his hand tools and belongings into the back of a lorry. There would be canvas hangars set up, tents to sleep in and only a NAAFI van providing food.

He liked his creature comforts and wasn't looking forward to roughing it. As far as his mates were concerned everything was still the same. They didn't know that his life had changed – that he'd spent the night with his future wife.

Probably not a big deal for most of them from what they bragged about – but for him it meant everything. There was comfort in the thought that whatever happened at the end of this bloody war he and Nancy would be together. How many of the others had that security to keep them going during the hard times?

The next few hours were frantic as he and Ronnie had only been there an hour when Harry's squadron was scrambled again. The Jerries were over in force today. The kites were backwards and forwards, constantly being rearmed and refuelled and whilst this was happening it was the ground crews' job to check for damage and repair anything that could be done on-site.

Harry looked knackered, engine oil ingrained in the lines of his face, and there was none of the usual banter. Those flyers stationed at Rochford had no time off; they just kept going, flying sortie after sortie and snatching food and rest when they could. Those at Hornchurch were doing the same. It wasn't much better for ground crew – he and Ronnie snatched a bite when Harry was airborne and tried to get a bit of kip in between sorties.

The Spits and Hurricanes no longer flew in formation; they came in and out on their own mostly. Either he or Ronnie had to keep an eye out and when they saw Harry approaching the runway, they were ready to run out and help him out when he taxied to his position on the edge of the grass strip.

It was Saturday, 9 a.m. The weather was perfect: fine and clear. He and Ronnie were chatting to Harry when the order came to scramble to intercept a huge raid heading from Cap Gris Nez towards Dover. He stood back and watched all the flights take off to intercept the bombers coming in.

The bloody Jerries came in a second raid later that day and dropped bombs on Hornchurch. The 264 squadron of Defiants were caught on the ground, he heard later, and two kites collided in the rush to get off the ground. He was worried about Nancy but none of the buildings were hit by bombs so she was obviously unhurt.

Being at Rochford meant they avoided attacks from German bombers but Hornchurch continued to get regular visits. So far the damage had been minimal. The number of casualties amongst the pilots and aircrew continued to grow. He and Ronnie stopped counting the kites back as it was too depressing.

'We're winning this battle against the Luftwaffe, Tommy. Might not seem that way but their losses are greater than ours. You blokes are the backbone of the wing. You carry on regardless – refuelling, rearming, doing running repairs – whilst the bombs and the bullets are flying around your heads. We couldn't do it without you.' This was the longest speech Harry had ever made and he and his mate appreciated it.

'Doing our bit, Harry. We don't put our lives on the line like you flyers, so least we can do is keep you airborne. I'll fetch you something to eat from the van. Grab a couple of minutes' shut-eye under the wing whilst Ronnie patches up the hole in the fuselage.'

3

Nancy heard the wail of the air raid siren whilst she was on her way to the dispersal points with the baskets of sarnies and tea. Bloody hell – them Germans were back again. Should she head for the shelter or carry on and deliver the food?

She did neither but steered the van into an empty hangar. There were no ground crew in it so they must all have buggered off already. It was too late to go to the air raid shelter herself so she jumped out of the van and decided to watch what was going on.

The bastard bombers were already coming over the horizon and still half the bleedin' planes was on the ground. Why wasn't they scrambling? They were sitting ducks where they were. Suddenly one of them took off. A few moments later it was followed by three others. Some silly bugger was holding them up – if they didn't get a move on then they'd be too late.

The sound of the ack-ack guns from a gun emplacement

near the farm added to the general chaos. There was so much dust in the air from the bombs she wondered how the gunners could see what they were doing.

She watched in horror as the three Spitfires were caught in the blast. The planes disintegrated – wings went in one direction and fuselage in another. She couldn't watch any more and backed into the gloom of the hangar and pressed herself against the wall as if that might keep her safe.

When it was over and the all clear sounded she scrambled back into the van, not sure whether to go back to the mess or try and find some officers to give the food to. She reversed carefully out of the hangar and as she did so several planes came into land. There was craters in the runways but somehow they got down safely apart from one or two of them, which was stuck in the middle of the runway.

Two men raced towards her, shouting that they needed the van. One of them were carrying some rope.

'Lend us your van, love. We need to tow the Spits out of the way or no one else can get in.'

'Righto, I'll sit in the back with the sarnies so's I can give them out when you're done.'

The bloke what jumped behind the wheel were a better driver than her and put his foot down and they sped across the grass lurching and bumping and she were almost catapulted out the back.

Whilst they were tying the rope to the first plane she sat tight. She was too short to be much help. They managed to move the first plane to the edge of the runway and she jumped out and had time to remove both baskets before they were ready to roar off and collect the second Spitfire.

The pilot from the plane saw her struggling and picked

up one of the baskets. 'Manna from heaven, sweetheart. There are a lot of chaps going to be delighted to see you.'

Eventually she returned to the Officers' Mess and as she was the senior WAAF present decided to make her own decisions about what she should do next. The other girls were finishing serving lunch. 'It don't look too clever. I reckon you'd have to be starving to eat what you're giving them,' she commented.

'It ain't our fault, Nancy. We was down the air raid shelter for an hour. Beggars can't be choosers. There's a war on, ain't there?' One of the girls grinned as she carried out a tray of cold cabbage, cold fried potatoes and some sort of chicken in congealed sauce.

'I'm going to make another load of sandwiches and flasks of tea. Then I'll do the rounds again.' The sound of the siren wailing meant another raid was coming in. They abandoned what they were doing and raced for the air raid shelter.

It was crowded, dark and full of all sorts, not just WAAF girls. The sergeant closed the door and a few minutes later someone hammered to be let in. The sarge opened it and from where she was standing, she could see it was the driver of a fuel bowser.

'Sod off, take that bloody thing with you and park it somewhere else before you blow us all to pieces,' the sergeant yelled. Quite right too – the silly bugger had parked the vehicle, full of petrol, right outside the shelter. He wasn't let in until he'd parked it further away.

The all clear went for the second time and she spent the remainder of the afternoon making and delivering food to the pilots and their ground crew. She'd just knocked off at six o'clock when there was another raid. This time it was just the runways and a few aircraft – none of the buildings were damaged apart from the new Airmen's Mess, which was about to be opened. She heard later that bombs were dropped on Elm Park residential housing – no one was bleedin' safe in this war.

The raids continued and Tommy didn't get more than an occasional kip. When the kites were grounded he and Ronnie had to check the engines and patch up anything that had bullet holes. Harry would sleep where he fell. He looked really rough, unshaven and filthy. They weren't any better. Personal hygiene and shaving were forgotten in the shitstorm they were enduring.

The kites couldn't fly for more than an hour and a half without needing to refuel. Harry had gone out earlier and should be back by now. Ronnie was asleep, oblivious to the noise. It was Tommy's turn to watch for returning kites.

'Ronnie, mate, Harry's been hit. There's smoke pouring out of his engine. On your feet – this isn't going to be good.'

The fire tender and ambulance were racing towards the runway. It was his and Ronnie's job to get Harry out and so they joined the general rush to help.

The Spit didn't have the landing gear down – it was going to be a bad one. Harry had had one prang and reckoned he was a dab hand at coming in without an engine or wheels. He was right. The plane glided in and slid along the grass. So far so good. Then it tilted and one wing hit the deck, sending the kite sideways. Fortunately, this helped to stop its forward momentum.

Tommy was only twenty yards from the crash. Harry was hammering on the cockpit, trying to release it.

'Hang on a minute, mate, I'll do that for you.' Tommy clambered on the wing and the heat from the burning engine melted the soles of his boots. He had gloves on and had brought a crowbar – he wasn't daft. He shoved the metal end into the cockpit edge and heaved.

The Perspex flew off. Ronnie arrived beside him and between them they grabbed Harry's arms and dragged him out. The fire engine was shooting foam at the flames licking the wings. They slithered to the ground. A strong stench of burning leather and cloth filled his nostrils.

They were a few yards from the kite. One of Harry's arms was around his shoulder and the other around Ronnie's, when the Spitfire exploded. He was lifted from his feet. Something hit him in the back. Everything went black.

3rd September 1940

Nancy, being short, wasn't given the task of mashing the potatoes as this required someone tall. Sue, a long beanpole of a girl, had that job today.

'Blimey, that thing what you've got to mash them with is bigger than me,' she told her friend.

'It's a knack. It looks easy but it isn't. Can't be any lumps in the spuds for the officers. Unlike the food we get – there were bits of carrot in the custard yesterday.'

'My Tommy and I eat at the NAAFI when we get time off together. I bet they don't mix the custard in a bucket like happens here.'

'I bet they do. It all goes down the same way and comes out the same way – doesn't bother me what it tastes like as long as I'm nice and full. My mate Gladys works at the enlisted men's mess hall. She was telling me that you have to open the tins of evaporated milk with a cleaver and she cut right through one yesterday. What a laugh!'

'Going to ask for a transfer over there. More my cup of tea than this place,' Nancy said.

Pots and pans rattled as yet another flight roared overhead, making conversation impossible. Her job today was preparing the runner beans and peas – a lot easier than what Sue was doing. She wasn't too keen on fresh veg, preferred what came out of tins.

She was halfway through when an RAF officer appeared at the kitchen door. Deirdre, who was the NCO in charge today, hurried across to speak to him. Nancy's heart almost stopped when they looked at her. Did they know she'd been outside for a quick fag this morning? She didn't want to be put on a charge – she'd have to clean the bogs and scrub floors for days if she were.

Deirdre hurried across. 'You have to go to the adjutant's office, Nancy. I'll finish these for you.'

'Do I need to change out of me overalls?'

'Yes, but do it quickly.'

Ten minutes later Nancy was in her blues and ready to trek to the squadron offices. These was the other side of the bloomin' airfield. She didn't want to keep anyone waiting so rushed out, turned right in front of the technical store and then ran down the road between the workshops and the NCOs' mess.

She paused outside to catch her breath, straightened her skirt, adjusted her hat and marched in smartly. She wasn't sure where she should go as she hadn't been given the name of the officer she was to report to – she didn't even know if it was a WAAF officer or an RAF officer who wanted to see her.

No point in piddling about. She had a tongue in her head so would ask the first person she saw. She stopped a handsome young officer with a magnificent moustache.

'Excuse me, sir, I were told to report here but ain't got no idea who I'm to see. LACW 1377, Nancy Evans.' She saluted smartly.

'Haven't got the foggiest, but I'll enquire for you. Won't be a tick.' He smiled and dashed into the nearest office where she could hear him asking whoever was in there.

When he came out he was accompanied by someone more senior than him, an older man with a lot of stripes and gold braid on his shoulders. The young officer was no longer smiling. He nodded sympathetically and then vanished.

'Come in, my dear; take a pew.'

Her heart was thudding, her hands clammy. She didn't want to sit down. She wanted to run away and not hear whatever it was he'd called her here to tell her. But she did as instructed – it didn't do to disobey orders.

To her astonishment he poured her some tea into a fancy cup and saucer. He then put three lumps of sugar into it. She didn't want no tea; she wanted to know what the bad news was. Had one of her brothers or her pa been killed on the docks?

He leaned over and placed the cup and saucer in front of her. 'I've got some very bad news for you, my dear. I regret to tell you that your fiancé, Tommy Smith, was killed earlier today. He died a hero saving a pilot who had crash-landed.'

Nancy stared at him. The words didn't sink in for a moment. What had he just said? Tommy couldn't be dead – he didn't do nothing dangerous – he was ground crew not aircrew.

'Drink your tea, my dear. Don't try and speak for a moment.'

Obediently she picked up the cup and managed to swallow a couple of mouthfuls before his words sunk in. Her Tommy, the man she loved, the man she was going to marry in two days' time, was dead.

The cup rattled in the saucer. She wanted to scream, to throw the cup at the wall, but she was from Poplar. East End girls didn't make a fuss. Ma always said that everyone died sometime. It was up to the living to get on with their lives and not kick up a racket.

Somehow, she replaced the saucer on the desk without dropping it. Pushed herself upright. Saluted, about-turned, and marched out. Her eyes were blurred, her throat clogged, but she wasn't going to give in in front of this toffee-nosed lot.

Instinctively she headed for the guardhouse, marched through and by the time she was across the road and down Sutton Lane she was running. The dormitory would be empty. She needed somewhere private, somewhere she could cry in peace.

In her agony of grief she'd not stopped to think it through. The beds were all neatly stacked, the three square mattresses at the end of the bed with the blankets and pillow on top.

There were no chairs in the dormitory and it was strictly forbidden to make up your bed during the day.

Her space was at the far end, furthest from the door and from the central iron stove. Being last in meant she had the worst position. She stumbled down the centre of the long dormitory and slumped against the wall next to her locker. Slowly her legs folded and she ended in a heap on the floor.

They should have been getting married in two days and now it'd be a funeral not a wedding. She drew her knees up, dropped her head onto them, and wrapped her arms around her folded legs. She wanted to cry but couldn't. She rocked back and forth trying to make sense of this disaster. Tommy had said he were safe as ground crew. How could he be dead?

He died a hero – what bloody use was that to her? Better to have lived a coward. She'd never forgive him for leaving her when he didn't have to. What was that strange sound? Was there someone else here? She realised it was her making a strange whining noise. She clamped her teeth shut. Ma always said you had to get on with things. Be strong and carry on regardless.

How could she go on living without Tommy? He was her everything. He'd loved her and hadn't wanted her to be anything different. Her eyes were gritty, her mouth dry, her throat so tight it was hard to swallow.

The ack-ack guns began to fire. The noise was deafening and it released something inside of her. No one could hear over that. She flung her head back and screamed. Once she'd started she couldn't stop even when the guns were silent.

Vaguely she was aware of two people coming in. Then something sharp was pressed into her arm and things became blurry and welcome darkness took her away from the world she didn't want to be in any more.

Nancy woke up in the hospital wing. She was in a side ward. How could the sun be shining when Tommy was dead? She rolled over and curled into a ball, wishing someone would put her out of her misery too.

'Nancy, I'm so sorry about Tommy. I've got a twenty-four-hour pass and Oscar's parents have said I'm to take you to them. They'll look after you,' Jane said.

Slowly Nancy pushed herself up, feeling like an old woman. 'How'd you know to come?'

'You had my name down as first contact. Don't you remember doing it? I thought it should be your parents but you said you didn't want them involved with anything serious.'

'I'm glad you've come. How long have I been here? It's all a bit fuzzy.'

'They sedated you and you've been asleep for a day.'

'Where's me clothes? I need a wash and to get dressed. I want to know what happened and I don't want to miss the funeral.'

'You won't. It's this afternoon. His parents aren't coming. Did you ever meet them?'

'No, I didn't. Tommy never got on with them. I'm ever so pleased to see you. I don't reckon there's anyone else I want right now.'

Her friend smiled. 'Do you need my help getting to the bathroom? I've got your kitbag packed and there's clean underwear and stockings on the chair with your uniform.

You've got a week's compassionate leave starting from the funeral.'

Nancy's legs felt wobbly, but she wasn't too bad considering. She had to pull herself together – there was a war on – civilians and servicemen alike were going to die so she bloomin' well better get used to it.

When she came back correctly dressed she was more in control. She was a WAAF like her friends Jane and Charlotte, and there wasn't no time for grieving and such. They had their duty to do.

There was a tray on the side table with two mugs of tea and a pile of freshly made toast dripping with real butter and marmalade.

'Blimey, I ain't seen either butter or marmalade for months. I didn't think I were hungry but I am.' They shared the food and when it was gone, the butter licked from her fingers, she was ready to face the world.

'Being married suits you, Jane. You must be worried sick about your Oscar up there all the time fighting them Jerries.'

'I am, but there's nothing we can do about it. I've only seen him three times since we were married.'

'Are you sure the vicar and his wife want me to stay with them?'

'Absolutely certain. Obviously, I've not been able to speak to Oscar – he's on permanent duty at the moment – but I rang the vicarage and my in-laws are only too happy to offer you refuge for a few days. You certainly don't want to go back to Poplar at the moment. It's far too dangerous.'

'I don't know, I reckon I'd be better staying here and working; keep me mind off things, like.'

'You can make up your mind after the funeral. Shall I tell you what happened?'

Nancy nodded. 'Everyone else knows, so I'd better hear it too. I know he were killed trying to rescue a pilot. Were he killed an all?'

'No. It was just rotten luck. A piece of shrapnel from the Spitfire hit Tommy in the back. Ronnie, his friend who was helping, and Harry, the pilot, just suffered from the blast but aren't seriously hurt.'

'Ta for telling me. Hang on a minute, if he ain't going home to be buried where's he going to be put?' She reckoned she sounded all right but it was becoming harder and harder to speak at all through her tears.

'Tommy will be buried in the RAF Cemetery along with the others who've lost their lives. There's a car waiting outside to take us.'

4

The graveside service was brief. The coffin with her beloved Tommy in it was draped with a Union Jack and carried on the shoulders of his friends. Nancy only recognised one of them, Ronnie, who she'd met the first day she'd arrived.

Thank God Jane was at her side with her arm through hers. She wouldn't have got through it otherwise. Seeing the box being lowered into the ground was the worst part. It wasn't only her Tommy being buried here today – there were others. There'd been one funeral before this one and two more to follow.

Her friend guided her to a waiting car. She wasn't sure where they were going. She just wanted to get away from here – just looking at the blokes in blue was tearing her apart. She slumped into the corner of the seat and closed her eyes, wishing she were in the ground with him.

She must've nodded off because when she woke up she was at Chalfont Major where Oscar's parents lived. She'd met Jane's in-laws at the wedding but never spoken to them for very long. She didn't hold much with God-bothering – and the dad was a vicar.

'I ain't sure I want to be here, Jane. It's nice of you to

bring me but I reckon I might be better in London with me own folks.'

'Well, you can decide that in a day or two. We're here now and I don't have time to take you back to London. Come on – let's get you inside. You can have a nice hot bath and go to bed. It'll be easier waking up without hearing the aircraft thundering backwards and forwards all the time.'

She was right about that at least. 'You know what it's like, don't you, Jane? When you came here first it was to tell them that Oscar had died.' She gulped and bit her lip to stop herself from sobbing out loud. 'But your man wasn't dead, mine is.'

What happened next was a bit of a blur. Jane give her a hug and then rushed off as she had to be back on duty that evening, leaving her alone with a couple of folk she didn't know. She was so wretched it didn't matter where she was. Her Tommy was gone and she had nothing left to live for.

She cried herself to sleep and next morning only got up to use the facilities and then crept back into bed. The vicar and his wife didn't try and make her get up. They came in regular like with trays but she ignored them. Maybe if she refused to eat or drink then she'd fade away and could be with Tommy wherever he was.

With the blackouts down all the time night blurred into day, and she'd no idea what time it was or how long she'd been huddled in bed hoping she'd die.

This time when the tray, again without comment, arrived she crawled out of bed and collapsed on the floor beside it. First, she drank the tea, then before she realised, she'd eaten everything and felt a lot better for it. Tommy was dead but she wasn't and she'd better get used to the idea of living without him. Ma would be disgusted with her giving in like this.

She crept to the door and pulled it open an inch – sunshine filled the passageway. The bathroom was empty and she filled the tub with the regulation five inches and when she got out she was feeling a lot better.

Wrapped in a large towel she hurried back to her bedroom and got dressed. Her hair was a mess, needed washing, but once it was up it didn't look too bad. Her stomach gurgled loudly. Her appetite was back with a vengeance.

Carrying the tray downstairs had proved more difficult than it should. Her head were still a bit swimmy and her legs had a mind of their own. She'd not been inside the vicarage before, as at the wedding she'd only been in the church, the village hall and the garden.

The kitchen would be at the back of this grand house so she headed in that direction. When she pushed open the door Mrs Stanton smiled warmly. There were boxes taped up and labelled lining the passageway and she wondered if the vicar and his wife were about to move somewhere. She was too dispirited to ask.

'Good, I'm so glad to see that you're up, Nancy. Thank you for bringing the tray down and I'm glad that you've eaten everything. Sit down at the table and I'll make you something more substantial.'

'How long have I been up there feeling sorry for myself?'

'Two days – it's the 5th of September today.'

Nancy gripped the edge of the table. It should have been their wedding day. Tears trickled down her cheeks but she couldn't wipe them away, because if she removed her hands she'd collapse on the floor.

'I'm so sorry, you were going to get married today. Sit down, my dear, and catch your breath.'

Nancy subsided onto the nearest chair and drank the glass of water she was handed. No questions were asked, nothing was demanded of her and, after a few days, she began to feel she would be able to get through this eventually.

Jane had telephoned the day after her arrival but she'd not been up to speak to her. This time she had no excuse although she didn't want to talk about Tommy.

'Nancy, I'm so glad that you're now up and about. Things are frantic at the moment or I'd come and see you. Two girls here have lost their partners; both of them have carried on working.'

'I should've done the same. I've let everyone down and am going back to work tomorrow.'

'No, I'm so sorry, I wasn't implying that you should do the same. The catering department can manage perfectly well without you for a bit longer. It's not the same for us.'

'I know it ain't. I was never as good as you or Charlotte. Ta ever so for ringing but you don't need to bother about me.'

Nancy put the receiver down feeling even more wretched than before she'd spoken to her friend. Being so immersed in her own misery she'd forgotten she was supposed to be back at the base by now. That evening she mentioned this to the vicar who was a nice sort of bloke.

'I took the liberty of ringing Hornchurch and speaking to your CO, my dear. I told them you were in no fit state to resume your duties but would return as soon as you were well.'

'I'll be put on a charge. I'm AWOL and that ain't good.'

'You are also in a position to resign if you should wish to as for some reason you haven't signed on for the duration as yet.'

'I did get a letter but I never read it. Do that mean I ain't got to go back if I don't want?'

'Why would you wish to do that? Being a WAAF is a great help to the war effort and if you don't stay in the services what else will you do?'

'I ain't ready to return to Hornchurch right now. All them bombers and fighters overhead are bad enough here but there it'll just make me think of Tommy all the time.'

Talking about him was difficult and she needed to pull herself together. Other girls lost their men and they didn't carry on the way she was doing.

She'd been at the vicarage for more than a week and was still feeling right peculiar. Her head kept spinning and she couldn't swallow nothing. She'd hidden this from the Stantons as she didn't want them fussing and worrying over her.

'I'm going for a walk, Mrs Stanton. I need the fresh air and time to think. I know I've got to go. This might be the last chance I get to spend time in the countryside.'

'Of course, Nancy, you take as long as you want.'

She strolled through the churchyard, hopped over the wall at the back and into the fields beyond. She walked briskly enjoying the autumn sun on her face. Then suddenly her head spun and her knees gave way and she toppled forward onto her face.

The grass was warm; the sun beat down on her back. She

closed her eyes and let the blackness take her. Something cold and damp pressed against her cheek. Then a hot wet tongue slathered her face. She wanted to tell the dog to go away but remained still. Then someone knelt beside her. She didn't have the energy to move, to ask them to leave her alone.

'I'm a doctor. I'm going to check to see if you're injured. Don't be alarmed when I put my hands on you.'

She lay passive whilst this doctor checked she'd broken nothing. She should turn over, speak to him, but she didn't have the energy.

'Okay, I'm going to pick you up now.'

He gently rolled her onto her back but she kept her eyes closed. Then he scooped her up and began to carry her across the field. That would be a good time to say she was staying at the vicarage but her head hurt, everything felt heavy and she went back to sleep.

Doctor David Denny shouldered his way into his kitchen and yelled for his housekeeper. 'Ava, I need you. I've got an unconscious WAAF I found in the field when I was walking Polly.'

'My word, whatever next. It must be the one staying at the vicarage. The bed's made up in the back bedroom – why don't you put her in there for now?'

He followed her upstairs and waited, with the worryingly quiet girl in his arms, whilst the covers were pulled back.

'There you go.'

'I'm going to fetch my bag. Would you stay with her, please. I need to examine her before I decide if I have to call for the ambulance.'

When Julia had died three years ago, he couldn't bring himself to give away her clothes. What Ava had called the back bedroom had once been the room he'd shared with his wife, and this WAAF could benefit from his inability to move on, to accept that he'd lost his beloved wife.

Ava remained beside the bed as chaperone. The girl's pulse was shallow, but regular. She had no temperature – didn't have any sign of a head injury. He stepped back and looked down at the seemingly comatose young woman. She was tiny, no more than five foot, but quite definitely an adult. He stared dispassionately at her rounded breasts, her small waist and the curve of her hips.

Julia dying had also killed his interest in other women. Despite the fact that this young woman was quite definitely beautiful it didn't move him. He smiled wryly. This was a good thing. Being a doctor, anything but the most professional attitude towards her could get him struck off.

'What's wrong with the girl, do you know?' Ava asked when he returned a few moments later.

'I've no idea what made her collapse, but I'm hopeful that she's not seriously ill. I think it must be some sort of emotional trauma. You said she's staying at the vicarage so I'll give them a ring and let them know their guest is here.'

The vicar had a son who was a fighter pilot and he'd married a WAAF in the summer. He'd been invited to the wedding but had declined as he didn't socialise any more. It was probably no coincidence that this nameless girl was staying there. No doubt she was a friend of Oscar's wife.

The operator connected him and Mrs Stanton answered. 'I was wondering if you know anything about a young WAAF...'

'Oh, thank God, we've had the search parties out. Nancy Evans is a close friend of my daughter-in-law and sadly her fiancé was killed two days before their wedding. Jane brought her to us to recuperate ten days ago. I thought she was doing so well. Is she all right?'

'I found her unconscious in a field and she's now asleep in a spare bedroom.'

'She was having a last wander about before going back to Hornchurch. I've no idea why she might have fainted.'

'I'll keep her here until I'm sure she's well enough to leave. I think there's more to this than just being overwhelmed by grief. Better to have her here where I can keep an eye on her. I'll ask Ava to collect her things.'

'If you're quite sure that's not an inconvenience, then you must do what you think is best.'

He disconnected without saying goodbye and he asked his housekeeper if she would be prepared to fetch the girl's kitbag.

'It's only down the road a few minutes. It won't take me long. I'll nip into the butcher's whilst I'm out as he said he would have offal this afternoon and I don't want to miss out on a nice bit of liver for your tea.'

The only reason she wanted to go out was to spread the gossip. He appreciated Ava's invaluable help in the house but not her tendency to tittle-tattle about anything she heard. Jill Andrews, his receptionist, had to be very careful that the door to the waiting room was closed when she was talking to patients.

He was fond of Jill, a widow whose husband had gone down with his ship somewhere in the Atlantic, but he had no intention of being more than a friend to her. If he showed the slightest partiality then the rumour mill would kick in and Stanton would be asking him when he wanted the church for his next wedding.

Since he'd curtailed her afternoon walk his dog was fussing around his feet, looking hopefully at the lead hanging on a hook by the back door. 'Sorry, old girl, you'll have to wait until after evening surgery. Go in the garden and play with your ball.'

Polly was a mongrel, but a pretty one, and had a lot of Labrador and spaniel in her, which meant there was nothing she liked better than chasing a ball and retrieving it.

He glanced at his wristwatch – two hours until his first appointment and he had no visits either today. The midwife, an excellent woman, dealt with births unless there was a complication. Without checking his records, he couldn't be certain there wasn't at least one infant due this week.

Ava bustled off with her shopping bag and he thought he'd better check on his patient. The girl had been upstairs for a couple of hours now and she hadn't been offered anything to drink or eat. It was possible her blood sugar was low, which could be the reason for her collapse.

He was quite capable of making himself a decent meal when he had to but enjoyed having someone taking care of the domestic chores so he could concentrate on his work. Ava came in to make his breakfast and left at six o'clock so she was home to make her own husband's tea. She always left him something in the slow oven in the Aga for when he'd finished work. She also organised the laundry and kept the house spotless.

The garden was his preserve and he spent all his spare time pottering about out there. He had half a dozen chickens, a few ducks on the pond and grew all his own vegetables. However, he preferred flowers to vegetables and was famous for his perennial border and his rose garden.

He made a sandwich, found a slice of cake in the tin and poured out a mug of tea. He put the three items on a tray, added a napkin, and headed upstairs. The door to the bedroom had been left open and he could see his patient was awake.

'Excellent, Miss Evans; I've brought you something to eat and drink. No arguments, please, doctor's orders.'

She managed a wan smile but said nothing. He placed the tray across her knees and she didn't protest. 'Ta ever so, Doc. I appreciate what you done for me. I ain't one for fainting and such. Didn't know losing me fiancé would make me like what I am.'

Good grief – from her accent and syntax she was an uneducated girl from the East End. Young Oscar's new wife had been a well-spoken young lady – how could this girl be a close friend of hers?

'Grief is different for everyone, Miss Evans. If you haven't been eating or drinking properly then it's hardly surprising you fainted.' He pointed to the door. 'The bathroom and WC are at the end of the corridor. My housekeeper has gone to fetch your belongings. Mrs Stanton agreed with me that it would be better for you to remain here as you appear to be rather unsteady at the moment.'

'It don't matter to me where I am. I just want to get back on me feet and get off to me job. I'm going back on the bus.'

'What exactly do you do in the WAAF, Miss Evans?'

'I'm LACW first class, 1377. I ain't Miss Evans any more,

I'm Mrs Smith – though you can call me Nancy if you want. What's your name?'

'I'm Doctor David Denny. Pleased to meet you, LACW 1377.' He smiled as she pulled a face at him. 'I beg your pardon, should I have mentioned "first class"?'

'Too bloody right. I earned the promotions. I'll be an NCO one day with any luck. I'm in catering – look after the officers like. I were in the stores before…' Her voice trailed away and her eyes glittered.

'Eat your sandwich, young lady, and drink your tea. I made them especially for you. I'm going down to eat my own belated lunch.'

Nancy obediently picked up the sarnie intending to take just one bite to show willing, but the bread was fresh, it was butter with actual chicken and pickle inside. She finished that and then demolished the cake and drank the tea.

So far no one had commented on the fact that she was wearing both a wedding and an engagement ring. Having both on, she realised, would tell everyone that she'd spent the night with Tommy. Why else would she be wearing it if it hadn't been to fool a landlady? She'd told the doctor she was married and Mrs Stanton knew that wasn't true and would probably have told the doctor that her fiancé had died before they could be married. She wasn't sure what had prompted her to do this.

She wasn't happy about being palmed off to this doctor bloke. Still, she was leaving anyway so she wasn't fussy where she was. She felt ever so peculiar, light-headed and wobbly-legged. She wasn't ever ill, was fit as a flea, bloomin' strange that Tommy dying had made her like this.

Just thinking about him choked her up but crying and such wouldn't bring him back. No – time to get on with her life – get back to work and do her bit. She'd been away from her duty for more than two weeks already and that just wasn't good enough. If there wasn't a war on, if she wasn't a girl from the East End, then she'd be able to grieve properly but things were different now.

This doctor wasn't exactly old, but he wasn't young neither. She'd only noticed his horn-rimmed glasses and his dark hair. She swung her legs to the mat beside the bed but didn't stand up until she was sure she wasn't going to pass out again. She wandered across to the chair and collected her uniform jacket.

It was strange being in his bedroom. Why hadn't she been put in a spare room? She opened and shut drawers, looking in the wardrobe, checking in the dressing table compartments. None of his things were there; it was all women's stuff. There were trinket boxes full of knick-knacks, necklaces, rings and bracelets. She held what looked like a diamond ring up to the light and froze.

She wouldn't be in here if Mrs Denny was around. His wife must be dead and he'd not had the heart to get rid of her things. She wasn't comfortable in here any more and she certainly wasn't going to sleep there.

Rushing about made her feel dizzy so she lay on the bed until things were back to normal. When her kitbag turned up, she'd wait for a bus and make her way back to Hornchurch.

Tommy wouldn't want her to shirk her duty just because

he was gone. When she'd gone for a walk earlier she'd not been wearing her hat. She couldn't go back without it or she'd be put on a charge.

Might as well go and fetch her things for herself. It was after three o'clock and she reckoned there might not be a bus to take her to the nearest town after four. She was halfway down the stairs when she went all peculiar again. She clung on to the banister. If she fell head first she might break her bleeding neck.

5

Nancy's hands lost their grip on the banister and with a despairing cry she fell down the stairs. The doctor caught her before she hit the floor at the bottom.

'You're making a habit of this, young lady. What on earth are you doing up?'

She wanted to tell him but her mouth was full of cotton wool and the words wouldn't come.

'You need to stay in bed until you're feeling better.' He carried her up the stairs like a parcel and headed for the room she'd just escaped from.

'No, no, not there.'

He stopped at the door. 'I'm sorry, I should have realised you wouldn't want to be in my dead wife's room. I've got two others – are you feeling up to making a selection?'

Her head had cleared a little and her tongue were no longer stuck to the roof of her mouth. 'Any other room, ta ever so.'

'This one's closer to the bathroom but the bed's not made up. I'll put you on top of the bedspread.'

He stepped back and looked at her thoughtfully then picked up a chair and brought it over. He sat, a yard away, his arms folded, staring at her through narrowed eyes. Then he leaned over and raised her left hand – saw the wedding ring and nodded.

'How long ago did you have intercourse with your fiancé? Have you missed your period?'

He was so matter-of-fact, no disapproval or judgement in his expression that she answered truthfully. 'It should have come more than a week ago. We went together two weeks before he died as we wouldn't be able to do it on our wedding night. Am I in the family way? I thought you couldn't get pregnant the first time.'

He smiled and it made him look younger, almost handsome. 'I'm afraid that's not true, Miss Evans. Fainting is not uncommon in the first trimester although it's unusual so early in a pregnancy.'

She closed her eyes, letting the information sink in. Tommy was gone, but she had a part of him inside her. She wasn't alone any more – she'd got a little one to think about.

'I ain't ashamed; I'm happy to be expecting. Are you sure that's what's making me so wobbly?'

'As sure as I can be. However, it can't be confirmed until you're further along. Are you normally regular?'

'Like clockwork. Four weeks exactly every month since I was eleven years old. I can't stay in the WAAF once they know – but I don't reckon I'll show for a few months yet.'

'What exactly do you do in the catering department?'

'I clean one day and cook the next. I make the sandwiches and tea and take it in the van to the pilots waiting at dispersal to be scrambled.'

'Then I'm sorry but I can't allow you to return to duty,

Miss Evans. You would be a liability to yourself and to the service at the moment.'

'Then will you write me medical note and I'll post it to them?'

'Where will you go? Do you have family you can stay with?'

'I do. I'll tell them I was married before Tommy died. They won't know no difference, will they?'

He pointed to her ring. 'Have you been wearing that since you slept together?' She nodded. 'I'm surprised nobody mentioned it. What would your married name have been?'

'Smith – from now on I'm going to be Nancy Smith, like what I told you before. I'll not have no one picking on me little one for being a bastard.'

'Good for you. I don't want you to leave until I'm sure you're not going to pass out and fall under a bus or tram. I'll explain things to the Stantons.'

'Blimey, I'd not thought of that. How long will this fainting last?'

'It depends. In my experience both nausea and dizziness dissipate in the second trimester – around four months.'

'I ain't staying here until then, that's for sure. I'm no one's charity case. I'll take me chances.'

'If you want me to write you a medical certificate so you can be discharged from the WAAF then will you agree to remain here until I consider that you're well enough to go?'

'I don't need no note from you, Doctor Denny. I'll report back and the medic there can tell me what's what.'

'How are you intending to get back to Hornchurch?'

'I'll catch the bleedin' bus. I'm just waiting for me stuff

to come and then I'll be off. I'm ever so grateful but I can take care of meself.'

'When you feel well enough I can arrange for you to get a lift to Chelmsford. From there you can catch the train to Romford. Hornchurch base is only a couple of miles from there.'

She was going to refuse but reconsidered. 'Righty ho. The vicar spoke to them so they won't be expecting me back any particular day.'

'Good girl, a wise decision. Do you feel at all dizzy?'

'No, tickety-boo, ta very much.'

'Excellent. I'm going to take my dog, Polly, for a walk. Do you want to come with me?'

The noise of bombers flying overhead and the sound of dogfights interrupted their conversation. They might be out in the middle of nowhere, nothing but trees and grass and such, but you couldn't get away from the fighting in the skies. She swallowed a lump in her throat. Going back to the base was going to be so difficult. She dreaded seeing the sympathetic faces, the knowing looks, and decided right then that she would ask the doctor to write to her CO and get her discharged immediately. She frowned. Why couldn't she make up her mind? She was like a bleedin' windmill at the moment.

'No, ta, I'll stop here. Need to have a bit of a think about things. Knowing I'm having Tommy's baby makes things a bit better, but I still can't believe he's gone. He should have been safe not being aircrew – it ain't fair.' Her eyes filled and she sniffed and rummaged in her pocket for a hanky.

'There's nothing fair about death. It's indiscriminate.' He whistled to his dog and walked off without another word.

He was a grumpy old sod but had a kind heart and seemed like a good doctor. He was taller than Tommy and broader in the shoulder and she wasn't that keen on a bloke who was a head taller than her.

She didn't like sitting about doing nothing so she'd go in search of sheets and pillow slips and get the bed made up in the room she was going to use.

David wasn't sure having Nancy staying was a good idea, although he wasn't going to change his mind and send her back to the vicarage. Having a young girl under his roof unchaperoned would cause a lot of speculation. Too bad – he didn't give a damn what anyone thought. He was his own man and always had been.

When his wife, Julia, had finally got pregnant after many years of trying they'd both been delighted. She was considered an elderly primigravida being twenty-nine but she was healthy and neither of them anticipated any problems. How wrong they'd been. Everything had been fine until she was in her third trimester and then things had gone disastrously wrong. She'd gone into premature labour. He'd driven her to hospital like a madman but, on her arrival, she'd haemorrhaged and both his unborn child and his wife had died.

He should have realised things were going awry. He was a doctor for God's sake; she shouldn't have died like that. If he had taken her to hospital sooner… if… if.

He scowled and slashed at the nettles along the path with the lead, making his dog bark in surprise. Julia had died three years ago and he still blamed himself. This was one reason the bedroom they'd shared had been left unchanged. He'd got rid of the baby things – he couldn't bear to have them in the house – but he still wandered into the room upstairs occasionally and looked through her possessions.

This unwanted guest had brought home to him that it was macabre and unhealthy not to have given away her things. There was a war on and rationing meant that everything was in short supply. Better that these garments were worn by someone who needed them than left mouldering in the wardrobe and chest of drawers.

On his return he could hear Ava yelling. The sound carried through an open bedroom window. The wretched girl had only been under his roof for a few hours and was already causing chaos. He tossed the lead onto the table and took the stairs two at a time.

'You've no right to interfere, miss. Who do you think you are to come in here and make up a bed as if you owned the place?'

'I were only helping out. No need to take on. You fetched me things, seemed only right to do this for you. I ain't an invalid. I just lost the man I loved and it's knocked me sideways.'

'I don't care who you lost…'

'Enough, Ava. I could hear you in the garden and I expect most of the village could. Nancy should be thanked for helping. You're out of order. I suggest you go downstairs and get on with your work.'

The woman pursed her lips, seemed to swell. Bright spots of red appeared on her cheeks. 'I won't stay here and be spoken to like a servant. I've looked after you since Mrs Denny died. She'd be turning in her grave to think you've got a floozy under your roof.' She glared at Nancy. 'I know your sort – where you come from all girls are the same.'

'Your employment here is terminated. Get out.' She took one look at his face and didn't argue. She scampered down the stairs and he heard the back door slam behind her.

'Blimey, that were something else. You didn't have to sack her on my account. I've been called worse in me time.'

His anger passed as quickly as it had come. 'I'm so sorry. That shouldn't have happened. Don't look so concerned, Nancy. I'm actually relieved that I've got rid of her. She was very efficient but an inveterate gossip and ignored anything I asked her to do if she didn't want to do it.'

'You ain't got the time to look after the house as well as do your doctoring. The least I can do is take over until I leave. Remember, that's me trade – catering and cleaning.'

'Then, thank you, I accept your offer. However, I don't think you should act as my housekeeper wearing your uniform. It doesn't seem appropriate somehow.'

'Well I jolly well ain't wearing anything in that room. I'll put a pinny on over me things. That Ava's twice me size so I reckon it'll wrap around me nice.'

She wasn't wearing her uniform jacket – that was hanging neatly over the back of a chair. Her kitbag was leaning drunkenly against the wall.

'Surgery starts in half an hour. Are you sure you feel up to making our evening meal?'

'Bleedin' hell, Doc, cooking for two ain't nothing after what I've been doing.'

How was he going to say this without offending her? 'Look, Nancy, I'm not comfortable with you swearing.

Do you think you could stick to blooming and blimey in future?'

She grinned. 'I'll do me best. Jane Stanton, one of me best friends, is always saying the same. I wish I could talk proper – I ain't stupid you know but every time I open me mouth people think I am. I can't read good either.'

'Then in return for your help in the house I'll help you with your reading and so on. How's that for a deal?'

'Sounds tickety-boo to me. I'm not stopping long but every little helps, don't it? I ain't too clever with writing neither – I don't suppose you could help me with that as well? I hated school and only went when I had to.'

'First lesson – try to say *I'm not* instead of *I ain't*.'

'Righty ho. I'll get me stuff stowed away and then get started. I ain't... I'm not going to unpack everything. It don't seem worth it.'

'That's up to you. I think Ava got some liver for supper. It will be in the meat safe in the pantry.'

'I love a bit of liver. I'll do onion gravy and mash to go with it.'

Whilst he was changing his shirt and finding a tie and jacket he was beginning to have second thoughts about this new arrangement. His ex-housekeeper would no doubt be spreading venomous gossip already. He didn't care for his own reputation but Nancy didn't deserve to be vilified. Maybe it would be better if she did return to the vicarage, but then he would have to make his own meals, tidy the house and do the laundry.

Good God! Washing his underpants was one thing he wasn't going to let Nancy do for him. There wasn't time to speak to the vicar's wife, but he'd ring her after surgery and see if she knew of anyone in the village who would be happy to take on the job of doing his domestic chores and cooking for him. Nancy seemed determined to leave but he'd no intention of letting her go until he was sure she wasn't going to pass out under a passing trolleybus.

Nancy was able to push her misery aside whilst she was busy in the kitchen and around the house for the rest of the day. The dog, Polly, had taken a shine to her and was constantly under her feet. Twice she'd had to sit down when her head spun but she hadn't fainted again.

The surgery was in a separate annexe with a door what led from the house into it. The patients what attended went round the front and straight in so she never saw how many came. David – he'd insisted she use his name – said he'd be done by seven o'clock.

There were a dining room and she wasn't sure if she were supposed to lay up for him in there. Seemed daft to do that so she found a pretty floral tablecloth and shoved it on the kitchen table instead. She wasn't his real housekeeper, more a guest like, so decided she'd eat with him.

She'd fed the dog with the scraps plus some spuds and a dollop of gravy without the onions. Polly had gulped it down wagging her tail whilst she ate.

'Something smells tasty. It seems a long time since I had that sandwich.' David came in having removed his jacket and tie. He looked ever so smart even with his shirt open at the neck.

'I weren't sure...'

'I wasn't sure...'

'Blimey, you've got your work cut out if you hope to make me sound like someone posh.' She put his plate on the table in front of him. 'I *wasn't* sure if you preferred to eat in the dining room.'

'No, in the kitchen with you.' He waited until she'd served herself and sat down opposite before he picked up his cutlery. 'My heart sunk when Ava said she was going to get liver for supper – I don't like it as a rule but this is quite delicious. Is that an apple crumble I see lurking on the dresser?'

'It is. Do you want your tea now or after?'

'Afterwards. You don't have to wait on me – you're not my employee but a guest helping out.'

She ate a few mouthfuls but then her throat closed up and she couldn't force any more down. She should be sitting with Tommy eating supper, not with this stranger. She pushed the food around her plate for a bit hoping he wouldn't notice she wasn't eating.

'Leave it, Nancy. Polly will be happy to finish it for you. You've had something and hopefully you'll eat a little of the dessert as well. Have you had any more dizzy spells this afternoon?'

'I… I haven't, not really. Had to sit down twice, that's all.'

'Excellent, don't stand up too quickly, don't rush about and you'll be fine.' He put down his knife and fork with a satisfied sigh and then immediately stood up before she could move. 'I'll clear; you stay where you are.'

He scraped her food into the dog's bowl, including the onion gravy, but Polly didn't mind and ate it with as much enthusiasm as before. He then dished up the afters, added some evaporated milk, and brought it to the table.

'Very small portion for you; eat what you can. Please don't comment on the size of mine – crumble is my weakness.'

After doing the washing-up she made the tea and arranged it on a tray with cups and saucers, sugar and everything. He'd gone off to the sitting room. She wasn't going to sit with him. That wouldn't be right. Anyway, she wasn't up to socialising.

'I'm going to bed, David. What time do you want breakfast ready?'

'Whenever you like. Don't get up especially for me as you need to rest. I only have toast and tea anyway. Morning surgery is at nine o'clock and is usually over by midday.'

'Okay then, I'll say good night and ta for taking me in like this.'

He was already engrossed in his paper when she left. She'd been all right until she went to bed then grief overwhelmed her. The constant sound of bombers and fighters overhead was too much for her. It reminded her of what had happened.

She cried into her pillow until it was soaked. Eventually she fell asleep, but not for long. She woke in the middle of the night, her heart racing, not sure where she was. For a second she forgot why she was there but then she remembered Tommy was dead, that she'd never see him again and she didn't think she'd be able to go on without him.

She curled up in a ball, biting her lip to stop her sobs being heard in the quiet house. She wasn't quiet enough as unexpectedly he was sitting beside her on the bed.

'You'll make yourself ill, Nancy, crying like this. Take a deep breath through your nose and then breathe out slowly.'

At first she couldn't do it but then slowly she regained control.

'There, that's better. Here, drink this. It will make you feel better.'

A glass was pressed against her lips and she took a swallow – it was medicine of some sort but didn't taste too bad.

'I'll sit with you until you go to sleep.'

When she opened her eyes next the sun was up. She didn't want to get out of bed but she'd a job to do and she wasn't a shirker. Tommy would be proud of her. She'd learn how to read and write properly for him and for the baby he'd given her. She didn't want him or her to be ashamed of her.

Getting up slowly meant she didn't feel dizzy; could stand safely. She collected her toilet bag and towel and put her ear to the door. Not a sound. No clock in the room so she didn't know the time but guessed it was still early.

The dog greeted her with small yelps of excitement, turning in circles around her feet. 'Blimey, it's only six o'clock. Shall we go for a walk, Polly? I could do with some fresh air.'

She unhooked the lead but didn't clip it to the dog's collar. David hadn't put it on so she reckoned it would be safe not to use it. The air was damp and cool, a bit of a nip to it. Autumn was on its way.

David's house had a large garden and everywhere she looked there were flowers and such. The dog dashed ahead of her towards a hen coop and the vegetable garden. The birds clucked and fussed when they went past, obviously hoping to be let out.

Polly stopped at a gate at the end of the path and Nancy

opened it. It led into a narrow track with trees on either side. The dog ran off following a scent of some animal or other. She followed more slowly enjoying the peace and trying not to think about Tommy. David had said too much crying was bad for her so from now on she'd try not to break down.

Another dog, a mastiff of some sort, burst through the undergrowth. It headed straight for her, teeth bared, and ears flat.

6

David heard Nancy go out with the dog and decided he'd get up as well. The window overlooked the garden and he watched her stop and smell the roses and for some reason this pleased him. She was an East End girl. Gardens didn't feature there, but she obviously enjoyed being in the country.

He fetched four large suitcases from the attic and gritted his teeth. Today was the day he was going to clear the room of Julia's belongings. He would keep the jewellery; he might one day marry again and everything he'd given her had come from various family members so it made sense to hang on to it.

It took less time than he'd expected to clear the wardrobe, dressing table and chest of drawers. He fastened the suitcases and hefted them downstairs and left them by the front door. Mrs Stanton would know who to give them to.

He checked his watch and was concerned that Nancy had been gone for more than an hour. He decided to go in search of her in case she'd fainted again. As he approached the back gate leading into the woods that ran along the back of his garden he could hear her talking to someone.

'I better get back; the doctor will think I've got lost. I a...

I'm not a country girl. I thought this old boy was coming to attack me.'

'Not Jasper – he's as soft as butter. I'm glad I got to meet you, Mrs Smith. I can put a few people straight about things.'

He recognised the other speaker as Joan Butler, the landlady of the local pub.

'I can't believe anyone would think there might be something going on between us. Even if I wasn't grieving for my poor Tommy, I wouldn't be interested in a man old enough to be my pa.'

He backed away hastily, not sure if he was upset or relieved by what he'd overheard. Good God – he couldn't be more than a dozen years older than Nancy so she must think he was in his late forties, not his early thirties.

Polly came in first wagging her tail and Nancy followed. 'Sorry I were… was so long, David. I met a nice lady – Joan something or other – and we had a good old chinwag. You wouldn't believe what your old housekeeper has been saying about us.'

'I can guess. I'm sure you put Joan straight. If you don't mind making the tea and toast, I've got to phone the vicarage.'

She nodded, her smile slipping a little. 'I understand. You want me to move back there to stop the gossip.'

'I certainly don't. I'm hoping Mrs Stanton might have someone in mind to replace Ava. I've also got several suitcases of clothes and so on for her to distribute to the needy.'

'Fair enough. Before you start your surgery, David, would you please write my medical note and send it to

Hornchurch?' She was talking in a slightly stilted way, obviously trying to avoid misusing words.

'I'll do it immediately I've finished my telephone call. It will get easier you know. Good for you.'

The telephone sat on a small hexagonal table in the hall so he could answer it in the middle of the night if necessary. There was also an extension in his surgery, which his receptionist answered for him when she was there. As the two were connected he was certain Ava used to eavesdrop from the one in the hall.

Nancy's arrival had prompted him to sack Ava – something he should have done years ago – and clear out Julia's room, also something he should have done a long time ago.

The vicar's wife answered the telephone as she always did even when her husband was in the house. 'Good morning, Mrs Stanton. I've got three suitcases of clothes and other personal items for you to collect at some point.'

'Not before time, if you don't mind me saying so, Doctor Denny. Jim, our gardener, is taking several boxes of things into Romford later today so he'll call for them before he leaves, if that's all right?'

'Excellent. You've probably already heard on the village grapevine that I'm in need of a new daily. Do you know of anyone who might be interested who will be a better fit than the previous one?'

'Mrs Arbuckle would be ideal. Her children are old enough to take care of themselves when they're not at school.'

'I don't know why I didn't think of her myself. I'll go round and see her later, thank you.' He paused, waiting to see if she would mention anything about Nancy but she didn't. His temporary guest was a close friend of their family, which meant it was unlikely they would believe any of the nonsense Ava was spreading. 'By the way, it's Mrs Nancy Smith, not Nancy Evans.'

'I understand perfectly. I'll refer to her as Mrs Smith in future.'

He sat at his desk and unscrewed the cap of his fountain pen. It didn't take him long to write a brief letter to the doctor in charge of the hospital wing at Hornchurch. He included a medical certificate, signed both, blotted them and was about to fold them and push them into the envelope when he remembered that she would be known by her rank and number, not her name. There was ample room beneath the address for him to print that when he knew it.

The sound of singing echoed down the passageway. She had a lovely voice and he was impressed by her resilience. He hadn't even smiled for months after Julia died and yet Nancy was able to sing and not let her grief interfere with her duty. She would be a loss to the RAF and if she'd been able to stay no doubt would have been promoted, but her lack of education precluded her ever becoming an officer.

He tapped his pen on his teeth. An annoying habit, so his wife had told him, that she'd insisted he eradicate. He hadn't done it for years. What sort of future did Nancy have without a husband to support her, no income, and a baby due next May?

The house rattled as wave after wave of German bombers flew overhead hotly pursued by Spitfires and Hurricanes. If the RAF was destroyed then the war would be lost and in a few weeks there would be jackbooted Nazis marching down the streets of London. God help them all if that happened.

Everyone in Chalfont Major had been preparing for a possible invasion and there were stocks of tinned food being stored at the vicarage, in back gardens and in the church. The wells that hadn't been used since mains water was connected a few years ago were fully functioning just in case the pipes got broken. He hoped the day that Germans marched through England never came.

Nancy stopped singing, shocked that she was doing so just two weeks after Tommy had died. She should be sitting in a heap in a corner, not rushing about some bloke's kitchen making his breakfast as if nothing had happened. She was devastated, but moping about wouldn't do her any good and Tommy wouldn't want her to, not with a baby on the way.

East End women were a tough lot – they had to be as there was rarely enough housekeeping to make ends meet. She'd burnt her boats by asking David to get her dismissed as unfit for service. She had a few pounds in her post office savings book but it wouldn't last long. If she'd really been married to Tommy then she'd get a widow's pension. It wouldn't have been much but it would have been better than nothing.

She'd go home for a bit and find a job somewhere until she was showing. It wouldn't matter if anyone knew she was in the family way as they'd all think she was married. What about when it came to registering the baby? She'd have to show her wedding lines then. Pa would throw her out, baby and all, when he found out. He wouldn't hold with "little bastards" of any sort even if they were his own grandchild.

Her eyes filled and swallowing was difficult. She sniffed, straightened her shoulders and started singing again. She was doing her best but her voice wobbled, stopped and her head dropped. She gripped on to the handles on the Aga trying to regain control.

'Sit down, my dear. However hard you try to push it aside grief will sometimes crush you. Pretending nothing's happened is as bad as wallowing in your misery for years.'

His hands were firm on her shoulders and she was guided to a chair and gently pressed onto it. A clean, ironed handkerchief was pushed between her fingers and she held it to her face. Her shoulders shook and his hands remained resting on them until she was able to stop crying. Only then did he move away and she watched as he made the tea and then put pieces of bread on the toasting forks and held them in front of the open range.

She blew her nose, drank half the tea he'd put in front of her and began to feel more in control. 'Why ain't... haven't you got one of them posh gas cookers? Ever so much easier than that old thing.'

'I really don't know. My wife wanted it and as I had nothing to do with the domestic side of things, I made no objection. Dammit! The toast's burning.'

'Here, let me. I'm a dab hand at toast.'

Having something to do made it easier not to think how different her life would have been if Tommy had still been alive. What was the future facing her and her unborn baby?

'I need your rank and number and then the letter's ready to go.'

She told him and watched him writing with admiration. 'You've got lovely handwriting, David. Ever so clear and neat.'

'Having this pen helps. I defy anybody to write badly using one of these.' He passed it across the table and she looked at it with interest.

'I've seen them but never held one. Real clever having the ink inside so you don't have to keep dipping and dripping all over the shop.'

He licked the envelope and stuck it down. The telephone rang shrilly in the hall. 'Excuse me, I have to answer that. Here, if you go after breakfast then you'll catch the first post. The post office is in the High Street about half a mile from here.'

He was back almost immediately. 'Complications with a delivery. Jill Andrews will be here in half an hour. Will you tell her to cancel as many of this morning's appointments as she can?'

Then he was gone, his big black medical bag swinging from one hand. She'd expected to hear a car start but she didn't. She hurried to the front room and saw him pedalling a battered lady's bike with the bag stuck in the basket at the front of the bicycle.

What would she do if the telephone rang again? Should she answer it or would that give the wrong impression to whoever were on the other line?

Mrs Andrews was fierce and reminded her of a schoolmistress. She was tall, posh-looking but quite pretty for an older lady. Nancy expected to be sneered at, looked down on, but the reverse was true.

'My dear Mrs Smith, I'm so sorry for your loss. To have been married only one day and then lose your beloved husband. It doesn't bear thinking of.'

'Ta, kind of you to say so. The doctor's rushed off to a complicated delivery. He never told me where he was going but I suppose you know. He said for you to cancel his morning appointments.'

'I'll try and do that but most people don't have a telephone. I'd love a cup of tea if you're making another one soon.'

'I've got to nip down to the post office first but I'll do it when I get back.'

Polly appeared at her feet, somehow knowing she was going out. Nancy swore the dog was looking at the lead and back again as if telling her to pick it up. It was hard to be sad with a dog bouncing around. 'I think I'd better put you on the lead, don't you? Can't have you running off in the street.'

Nancy flinched every time an aircraft flew overhead, however high it was. When she'd been living on base they'd not bothered her. Her Tommy hadn't even been bombed, or machine-gunned; he'd been killed by a piece of exploding Spitfire whilst trying to save a pilot's life. It just wasn't fair.

There were several cyclists, a few folk on foot and a horse and cart, but no motor vehicles at all. She was so lost in her own thoughts and didn't notice if anyone was giving her sideways glances. She didn't care if they were – she'd not be here much longer.

She didn't have to go in as the envelope had a stamp so

just shoved the letter in the post box and began the return journey. She almost collided with two ladies.

'I beg your pardon, I wasn't looking where I was going,' she said with a polite smile.

'I expect you're too busy planning how to ensnare the doctor to notice other pedestrians,' the older of the two – the ma, as she was a matching pair to the other one – said with a sneer.

'I've not got time for your nonsense, madam; kindly let me go by.'

If looks could kill then the one she was getting from the younger one would have finished her off. 'Doctor Denny is too kind to tell you to leave. You're a disgrace, trying to get your claws on him when your own husband's only been dead a couple of weeks.'

Nancy's hand tightened on the lead and Polly growled. That hadn't been her intention but it did the trick. Suddenly there was room for her to walk through between them and the dog didn't stop snarling until they were well away from the nasty pair.

She hurried around to the back door and into the kitchen, not wanting to cry outside. She remembered what David had said and took several deep breaths. After a bit she was all right again. How dare they mention Tommy's name like that? They must be friends of that nasty bitch, Ava.

The dog was sitting patiently by her feet waiting to have the lead taken off. 'Good girl, you soon saw them off, didn't you?'

The phone rang twice whilst she was preparing a tray for Mrs Andrews. She wasn't sure if she should make sandwiches and wrap them in greaseproof paper and put them in the larder for when David came home or wait and do it when he arrived.

The letter needed to get there first and then she'd leave on the bus. She didn't want to put the doctor to the bother of finding her a lift. After what happened when she was out she wasn't sure if she should stay another night.

She was going to do bubble and squeak with fried eggs for tea and then he could finish up last night's apple crumble for afters. He'd said he didn't want her to do any housework but if she didn't go around with a duster, the carpet sweeper and such then it wouldn't get done.

The receptionist cleared a space on her desk for the tray. 'Thank you, Mrs Smith, most welcome.'

'Have you got a few minutes spare? There's things I need to ask you.'

'I'm not busy really. The accounts have been written and I'll hand-deliver them myself when I go home. As there's no surgery things are much quieter. What did you want to know?'

'I'm not sure if I should be making sandwiches and putting them ready for when he comes back. Also, he said he didn't want me to do any housework but it won't get done if I don't do it. It's my fault that Ava left.'

'She didn't leave, she was sacked. About time too, if you want my opinion. There aren't many unpleasant people in this village but I'm afraid she's one of them. All sweetness and light as long as you stay on the right side of her.'

'I think I met two of her mates outside the post office. A mother and daughter, I reckon. Both had fair hair, piggy eyes and big bosoms.'

Mrs Andrews laughed. 'Your description's perfect, my

dear. You've got them to a T. Mrs and Miss Davenport. Celia Davenport, the daughter, has her eye on David so wouldn't be happy having you living here.'

'They must think I'm a nasty bit of work if they believe I'd be interested in anybody so soon after my man died a hero.'

The more Nancy thought about things the more she regretted agreeing to stay. She didn't want to make things difficult for no one so would leave immediately and not cause the nice doctor any more trouble.

David returned at a more sensible speed than he'd departed hours earlier. The baby had been breech, but had delivered safely. His expertise hadn't been needed as the midwife could have delivered the baby without his help. Mother and child were doing well. He didn't deliver many babies as the local midwife was excellent and only called him in when there was an emergency. Fortunately, this didn't happen very often.

He'd not had time for breakfast and it was now almost two o'clock. An appetising aroma of vegetable soup greeted him when he entered the surgery. Jill was talking on the telephone.

'Mr Bevan, the doctor has just walked in. Would you like to speak to him?' Luckily the patient was content with making an appointment for afternoon surgery, which allowed him to check the notes written in Jill's immaculate handwriting.

'Two house calls, I'm afraid. I said you would be there as soon as you were able. Mrs Smith has your luncheon waiting. It certainly smells delicious.'

The kitchen was empty and the table laid for one. The saucepan of soup was keeping warm on the back of the range. There were a couple of salad sandwiches neatly wrapped and waiting in the pantry. Nancy must be resting. He'd eat first and then go in search of her.

He had two helpings of soup and devoured both sandwiches. The kettle was steaming, the teapot warmed and the tea leaves already in it. All he had to do was to pour the water in.

Jill had left but would be back at five o'clock when he had a dozen or more appointments to get through. Before that he had to make the house calls. He called up the stairs to tell Nancy he'd made some tea but got no response.

He didn't want to wake her if she was sleeping deeply. She'd had a bloody horrible time and the more sleep she got the better. Both the patients he visited after lunch were housebound, but neither of them required anything more than reassurance.

Eventually he dumped his bicycle against the front wall of the house at four thirty. Just time for a cuppa and a freshen up before the first patient. He'd expected to hear sounds from the kitchen but there were none. He pounded up the stairs and walked into the room that Nancy was using.

Her kitbag was gone. The bed was neatly made and there was a note on the mantelpiece addressed to him.

Deer Daved
I've got the bus to Chelmsford. I'm going home. Ta ever so for taking me in but folk don't like me being here.
Nancy

He'd heard the bus go past whilst he'd been eating his lunch. If he'd bothered to look for Nancy then he could have stopped her. Something must have happened when she'd gone to the post office to make her change her mind. He bitterly regretted his lack of thought as the East End wasn't going to be a safe place for anyone, and especially not someone as vulnerable as her.

7

Nancy hid in the shadows waiting for the bus to come, not sure in which direction David would return from his emergency call. He was a good man and she didn't want to make his life difficult by staying with him any longer. She had a home in Poplar and that's where she was going.

Her family didn't know Tommy was dead or that he'd died two days before their wedding. As far as she was concerned, she was now Mrs Smith and the baby would be legitimate. The only problem was that they'd expect her to register the baby and have money from the government and she wouldn't get anything.

She'd hardly spent any of her wages since she'd signed up last year and had almost thirty pounds in the bank. If she could find a job then nobody would ever know the true circumstances. Despite feeling so wretched about everything she was chuffed with herself. She reckoned from now on she could talk better – certainly she wouldn't get *was* and *were* confused no more.

People made assumptions when they heard her speak. If she made a bit of an effort she wouldn't be immediately identified and considered common and spoken to like those nasty pair in the village had done.

If David hadn't pointed it out to her then she'd never have made the effort. There must be work somewhere in one of the factories that produced clothes and such. She'd been a decent seamstress before she'd joined up so maybe Mr Hyam would take her on again until she was too big to work.

Eventually the bus trundled up and she hefted her kitbag over her shoulder and scrambled on.

'Here, love, put your bag in this space with the others. You don't want to drag that all the way down the bus. There's a couple of seats at the back.' The conductor looked old enough to be her granddad but was sprightly enough.

'Ta, it's almost as big as me.'

The bus took off whilst she was still negotiating her way. Being in uniform meant people nodded and smiled as she went past. The first available place was next to a fat lady who took up more than her fair share of the seat. No wonder no one else had sat there. Good thing she was a little one herself.

'You based at Hornchurch, dearie? My Trevor's on the guns there.'

'I am. Been on leave but going back today.' It was none of anyone's business what she was actually doing. Pretending she was a normal WAAF made things easier.

The bus lurched and bumped, a few more people squeezed on, and then it arrived in Chelmsford. The conductor hadn't asked her to pay – maybe service personnel travelled free. There was a London train due in half an hour.

Again, she was waved through by the guard and found a corner to prop her kitbag and then sat on it. Bloody hell! Everything in her kitbag had to be returned and signed for or she'd be charged for the lot. She wasn't entitled to wear this uniform she'd been so proud of so had no option but to cross the station and catch a train to Romford. From there she'd walk if she didn't get a lift.

Being a small girl with a large kitbag meant an army lorry stopped to offer her a ride before she'd gone more than a hundred yards. The driver leaned out and grinned.

'Hop in the back, love – that's if you can get over the tailgate. There's half a dozen blokes inside will give you a hand.'

'Ta ever so. Save me the walk.'

When she arrived at the back two young soldiers jumped out, one grabbed her kitbag and threw it over the tailgate, the other picked her up and dropped her inside as if she was no heavier than her bag. They vaulted into the lorry just as it pulled away and both of them sprawled face first, making their mates laugh.

There was scarcely time to get settled before the lorry screeched to a halt outside the gates and the soldier who'd lifted her in reversed the process and the other one tossed her bag out after.

'Ta, boys, much appreciated.'

She showed her pass to the guards and then trudged across to the admin buildings. She ducked instinctively every time a plane landed or took off. Her hands were clammy and her heart was pounding. She staggered into the building and dropped her bag. Several RAF and WAAF members looked at her curiously. She tried to stand tall, march across the lobby, but everything was swirling around her. Her knees buckled and she slid to the lino and from a distance heard voices and then nothing at all.

'LACW 1377, wake up. Can you hear me?'

Nancy opened her eyes. She was stretched out on the floor in an office. Someone had put a folded coat under her head. 'I felt a bit faint...'

'You certainly did, young lady. Now, up you come. You can't lie around on my floor any longer.' The speaker was an officer and Nancy tried to salute from where she was. 'Not necessary, silly girl. Can you stand without help?'

There was no one else in the room. She'd been carried in and dumped on the floor like a sack of spuds. 'I can, ma'am. Sorry to be a nuisance.'

It took two attempts, but then she was upright, still a bit wobbly, but otherwise nothing damaged apart from her dignity.

'Sit in that chair and tell me what you're doing here. As far as I'm concerned you're on sick leave.'

Nancy explained about the medical certificate but was too embarrassed to mention the contents. 'I were... was on me way to London when I remembered I had to hand all me stuff back so I came here.'

'I see. The letter from your doctor hasn't been logged as yet. Do you feel well enough to take your things to the stores and get them signed in?'

'Yes, ma'am. I ain't... I haven't got any civvies so what do I wear after?'

'Good heavens, child, we let you keep what you're wearing. You can hardly walk out of here in your birthday suit. Now, off you go, and I'll see what I can do about the paperwork. I think it unlikely you can be discharged today.'

'Could I see the doctor here and get him to supply the certificate, ma'am?'

'Wait outside. I'll check first if it has arrived from this Doctor Denny.'

There were no chairs in the passageway and Nancy wasn't sure she would be allowed to sit on her kitbag. Then she did so anyway – she wouldn't be in the WAAF much longer so it didn't really matter what anybody thought. Nancy had just got comfortable when the officer called her back.

'Good news. The letter from that doctor of yours arrived this morning. I'll expedite matters as I'm sure you don't want to remain here any longer than you have to.' She cleared her throat. 'I'm sorry for your loss, LACW 1377. Most unfortunate. Dismissed.'

Nancy saluted and marched out. It took two hours to dispose of the contents of her kitbag but at the end of that she had the necessary paperwork to say she'd returned everything and didn't owe the RAF a penny.

She hadn't eaten since breakfast but had no intention of venturing any further than the admin building in case she bumped into anyone she knew. As long as nobody mentioned Tommy's death then she'd be okay.

At five o'clock she left Hornchurch for the last time, looking like a WAAF, but no longer a member. It had been a pleasant surprise to discover she had a few pounds owing to her as well as another three pounds' discharge pay. They'd allowed her to hang on to the canvas haversack and all her worldly goods were inside. Her toilet bag, her sewing kit, plus a few photographs of her and Tommy, and her discharge papers.

If only she wasn't in the family way then she could have stayed in and asked for a transfer. Had she made a real error believing what the doctor had said without any actual proof? She'd burnt her boats so couldn't go back now even if she wanted to. Tommy would be disappointed that she'd given up so easily. She blinked, trying to hide the tears.

She marched out not looking back and walked the two miles to Romford station. This was no problem now she was no longer burdened by her heavy kitbag and wasn't as dizzy as she'd been earlier. Being waved through by the guard for the last time brought a lump to her throat. Her life was going to be different now, not how she thought it would be, but she was going to do the best she could for Tommy's baby.

London looked different from the last time she'd been there. Barrage balloons everywhere, more people in uniform than out, and even more signs on every corner directing you to the air raid shelters. These had been built before she left last year but there hadn't been all the signs and things. She hesitated at the steps that led down to the underground and then decided to take the trolleybus back.

She gazed out of the window, looking but not really seeing anything. Her head was full of what-ifs – what if she had made an error leaving Hornchurch when she might not have had to?

She wasn't looking forward to turning up at home and announcing that Tommy was dead, that she was expecting and was no longer in the WAAF. Ma might be sympathetic but Pa would immediately think she'd had to get married because of the baby. He wouldn't understand that sometimes a doctor could be sure of his diagnosis even after missing only one monthly.

Ruby, her good friend who'd come with her to sign up last year but then changed her mind and stayed at home, was the first person she saw as she turned down Cottage Street.

'Bloomin' heck, Nancy Evans, never thought to see you here.'

'It's Nancy Smith now.' She held up her hand showing the new wedding band and her eyes filled. She was unable to continue.

'Is your Tommy dead?'

She nodded and when Ruby took her hand and pulled her along and into Poplar High Street she didn't protest. There was a little caf they'd used to go to and it was still open.

'You sit down, Nancy love; I'll get us both a nice cuppa and a bun, if they've got one spare.'

This gave her a precious few moments to find her hanky, wipe her eyes, blow her nose, and try and push the misery back where it belonged. She had to get her facts right – she'd been married on Saturday, the last day of August. Tommy had been killed on the 3rd of September. How could it only be two weeks since he'd died? It didn't seem real, none of it did. A while ago she'd been looking forward to getting married on the 5th and now she was out of the WAAF, in the family way and Tommy was dead.

'Here you are. You don't look too clever; get this down you before you tell me what happened.'

Nancy ignored the iced finger but drank the tea. Strong and sweet, just how she liked it. She took a small bite of the cake but despite chewing it a hundred times it refused to go down. Eventually she got rid of it with a mouthful of tea.

'We were married just over two weeks ago and he was killed three days later.' She gripped the edge of the table, took a deep breath and continued. 'We spent the night together two weeks before we got married and I'm expecting. I've left the WAAF and need to find a job.'

Ruby reached out and squeezed her hand. 'There was bombs dropped the other week, Nancy. You don't want to be here once it kicks off. Not in your condition.'

'I've got nowhere else to go. I need to work – I'll only get a pittance from the government and it won't be enough to keep me and the baby when it comes next year.'

'How'd you know you're expecting? Can't be sure for another few weeks.'

'I've missed me monthly and I'm regular as clockwork. I also keep fainting and Doctor Denny was certain enough to write me a letter so I could be discharged from the WAAF.'

'Who's this Doctor Denny when he's at home? Someone where you was based?'

'Jane – you remember I signed up with her – took me to her in-laws in the country somewhere in Suffolk. He's the doctor there. I fainted in front of him, which is how he got involved.'

'All right then. I reckon I can get you into the factory with me if you want.'

'I'm hoping Mr Hyam will take me back until I'm too big to sit behind a sewing machine. I was good at me job and I know he was fed up about me leaving.'

'They ain't making frocks no more – it's shirts for sailors or somethink like that.'

The siren went off and Ruby grabbed her arm. 'There's that public shelter a few doors down – we'll have to go there.'

Outside, people were panicking. ARP wardens were

running up and down, blowing their whistles and shouting for people to take cover. They followed the stampede towards the shelter, stumbled down the steps, and the warden slammed the door after the last person.

It smelt damp and nasty. She reckoned no one had emptied the Elsan. She hoped she didn't have to use it whilst they were down there. There were candles in jam jars positioned on a shelf at head height. Even the smell of smoke was preferable to the contents of the bucket.

There were spiders on the ceiling and one or two ladies were complaining. Then the bombs started exploding. The shelter shook and dust and dirt came down in a shower along with the spiders and cobwebs.

The guns were firing at the bombers. The distinct noise of planes flying overhead added to the horrible noise. There wasn't any room on the benches so she and Ruby stayed up near the door, pressed against the slimy corrugated iron that lined the shelter.

It seemed like hours before the all clear was sounded. Being at the front of the shelter meant that they emerged first. Nancy blinked in the sunlight and looked around. The street was packed with ambulances, fire engines, all of them clanging their bells.

'Someone's copped it – God – I hope it ain't Cottage Street,' Ruby said.

The gutters were running with water filled with soot. The oil had rainbows in it and reflected the dark red glow from the sky caused by burning buildings a few streets away.

'Hurry up, those buggers might be back in a minute. We need to get home and see that everyone's all right.' Ruby grabbed her arm and pulled her in the direction of home.

The Spitfires and Hurricanes were doing their best to shoot down the bombers. The battles were taking place thousands of feet above them – the vapour trails from the fighters crisscrossed the sky. Nancy prayed that her family hadn't been killed in the raid. She'd already lost Tommy – she didn't think she could cope if she lost anyone else.

They dodged around the wardens, firemen and ambulance drivers, ignoring their instructions to stay where they were. Just as they arrived to see, with considerable relief, that no bombs had dropped in their own street, the siren went off again.

'Where do we go? No one here has an Anderson shelter. We'll have to run back to the one in the High Street,' Nancy shouted above the racket.

'There's one for us now at the other end, on the corner. Quick, they sound real close.'

They were the last to tumble down the steps and the door slammed behind them not a moment too soon. For the second time she was standing in the space at the bottom of the steps. There was plenty of room to sit down but she hoped they wouldn't be in there very long so didn't bother.

This shelter was bigger than the other one, was lit by oil lamps as well as candles, and there was a curtained-off area at the far end for anyone caught short. There were rough benches running down either side and a narrow gap between them. Apart from the smell of unwashed bodies it wasn't too bad down there compared to the other one.

Once her heart stopped hammering and her eyes adjusted to the flickering light she began to recognise voices and faces.

'I can hear me ma down there. I can't hear me brothers or

me dad. They must be at the docks.' She'd had to shout to make herself heard over the noise of the bombs dropping. Unfortunately, everyone else was doing the same and she doubted anyone could make sense of anything that was being said.

'I can see her, and me own ma and me nan and two little sisters sitting at the far end. Don't you want to go up there?'

'No, not worth the effort. I'll see her soon enough. This bloody air raid can't go on forever.'

The noise from the bombs dropping, the ack-ack firing and the Spitfires and Hurricanes trying to shoot down the Germans continued for an hour. It had been impossible to ignore the fact that ma was at the other end of the shelter. Nancy had waved but remained where she was.

She and Ruby had found themselves a place on the end of the bench. 'Bleedin' hell,' Ruby said loudly. 'I've got splinters in me arse from sitting on this.'

An old man, snot dripping from his nose, no teeth at all, heard her comment. 'Think yourself lucky you've got anything to sit on, girly, and stop moaning. There's a war on, you know.' He wiped his nose on his sleeve and continued to mutter under his breath.

The lady sitting next to him smiled apologetically. 'Me pa ain't himself. All the banging and such reminds him of the last lot. He were down the trenches in Flanders; never been the same since then.'

'No need to apologise, missus. He's done his bit. He can say what he likes; he won't cause no offence to me.' Ruby's shouted reply was heard by a couple of others sitting on the opposite bench who nodded and agreed.

Several times the shelter shook but the explosions weren't

that close. By the time the all clear sounded Nancy was desperate for a pee and wasn't going to use the communal bucket, not for anyone.

'I'm going to make a dash for home, Ruby, before I wet me knickers.'

8

Nancy was the first out of the shelter and her need was so great she didn't stop to see if any of the houses close by had been hit. The smell of burning, of smoke and cordite, caught the back of her throat as she ran. The front door was never locked and she hurtled through it and out the back where the bog used by the three families in the terrace was situated.

Even though more than a dozen people shared this one WC, it was always clean and neatly cut squares of newspaper threaded onto string were always hanging on the hook inside the door. Having spent the past year using the immaculate ablutions in the WAAF she realised this primitive arrangement wasn't as fresh as she'd remembered. Her standards had improved since she'd last been home.

As she emerged three others burst through their back doors into the yard with the same look of desperation on their faces. She nodded and smiled but didn't stop to talk and was inside in the scullery washing her hands when her mother rushed in.

'Nancy, I couldn't believe my eyes when I saw you. Why are you home, lovey?'

She had rehearsed what she was going to say but instead

she flung herself into her mother's comfortable arms and sobbed. There was no need for her to explain. Ma understood immediately.

'Here, don't take on so, Nancy. Sit yourself down and I'll make a nice cuppa. Your Tommy's bought it? You can tell me how when you feel more the ticket.'

Sometime later the untrue version of events had been shared. Now Ma was in tears. 'Married only three days before he died? Would have been better if you hadn't been married at all.'

Nancy had decided not to say that she was pretty sure she was pregnant because if she did it would only cause complications. Better to wait until she'd missed another monthly and be sure.

'When do you have to go back, Nancy?'

She was about to say that she'd left but then decided to keep that news for later. 'I'm thinking of leaving. I'm a volunteer, Ma, I never signed on for any length of time so they'll let me go.'

'Leave? What do you want to do that for? You've your meals and clothes supplied, get paid every week. Why would you want to come back here and have bombs dropped on you?'

'You're right. I'll get me head together and then go back. I've got to report later tonight. I just wanted to tell you in person.'

'Course you did, lovey. I'm your ma. Who else would you come to? Have you got a couple of quid I could lend, lovey? I'm a bit short in the housekeeping this week what with the bombing and all. It's going to be hard to find anything to put on the table.' Her mother nodded. 'I reckon you don't have much to spend your money on, do you?'

Nancy had a wad of notes and a purse full of coins. She wished she'd stopped to pay them into her post office savings account because if anyone in the family knew she had it they'd take it from her, by force if necessary. Coming home had been the wrong thing to do. There was no life here for her and the baby, especially now that the Germans had begun to drop bombs on the East End.

'I don't have much, Ma, but I can give you something. You don't have to pay it back. What time are the boys and Pa off work? I could go and get us all some nice fish and chips for tea – if the chippy's still standing.'

'They'll be home in half an hour if they ain't been blown up. I reckon there'll be a big queue so you'd better get off.'

Outside the air was acrid. She could smell houses burning not that far away. This was no place to bring a baby into the world. Her plan to find a job as a seamstress again, to live at home, were abandoned. She hurried to the end of the street and out into East India Dock Road. Although there was smoke billowing into the sky there was no apparent damage to any houses, shops or businesses close by.

She joined the queue waiting outside the fish and chip shop but avoided conversation. She knew most of the people in front of her and they probably thought her stuck-up in her posh uniform, but she didn't care.

She carefully extracted two pound notes from her store and pushed the rest inside her brassiere. It should be safe enough in there. If she'd got it out in front of her mother then she'd have lost the lot.

With her arms full of hot, vinegary fish and chips

wrapped in newspaper, she hurried back. Her brothers rarely spoke and they didn't even acknowledge her. Her father nodded and smiled but continued to smoke his fag and stare into space.

They ate their food from the paper and washed it down with more tea. They'd just finished when the siren went off again.

'I won't come down the shelter with you; if I don't go now then I'll be late back and get into trouble.' She slipped her ma the money and then dashed off in the opposite direction to her family who were running, along with everyone else in Cottage Street, towards the shelter nearest to their home.

She raced to the one in Poplar High Street that she and Ruby had used a few hours ago. The door was shut. There was nowhere to hide from the bombs apart from in a shop doorway. If one had her name on it then so be it. There was nothing she could do about it now.

The German planes were almost overhead and she saw bombs falling like black sticks towards the unprotected houses. It was the docks that were getting the worst of it. Not surprising as there was a lot of freshly cut timber stored down there as well as other things – ideal for the incendiary bombs.

This time nothing fell in Poplar as far as she could see and when the all clear sounded she was already halfway to the underground station at Stepney Green. The one at Mile End would have been closest but it was closed, no trains running along that track, and she'd heard that people were already going down there to hide from the air raids.

She'd no idea where to go. Without civilian clothes, and with only her precious savings book and the money stuffed down her bra between her and poverty, she began to regret her hasty decision. Her head spun and her legs were a bit wobbly so to be on the safe side she leaned against a shop window. It was crisscrossed with brown tape and this was supposed to stop the glass blowing out and killing someone passing by. No – she had more money than her ma had ever had in her life. Whatever happened she'd be fine; she might not be like Jane or Charlotte but she was just as strong as they were and just as independent. She couldn't hang about here as it would be dark soon.

She passed a telephone box and decided to call Mrs Stanton, the vicar's wife, as she might have a helpful suggestion. She didn't regret her decision not to stay in Poplar – she might be an East End girl but she no longer felt comfortable here.

She lifted the receiver from the handset, sorted out a pile of coppers to push through the slots, and then dialled the operator. There were clicks and whirrs. She was asked to put in the money and then the phone was answered and she pressed button A. The money fell into the box and she was connected.

'Mrs Stanton, it's Nancy Smith. I'm ever so sorry to bother you but I don't know what to do. There's bombs dropping everywhere and I can't stay with my family. I've left the WAAF. I was hoping you might know where I could stay – a church hostel or something.'

'My dear girl, you must come back at once to Chalfont Major. Jane was horrified when she heard that you'd gone back to Poplar and insisted that if you contacted me I should persuade you to return at once where you can be safe.'

'I'm expecting, Mrs Stanton, and although I'm calling myself Mrs Smith, we both know that ain't... that isn't true.'

'As far as I'm concerned it's a small technicality, Nancy. If your Tommy hadn't been killed you would now be married. Nobody knows apart from Doctor Denny, my husband and I. It's not safe for you and the baby in London.'

'I can't stay with the doctor as people are already gossiping.'

'Of course you can't. You can stay here as originally planned. We have more than enough room for both you, and the baby when it comes. Did you know that Charlotte is now based near Felixstowe? She gets thirty-six hours free every now and again and she's coming to stay the night here next time.'

'I never knew that. Last time I heard from Charlotte she was in the north somewhere. I don't know when I'll be able to get the train and that. I'm going to find a B&B and come in the morning. Ta ever so. I should never have left.'

'No, my dear, you shouldn't have. You must consider this your home for the foreseeable future. I can assure you that you'll have plenty of useful war work to occupy your time. An extra pair of hands is always appreciated when it comes to knitting balaclavas and gloves for the sailors, rolling bandages and so on.'

The beeps went. 'No more coppers, Mrs Stanton. I'll see you tomorrow. TTFN.'

The closer she got to the vicarage the more worried Nancy was about her lack of possessions. She shouldn't be wearing this uniform but had nothing else to put on. Having enough coupons in your ration book didn't mean you could actually buy what you wanted. Though to be fair, clothes weren't rationed at the moment. But there was not even a pair of drawers to be had in Woolworths. God knows how she was going to manage. It was right embarrassing to arrive with nothing as the vicar's wife would then feel obliged to provide what she didn't have.

At least she'd managed to buy a few yards of fire-damaged cotton – more than enough to make herself a frock once it had been washed. Good thing she was a trained seamstress and could make her own clothes. It was underwear she needed. She'd been wearing the same knickers for days and soon they'd begin to pong.

Maybe when they were clean she could turn them into two pairs. They came down to her knees and she reckoned if she made them French knicker length there'd be ample material for at least two. In a few months she'd be needing a maternity smock and then there was the layette for the baby.

She wasn't going to cry. Tommy would want her to be strong and not give up because he'd gone. There'd be thousands of people die before this lot was over and giving in would be like giving that bastard Hitler something to crow about.

The bus stopped a hundred yards from the vicarage. It felt nice, like coming home. Although she'd grown up in the East End she thought she might become a country girl given half the chance. She paused in front of the gate and took several deep breaths. The air smelt better, cleaner, fresher down here. There were birds singing in the trees above her head, the sun was out and she felt safe. Then the drone of incoming German bombers ruined the moment.

Should she go round the back or knock on the front door? There was someone in the garden so she decided to head in that direction. The old black dog shuffled up to her, wagging his tail. 'Hello, back again like a bad penny.'

Mrs Stanton called to her from the bottom of the garden where the vegetables and chickens were. 'Nancy, why don't you put your bag on the bench and come and help me collect the eggs.'

She removed her jacket and hat and put them with the bag. 'I need to use the bathroom first, if you don't mind?'

The vicar shouted through an upstairs window making her jump. 'It's the third door on the left, Nancy.'

She smiled and waved and rushed in just in time. There'd been no need for him to call out as she knew exactly where everything was – she'd stayed there for ten days. Must be something to do with her condition because she'd never had to go for a pee so often before.

Collecting the eggs was a novel experience but not one she enjoyed. It wasn't the smell – she didn't mind that – it was the chickens themselves. They fussed and clucked round her ankles and made her nervous. She was right glad to get out of the run.

'You'll get used to them, my dear. I'm going to make omelettes for lunch so needed some extra eggs.'

'I could do that for you. I'm a dab hand in the kitchen, remember. I'm trained and everything. The officers liked an omelette when we had fresh eggs but they weren't so keen when it was made with that dried stuff.'

'No need to help me with the cooking today, Nancy. We can discuss how things will work over lunch. Tomorrow is soon enough for you to start doing chores.'

'I'm not supposed to be wearing this uniform any more, Mrs Stanton, but I don't have any civilian clothes.'

'I thought that might be the case so have made provisions for you. I've put a selection of things in your wardrobe. There's underwear in the chest of drawers. Why don't you have a quick bath and get out of that.'

Nancy was a bit worried she might smell worse than she thought and once she was in the privacy of her bedroom she sniffed under her arms. Not too bad considering. It was going to be strange having her own room as, apart from the nights she'd been in the village before, she'd always had to share. Back at home, Pa had nailed an old blanket across a corner of the second bedroom and she'd had one side and her brothers the other.

There were three frocks, a couple of skirts and three blouses hanging up alongside a cardigan and a twin set. She rejected two of the dresses as a bit fancy and took the plainest one, navy blue with polka dots and a matching belt, and clean underwear and headed for the bathroom.

The bra was a bit loose but beggars couldn't be choosers and her front would get bigger later on. The drawers were fine. The dress was several inches too long but she had it the correct length in no time. She stepped into it, did the buttons up at the front and pulled in the belt.

There wasn't a mirror in the room but she knew she looked very smart – not at all like an East End girl. Jane had told her that her Oscar had two older sisters and these clothes must have belonged to them. She didn't have any stockings apart from the dirty ones she'd taken off but her sturdy shoes were comfortable enough with bare feet.

The vicar called out from the kitchen. 'In here, Nancy – as you know we don't use the dining room unless there are guests.'

She would have to get used to his unconventional behaviour. She didn't know much about clergymen but she was pretty sure yelling out of windows and so on wasn't usual.

David now had a more suitable housekeeper, Sally Arbuckle, and he was glad that the brief visit of the WAAF girl had precipitated this much-needed change. The house was more settled, comfortable again – not something he'd felt since Julia had died.

Giving away her clothes had probably helped as well – he no longer had the urge to wander into the back bedroom as it was now just another empty room. The house was too big for one person. It had been built as a family home and he decided to contact the organiser from the WVS – the Women's Voluntary Service – and offer to house evacuees. Now he came to think about it he was surprised he hadn't been sent some regardless of his wishes. Possibly because he didn't have a wife to take charge of them.

The East End was being bombed every day and already there were hundreds of casualties. Those children who had returned from the countryside after the phoney war would now be looking for somewhere else to stay. He didn't want children on their own – it wouldn't be suitable with no woman in the house.

His conversation with the efficient lady in charge of such matters was highly satisfactory. 'I'm getting several requests for housing for expectant mothers and those with young families. Would you be prepared to take someone like that?'

'Preferably not someone who is pregnant but certainly a young mother with small children would be acceptable.'

'Your house is perfect for a family. You have a large garden and plenty of space for them to run around. I'm certain I'll be sending you a family in the next few days. I'll ring and tell you who to expect as soon as I know myself.'

Sally was banging about in the kitchen and he could hear her two youngest, George, nine years of age, and Stan, a year older, playing football in the garden.

'There you are, Doctor Denny. There's a lovely slice of rabbit pie and mash for your lunch. My Bertie brings us back a rabbit most days.'

Bertie wasn't her husband but her lurcher – her husband was somewhere in Africa with the army.

'Delicious. I volunteered to take in an evacuee family. A young mother with small children will be coming later this week...'

Her face fell and for a moment he was puzzled. 'Good God, I don't expect whoever comes to replace you. I'm hoping you'll do a few extra hours and be prepared to cook for all of us.'

'I'd be happy to, Doctor. I read somewhere that the mum can only come if the children are under five. You'll need rubber sheets for the beds – there'll be a lot of wet ones. Will you know the age of the little ones before they come?'

'Yes, I'll be notified the day before.'

'You might need a cot as well. If you put them in the back bedroom, the big one overlooking the garden, there's room for a cot in there. They've probably come from overcrowded housing and might well prefer to sleep together in the same bed.'

'There's a small, single bed in the attic. I'll bring that down and perhaps you'd be good enough to make it up with these rubber sheets you mentioned. If the children are small then they can go top to tail.'

'I'd be happy to. Poor little mites. But wherever they come from it'll be a lot nicer for them here.'

'That's the idea. I assume they'll be bringing their ration books with them and will give them to you. I'm not quite sure how this works. Presumably the mother will take care of the children herself, keep her own room tidy and do her own laundry.'

'I should jolly well think so. It isn't a hotel. I expect whoever it is will find your laundry room an absolute marvel. An electric washing machine that heats the water and has its own ringer attached – I've never seen the like. Where did you get it?'

'I had it imported from America. My wife didn't want someone else to do our personal washing and I didn't want her to do it. This was the ideal compromise. There's still the old copper, the mangle and the deep sink and washboard. I know that sometimes it's quicker to do it the old-fashioned way – or so my previous housekeeper told me.'

'Would you mind if I gave it a try with my own things? If it's a good windy day I reckon I could get it dry and ironed before I go home and still get everything done for you.'

'It might be a good idea to see how robust it is before it has to deal with the laundry for a family of small children – possibly with nappies as well.'

He was smiling as he headed for the surgery and his first

patient of the morning. He'd just spent ten minutes talking about laundry. Not something he'd ever expected to do.

Several of the men he'd qualified with were now in the services. His was a reserved occupation, but if this war wasn't over by the end of the year he was going to volunteer. Having poor eyesight shouldn't matter for a medic as he wouldn't have to fire a gun. Whoever took over his practice could keep an eye on the evacuee family and his dog.

9

Nancy wasn't used to talking over a meal. In her family you ate first and then talked. She'd have to get used to the way things were done here if she was going to fit in.

'I thought you might like to join the WI and the WVS and come to meetings with me. It's not just old busybodies and do-gooders, if that's what you were thinking – all the young mothers are members of both of them. It's a way of doing our bit for the war effort when we can't actually join one of the services, work in a munitions factory or something like that.'

'I'd be happy to, Mrs Stanton. I never learned to knit or crochet but I can sew as good by hand as with a machine. Do you have a sewing machine?'

'There's one in the box room. I never got the hang of the pedal underneath that makes the needle go up and down. If you could take over the mending and so on that would be absolutely wonderful.'

'What about me laundry? I don't expect anyone else to do it even if you have someone in for yourselves.'

'I do the ironing. I find it very therapeutic especially since I've now got a lovely modern electric one and don't have to use the flat irons any more.'

'I'd be happy to do the weekly wash. I used to do it for me ma and with three men working on the docks it was hard graft, I can tell you.'

The vicar joined in the conversation. 'If you're going to do the mending and the laundry then that's it. I don't want Nancy to do anything else, Sylvia, is that clear? We must consider her as part of the family and as such we can't expect her to work like a servant.'

She held her breath expecting Mrs Stanton to be upset or cross by his ticking her off like that. Instead, she laughed. 'Giles, I have absolutely no intention of letting Nancy do our laundry. We have someone who comes in to do that for us and it would be depriving them of much-needed income. Taking on the mending is more than enough.'

'I don't want to be sitting about twiddling me thumbs. I like to be busy. I'll do whatever I can to help.'

'Thank you, Nancy my dear; we're going to love having you here. I don't suppose you sing, do you?' The vicar raised an eyebrow.

'I do. I've got a good voice.'

'Excellent, then you can join the choir. Choir practice is tonight. Mr Sibley will be delighted to have an extra member as it's sadly depleted since all the single men and women have now left to join various services.'

Nancy wished she'd kept her mouth shut. The only church she'd ever been in was a Catholic one and then only for weddings, funerals and such.

'I'm baptised a Catholic...' She remembered a priest kicking up a stink when the girl from the street had married someone from the Church of England.

'Did you go to mass and confession every week?'

'Never been to either.'

'In which case, my dear, we shall consider you a lapsed Catholic and free to attend whatever church you wish.'

It wasn't being a Catholic that had made her reluctant to join the choir but the fact that she couldn't read very well and wouldn't be able to follow the words, not of the hymns nor the prayers and so on.

'There's no need to harangue the poor girl, Giles. Nancy can join the choir when she's ready. Let's allow her time to settle in first, shall we?'

The vicar wandered off to his study and Mrs Stanton refused to let her wash up or even clear the table. 'Why don't you go for a walk, Nancy? You need to register at the grocer's so I can use your points when I do the shopping.'

'Will the post office be open this afternoon?'

'Early closing day in the village is Wednesday, so everything will be open today. If you're going there would you be kind enough to buy me some stamps?'

Paying the money into her savings book was a big relief. Nancy kept out a pound for incidentals. She counted the silver and coppers to pay for the stamps and then talked to a few locals who seemed friendly enough. They obviously weren't all like that nasty Ava and her friends.

She stepped out into the sunshine and came face to face with David walking towards his house. He nodded as if he didn't know her and was about to walk past but then stopped.

'Nancy, I do apologise, I didn't recognise you out of uniform. I hope you've decided to make your home here.'

'I have. I went to see my family and there were bombs dropping everywhere. I can tell you I was glad to get away.'

'Do you have half an hour to spare? I need to pick your brains.'

'I've got nothing to do at all. I prefer to be busy, so how can I help?'

'I've got a young woman with two small children arriving from Bow. Her house was bombed yesterday.'

'You're taking in evacuees then? I'm surprised you haven't got half a dozen already.'

David had reached his front gate and he stepped back politely to allow her to go in first. He was a real gent – such a kind man. Pity he didn't have a nice wife to share his life with.

'I've got a new housekeeper. You can hear her boys playing in the garden. She's prepared the bedroom for Mrs O'Brien and her children but I'd really like you to give it a once-over and see if we've got it right.'

'I don't know anything about children, not really...'

'I don't suppose you do at the moment. However, I don't want to overwhelm them, make them feel uncomfortable, out of place, so want to be sure we've set up their accommodation in a way that they're familiar with.'

Nancy's pleasure at having been asked faded. 'I see. You think because I'm from the East End that I'm the best person to ask?'

He frowned at her tone, not understanding why she was offended. 'I can't see the problem, Nancy. Have I upset you by asking?'

'I've just spent a year in the WAAF, Doctor Denny. I've moved on in the world and I'm sure that whoever this woman is she'll soon change her ways to fit in. It's insulting to her and to me to suggest that you should make her room like the back-to-back she's come from. Do you think that we like to live in overcrowded houses?

'Our homes might be small, but every step will be scrubbed clean and every window will be polished with newspaper and vinegar. We might be poor but we stick together, help each other out and don't turn our noses up at anyone.'

This was the longest speech she'd ever made to anyone and from the look on his face he was as surprised as she was.

'I've got this most dreadfully wrong, haven't I? Jumped in with both big feet – Julia always said I spoke without thinking first. I apologise. How can I make it up to you?'

'Mr Stanton wants me to join the choir but I can't read good enough. I'll help you with your family, make them feel at home, explain what's what, if you'll teach me my letters like we talked about before. I'm not stupid – I'm sure I'll get the hang of it quick enough.'

He nodded vigorously. 'Done. Please, I'd still like you to look at the bedroom and make sure everything is as it should be. Sally, my housekeeper, suggested they should all be in the same room as that's what they were used to, but I think that might be a mistake.'

The boys stopped kicking the ball and waved and David waved back. Their mum – the housekeeper – was a lot older than Nancy had expected – in her thirties at least. She had faded blonde hair, watery blue eyes but a lovely smile. David introduced them and she thought she might like her.

'I'll leave you two young ladies to inspect the

accommodation. I've got a letter to write. Nancy, I'll see you at the vicarage after surgery.'

He'd gone before she could say she didn't want to have the lessons there because the Stantons would know she was ignorant and uneducated, and she didn't want to disappoint them.

David had no letter to write; it had been an excuse to get away after his appalling *faux pas*. Both he and Sally had made assumptions about those who were forced to live in the East End. He ran his finger around inside his collar and loosened his tie. He should know better. He was a doctor, for God's sake, and shouldn't have made those suppositions.

He could hear the two young women moving about upstairs and he sincerely hoped Sally wouldn't make the same mistake he had. He rather liked Nancy and admired the way she was taking pains already to improve her speech.

She'd been attractive in her uniform but in that frock she was rather pretty. There was something familiar about her outfit and he couldn't quite put his finger on it. Then his eyes widened. She was wearing Julia's dress – one of the things that had been given to Mrs Stanton for those in need.

He supposed that Nancy qualified as well as the next person as she'd nothing at all to wear apart from the clothes she'd arrived in. He lurked in the surgery until he heard footsteps on the stairs and then emerged with what he hoped was a convincing smile for them both.

'Don't look so worried, Doctor Denny. Whoever's coming to live with you will be delighted with the way you've organised things. The little ones wouldn't be happy away from their ma and there's plenty of room for all three of them and then some over for playing.'

'I'm relieved that you approve, Nancy. I beg your pardon, I should have called you Mrs Smith.'

Her smile was genuine and for some reason he was pleased that she was no longer at odds with him. 'I'll see you later. Nice to meet you, Sally.'

For a small woman she was remarkably graceful even when wearing her unflattering ex WAAF shoes.

'I don't know how she's still smiling. If my Sydney died out in Africa I'd be all over the place for weeks.'

'You wouldn't; you would think about your children and get on with it. There were two young men from here lost at Dunkirk earlier this year and both families have accepted what happened and moved on.'

'That's what you think, Doctor Denny. They might put on a brave face in public but there's plenty of tears in private. Whatever you say, Nancy needs to grieve properly if she's going to get over something like losing a husband a few days after she was married.'

He could hardly tell her that Nancy was pregnant as the information was confidential. If she hadn't been then she would have remained in the WAAF and done her duty without a fuss. She was that sort of young woman.

At eight o'clock he went around to the back door of the vicarage and Nancy was waiting for him. 'We can work in here. It's quiet and Mrs Stanton has gone to visit a friend and the vicar's doing something at the church.'

'Good. I know you'd prefer to study elsewhere, but it

might be misconstrued if you come to my house in the evening when neither Sally nor my receptionist is there.'

'I was worried about them knowing I couldn't read very well but I'm not bothered now. I heard Mrs Stanton talking to him about pestering me to join the choir and saying that I needed time to get used to how things worked in church before I became part of it.'

'Makes sense to me. I found some simple texts, have got a notebook and pencils. I think it will work best if we combine your reading with writing.'

An hour later he was astonished at the progress she'd made. Her handwriting was neat and fluent; it had just been her spelling that was bizarre.

'I'd better get back in case there's anyone having an emergency. I'm the only doctor in the neighbourhood at the moment. God knows what they'll do if I enlist next year.'

Her hand jerked, sending the book she'd been holding to the floor. 'Why would you do that? You just said that there's nobody else to take care of your patients here. You have a duty to them first; that's what I think anyway.'

'I won't go unless I find a locum to take my place. I'm sure there are plenty of retired medics who'd be delighted to take over this rural practice for a year or two. I'm still relatively young and fit – apart from my eyesight. I'm not comfortable being on the sidelines indefinitely. Better that I go, as I'm a single man, than someone with a family.'

'I was hoping you'd be here to deliver my baby, or at least be available if you're needed, but that's selfish I suppose.'

'I can't promise as I intend to apply in the New Year. Of course, they might consider me a liability, as without my glasses I can't see anything worth a damn.'

She smiled and pointed at them. 'You could use sticky tape to fix them to your forehead. That way they wouldn't fall off whatever happened.'

'I'll suggest that to whoever gives me my medical. I'm sure he'll appreciate the suggestion.'

'The Stantons will be back in a bit and I said I'd have the kettle on to make the cocoa. Will you stay?'

He stood up and shook his head. 'Sadly, I must refuse. Bugger – I forgot my torch and it's Stygian darkness out there.'

She giggled. 'I ain't... I haven't the foggiest what that means but you can borrow me torch. I'll pick it up tomorrow.'

'My torch, not "me torch" – that's your next task. Thanks, I'll find something more suitable for you to read and you can take it with you next time and practise. How often do you want to do these sessions?'

'As often as you can. Hang on a tick, it's in me – it's in my bag.' Her footsteps echoed up the stairs and then she rushed back and handed it over. 'You told me not to swear but you just used a bad word yourself.'

'I apologise. Anyway, bad language doesn't sound so bad coming from a man.'

She turned out the central light and prepared to open the back door. They had a vigilant ARP who was revelling in the power of being able to shout at people for letting the slightest glimmer of light out into the darkness.

'Another thing, Doctor Denny, you didn't bring your gas mask with you. Black marks for that as well.'

'Good night, Nancy. I'm glad you're back.'

He was halfway home when he met Mrs Stanton

returning from her friends. 'How did the lesson go, Doctor Denny? We're so pleased Nancy wants to improve her literacy. She'll find life so much easier when her reading and writing is commensurate with her intelligence.'

'She's an able student and made remarkable progress. I doubt it'll take more than half a dozen before she's ready to join the choir.'

The vicar's voice boomed from the other side of the road. 'Good show. The verger's already sorted out a cassock and surplice that will fit her. Good night and thank you for your help.'

David couldn't remember enjoying an evening so much since Julia had died. He felt rather like Professor Henry Higgins from George Bernard Shaw's *Pygmalion* and Nancy was his Eliza. All they needed was a Freddy Eynsford-Hill to fall in love with Nancy and they'd have a full list of characters.

Nancy went to bed happy – well, happy was a bit of an exaggeration, but she was feeling less miserable. Somehow being away from Hornchurch, out of uniform, living somewhere completely different had pushed her old life into the back of her mind. She'd always love Tommy – he'd given her a baby to remember him by – but as long as she stayed away from anywhere that reminded her of him, she reckoned she could get through this.

She was up with the lark and washed out her smalls and also gave the fire-damaged material a good pummel in the sink using the washboard. It came out lovely and would make a smashing frock and a skirt as well if she was clever with the cutting.

During the morning she cleared a space in the box room so she could get at the sewing machine. It was a Singer treadle and in good nick. In fact, it was as good as new.

'There you are, my dear, I was wondering where you'd got to,' Mrs Stanton said as she came in carrying a cup of tea.

'Ta ever so, Mrs Stanton, but you don't have to wait on me. Give me a shout and I'll get my own tea from the kitchen.'

'I try not to shout, Nancy. Giles does more than enough of that for one household. Actually, I came to tell you that the evacuee family have just turned up at Doctor Denny's house. I rather think you might be needed as the young woman and her children are apparently not as impressed with their new surroundings as one might have hoped.'

'Blimey, I'd better get over there smartish and put her right. I reckon being bombed out and then dumped in the middle of nowhere, without her family, among strangers would be enough to set anyone off.'

'Drink your tea first, my dear. Things might settle down. Mrs Arbuckle is a competent young woman and it would take a lot to upset her.'

'What about the doctor? He's used to a quiet life and won't like a lot of ructions.'

'He vanished on his bicycle moments before they arrived. I'm not sure if that was deliberate or he'd had an emergency call.'

'More like running away, if you ask me. You've got everything here I need to sew, mend or refurbish things.

Your sewing box is bursting with reels of thread in every colour. It doesn't look as if it's ever been touched.'

Mrs Stanton laughed. 'That's because it hasn't. I hate sewing and always got somebody else to do it for me. There's an excellent dressmaker and seamstress in the village who's got more work than she can manage. I'm hoping you can make anything I want in future.'

'I certainly can. When my material's dry, could I lend your posh iron? Then I'll cut out a pattern and make meself – make myself a dress and a skirt and then you can see what you think.'

10

Nancy could hear the racket coming from the doctor's house when she was a hundred yards away. The noise was attracting attention from neighbours and passers-by who'd stop to gawp and gossip. The sooner she put a stop to the carrying-on the better. She reckoned David wouldn't return until things were calm again.

She headed straight for the back door and Sally's two boys waylaid her. 'Blimey, Mrs Smith, what's wrong with them kids? You'd think they were being murdered,' the older of the two said to her.

'I don't think you would be very happy if you'd been bombed out and then dragged halfway across the country, would you?'

The younger one joined in the conversation. 'Their mum should put a stop to it. If any of us made that sort of racket we'd get the slipper and really have something to cry about.'

'Go back to your game, lads; it's nothing to do with you anyway.'

She'd expected Sally to be trying to sort things out but instead she was busy in the kitchen as if there wasn't the most horrendous noise coming from upstairs.

'I was hoping you'd come, Nancy. I did my best but I

can't understand a word they say.' This seemed like a feeble excuse and Sally wouldn't meet her eye.

'I'll take a tray of tea, some orange squash and whatever cake or biscuits you've got handy.'

Armed with this she hurried up the stairs, balanced the tray on her arm whilst she knocked. She doubted Mrs O'Brien would hear her over the screaming children so she opened the door and walked in.

There was no sign of the mother. There was a toddler, a girl she thought but it was hard to tell underneath the matted hair and filthy face. The other one was definitely a boy about four years old. She could see crawlers in his hair from where she stood.

'Now then, Sonny Jim, that's quite enough of that noise. I've got biscuits and orange squash but not until you're quiet.'

The screaming subsided to an occasional sob. 'Where's me ma? I want me ma.'

'I'm sure you do. What's your name?'

'Billy and that's me sister Betty. She don't half stink, missus. Give us me drink then.'

She handed him the tin mug and a biscuit. There were nappies in a drawer so she'd clean the baby's bum before she did anything else.

Fortunately, there was a sink in the bedroom as from the smell she was going to need a lot of water. She found some rags and wet one under the tap. 'Here, Billy, let me wipe your face and hands.'

She thought he might object but he sat still and allowed her to take off the worst of the dirt. She would need to have him in the bath with a nit comb before he was allowed into his nice clean bed.

Betty was just grizzling. Both children were painfully thin and she hated to think what sort of home they'd been living in. There were no families like this in Cottage Street because the women would rally round and help out before things got so bad.

From the look of it the baby hadn't been changed for a long time. She could hear Billy munching through the entire plate of biscuits but at least it was keeping him quiet and occupied. The baby's bum was red raw in places and she reckoned David would have to do something about that, but a nice dry nappy would make her more comfortable.

If there was one thing she hated, it was nits. She was bound to be infested herself after this and she was certain that's why Sally hadn't done anything to help. But you didn't leave children in distress and the housekeeper went down in her estimation.

'Billy, I hope you left a biscuit for your sister.'

'I ain't left any.'

'Never mind, I'll make you both some lunch in a little while.' There was a second tin mug on the tray and she held it for the baby who gulped it down eagerly. Nancy wasn't sure if babies should drink squash or if they just had milk in a bottle but the poor little mite was obviously thirsty.

'Come with me, Billy. We're going to look for your ma.'

This was enough to get his cooperation. She snatched up half a dozen towels and pushed a bar of soap into her pocket and then picked up the baby.

Searching for Mrs O'Brien could come later – now she was going to give them both a bath. She just prayed there was a nit comb in the bathroom cabinet as she was going to need it. There was a slight sound behind her and the doctor joined her.

'Good God, they don't look in good shape. I'll give you a hand.' David had guessed where she was heading. 'I'll fetch what we need from the surgery.'

'I'll wait as it might be tricky for you to come in as the door will need to be locked. I'm going to help Billy and Betty look for their mum.'

He understood exactly that the little boy could well object violently to being put into a bath and the door would have to be locked as soon as she stepped into the bathroom with them.

'I won't be long. Check in the box room first.'

He didn't want the children anywhere near the bedrooms in use until they were vermin-free and she didn't blame him.

The box room wasn't full of junk piled in heaps all over the place. It was neat as a pin. There were shelves on both sides and everything was tidily stacked.

'What's in them boxes, missus?'

'Call me Mrs Smith, Billy. I've no idea and we mustn't touch them without asking Doctor Denny's permission. Why don't you go to the window and see if you can see your ma?'

He rushed past her and she almost gagged at the stench coming from his trousers. She remained by the door trying to keep her head away from the baby. She'd put it up today so maybe she'd be lucky and the little blighters would stay on the children's heads and not hop across to hers.

David threw the things he needed into an empty in-tray and

hurtled back up the stairs just as Nancy emerged from the box room, the baby in her arms and the small boy hanging on to her skirt with one grubby hand. She might not know much about children but was doing an excellent job with these two – far better than Sally. He was disappointed in his housekeeper's reluctance to get involved after she'd promised she'd do everything she could to help.

'Right, in we go, young man.' He opened the bathroom door and stood ready to slam it shut and push across the bolt before the child could escape. From the look of them they'd never had a bath in their lives.

'Betty has a really sore backside. Do you have something I can put on it after she's had a bath?'

'Thought that would be the case. I'll do Billy and you do Betty. Let's stand them in the bath. I'll put an inch of water in the bottom and hopefully the lice won't be able to hop off anywhere and then we can send them down the plug.'

'Have you ever seen one of these before, Billy?' Nancy asked.

'I seen one with coal in it. Why ain't there coal in this one?'

'We keep it outside in a special box. This is for us to use. Look, Doctor Denny is putting in the plug and he's going to turn the taps on and get some lovely warm water in the bottom.'

Betty pulled herself upright and was hanging on to the edge of the bath watching with interest. She gurgled and pointed and almost tipped head first over the edge and Nancy grabbed her.

'Wait a minute, baby. I'll take your clothes off. Billy, do you need to have a wee before you get in?'

'I bin in a bush a while back, Mrs Smith. I ain't taking my clothes off – not for no one.'

Nancy ignored the boy's comment and left him to work out a way of persuading Billy that he would feel more comfortable if he was clean and his head was no longer alive with lice.

David hesitated for a moment and then decided firm action would probably work better than prevarication and persuasion. The clothes the child had on would go straight into the boiler to be burnt. He grabbed the back of Billy's collar in two hands and ripped. The cloth was rotten and tore easily. The boy started to howl in protest but he ignored him and did the same with the malodorous trousers.

He then picked the screaming boy up and dropped him into the bath. 'Be quiet. I'll not have that noise in my house. Do I make myself clear?'

Nancy looked at him in shock and he winked. His fierce expression and stern words were enough to stop the noise.

'Right, young man, I'm going to comb your hair with this special comb and remove your livestock. I can promise you that you'll feel much better without them. Put your head forward, there's a good boy. Mrs Smith is going to do the same with your sister.'

After that it was surprisingly easy. It took half an hour to remove the lice but he was pretty sure the children were vermin-free – at least they had nothing alive in their heads now.

'If you pick up the baby, I'll hold Billy whilst the bath empties. I've got the worst of the excrement from his bottom so when we fill the bath again it won't be so smelly.'

Both children sat patiently whilst they had their hair

washed and then a solution of water and methylated spirits was rubbed in. As long as their heads were combed with the metal nit comb every couple of days this should get rid of any that hatched from eggs left on the hair.

'Stand up, Billy. Mrs Smith is going to let out the dirty water and clean around the bath and then will put in some more clean so you can splash about for a bit.'

Eventually both children were persuaded to come out. This time Nancy dealt with Billy and he made no objections to the change.

'Hopefully there's something they can wear in one of the drawers, Doctor Denny. There's a clean nappy on the stool with the pin.'

He smoothed on a liberal quantity of healing ointment and then expertly folded the square of terry towelling into the necessary triangle, pinned it neatly and added the rubber pants which hopefully would stop the urine and faeces leaking out.

'There you are, sweetheart, hopefully you'll be more comfortable now.'

Billy was smartly dressed when he walked into the bedroom and even had on footwear – a pair of almost new plimsolls that had been donated from somewhere.

'I've put out some clothes for Betty. People have been very generous. Have you any idea where Mrs O'Brien might be hiding? I'm sure she could do with a bath and a change of clothes too.'

'Let's get these two fed and watered first and then I'll go in search of her. She can't be far away. I should have been here when they arrived but old Mrs Tolley had a fall and I had to check if she'd broken anything.'

'I hope Mrs Arbuckle has got something ready for their lunch even if she wasn't prepared to do anything else.'

'I hope so too.' Nancy left with Billy who seemed happy to go with her and was no longer asking where his mother was.

The baby started to grizzle and was sucking her fist. 'I think you're hungry, my girl, so let's get you dressed and downstairs and then you can go into this lovely clean cot for an afternoon nap.'

Both children ate more than they should but he hadn't the heart to stop them. Sally still seemed reluctant to approach the children. This was going to be a problem as without her assistance this evacuation wasn't going to be successful for anyone.

Betty fell asleep on his lap and he carried her upstairs and put her gently into her cot. He pulled a blanket over her sleeping form and was about to tiptoe out when Nancy appeared at the door carrying Billy.

He was surprised that she pulled back the covers and didn't just lay him on top.

'He might wet the bed,' she whispered as she removed his trousers and plimsolls. 'There's a rubber sheet under him so only the bottom one will need to be changed if he does.'

They left the door open so they could hear the children if they woke and crept back downstairs. Sally had gone – an hour earlier than was usual for her – and this added to his concern about the future.

'We know Mrs O'Brien isn't in the house. I think one of

us must remain in earshot of the little ones and the other search the garden and outbuildings.'

'I'll stop here; you go and look.' She hesitated before continuing. 'I reckon she's long gone. She wouldn't put her kiddies in a home, but leaving them here? She wasn't coping and now she can go with a clear conscience, knowing her children are in a better place than they would be with her.'

'Good God! You think she's abandoned them? What the hell am I going to do with two small children?'

'I don't like to speak behind her back, but I wouldn't be surprised if that Sally don't come back either.'

'I fear you're correct, Nancy.' He'd noticed she was no longer using his name so maybe he'd better address her more formally. 'I apologise. Should I have called you Mrs Smith?'

'No, Nancy's all right with me. I didn't like to call you David in front of anyone else but when we're together, like, we'll stick to the arrangement.'

'Would you be kind enough to answer the telephone if it rings? If it's an emergency yell out of the back door. I won't be so far away I can't hear you shouting.'

She smiled. 'The vicar's a one for yelling and Mrs Stanton isn't too keen on that. I like that he does it – makes him seem a bit more like a normal person.'

'I won't be long.'

There were no phone calls and when she checked on the children they were still fast asleep. David returned and by then the washing-up was done, everything neat and tidy and the kettle hissing on the range ready to make another cuppa.

'No luck – she's definitely not in my garden. There were a couple of people walking along the path outside and I asked if they'd seen her. They hadn't, but promised to spread the word.'

'The bus would've come whilst we was busy in the bathroom. She'll have got on that.'

'I'm going to ring Mrs Arkwright, the WVS lady who arranged this. We need to know more about Mrs O'Brien's home circumstances.'

'I'm going to nip back to the vicarage and tell them what's what. I won't be a tick.'

He nodded and headed for the telephone in the hall. She had to go past the bus stop in order to get back and noticed an old bloke sitting in his garden watching who passed by.

'Excuse me, sir, did you see a young woman, a stranger, catch the bus earlier?'

'Three got on, no one got off, and I knew all of them. You lost that girl from London with the screaming kiddies?'

'We have. So, you're certain she hasn't gone past here?'

'I've not seen no one I don't know this morning.'

'Ta. Could you keep an eye out for her and let Doctor Denny know if you see her?'

The old man nodded but didn't answer. She rushed across the road and up the path to the vicarage. The front door was, for some reason, standing open.

'There you are. I was waiting for you. Giles found Mrs O'Brien in the church and brought her here.' The vicar's wife had met her in the porch.

'Thank God for that – we thought she'd done a runner.

We've sorted out her kiddies but I reckon she'll need the same.'

'Don't worry, everything has been taken care of. She's got a pretty frock on, everything clean and fresh and no unwanted livestock anywhere.'

'What's she like? Billy and Betty were half starved and not had a wash for weeks. She can't be much of a ma to them. You'd think her family or her in-laws would step in.'

'That's the problem, Nancy. Mrs O'Brien has no in-laws and her own family wanted nothing to do with her. The children have different fathers. Need I say more about her occupation?'

'Blimey! That'll give the gossips something to talk about, if ever they know. I've got to get back as I've left the doctor in charge and he's got surgery in half an hour. Is Mrs O'Brien coming with me?'

'I think the poor girl is at the end of her tether. Being bombed out was the last straw and she must have gone to the church to pray for help. Whatever her occupation in the past, this can be a fresh start for her and the children, and there's no need for anybody to know the truth.'

'Won't hear it from me, that's for sure. As far as everyone's concerned Mrs O'Brien's a war widow who lost her man at Dunkirk.'

'That's what we thought we'd tell everyone. Come and meet her. I'm hoping Doctor Denny will be able to help because I think she's having a nervous breakdown.'

'Not surprised with what she's been through. I think Mrs Arbuckle's going to leave. I was shocked at how she reacted to the children. It ain't – it isn't their fault they had nits and such. The doctor was really good with them but he won't be able to manage if Mrs O'Brien is poorly and his housekeeper's gone.'

'I think you must step in, Nancy my dear, and become his paid housekeeper. You will continue to live here and go there every day as Mrs Arbuckle has been doing. If you make the arrangement professional that will be easier for both of you and I'm sure being gainfully employed is exactly what you'd like.'

'If he asks then I'll do it but I'm not going to suggest it myself. Then I can pay for me board and lodgings and won't feel beholden.'

'Mrs O'Brien's given name is Violet. I warn you that she's very unresponsive.'

'If she's not talking then how do you know so much about her?'

'I got in touch with Mrs Arkwright and she told me in confidence. I think she's rather ashamed of foisting such a difficult family on the doctor without any warning.'

'No, I reckon she did the right thing. If Violet's not well then the best place for her is with him.'

Having been forewarned about what to expect Nancy didn't react badly when she saw the pitiful young woman huddled in a chair by the range. She was even thinner than her children but dressed in fresh clothes she didn't look too bad.

'Mrs O'Brien, I'm Mrs Smith, but you can call me Nancy. I've come to take you back to your children. They've been bathed and fed and are now sleeping but they could wake up at any time and Doctor Denny has his surgery to do.'

Violet didn't speak, didn't even nod, but pushed herself upright and waited to be told what to do next. Nancy put her arm into hers and guided her through the house and out into the street. Anyone seeing them wouldn't know how bad things were, that her companion was hanging on to her arm, barely able to support herself.

David was unsurprised when one of Sally's boys appeared with a hastily scribbled note saying that she was no longer able to work for him. His receptionist saw him read it and guessed the contents.

'Surely Sally hasn't handed in her notice? I thought she was so happy here and was certainly an improvement on Ava.'

'To say I'm disappointed is an understatement. She didn't like the evacuee family because they were lousy and filthy. Nothing a bath and a nit comb couldn't sort out.'

'It was the same thing for two of the families that took in evacuees last September. Just look at the children now. You wouldn't know they hadn't been born and bred here. They're going to find it hard going back when the war's over.'

'I can't come into the surgery until Mrs Smith returns – hopefully with Mrs O'Brien who, it seems, wandered off and ended up in the church.'

'Why don't you ask Mrs Smith to be your official housekeeper? As long as she lives at the vicarage then I'm sure no one will comment.'

'I intend to do so. From what I've been told Mrs O'Brien is

in a bad way mentally and I'm certain won't be able to cope with her children for a while. Mrs Smith was exceptionally good with the little ones and I'm sure she'll be happy to help out in that department as well.'

The telephone rang shrilly and Jill hurried off to answer it. He checked his watch – the children had been asleep for almost two hours and were bound to wake up soon. His first patient was due in twenty minutes so hopefully Nancy would be back by then.

He dashed upstairs to check and all was quiet in the bedroom. He reread the note and frowned. Sally had asked for her wages for the days she'd done this week, which he was disinclined to give her. She should have given him a week's notice and, both legally and morally, he could hold back her money in lieu of notice.

It might be his right, but he wouldn't do it. Sally needed the money and he sincerely hoped she'd find herself some other employment to make up the deficit. The pitiful amount she got from the government wasn't enough to feed a growing family. A serving soldier gave up a portion of his wages and this was paid directly to his family. It was up to the soldier how much he parted with and from what he remembered about Sydney Arbuckle, he would put himself first every time.

There was the crunch of footsteps on the path outside the kitchen window and his missing guest was led into the kitchen. The young woman, scarcely more than a girl really, was blank-eyed and he wondered if she might be better off in an asylum, but then decided she'd recover quicker with her children nearby, even if she didn't wish to interact with them at the moment.

'Sorry I've been so long, Doctor Denny, but you can see how things are. I think Mrs O'Brien, Violet, might be better on her own at the moment. What do you think?'

'I agree. I don't have time to go into details but would you be prepared to take on the role of housekeeper and so on? I'm really going to need your help and so is this unfortunate family.'

'I'd be happy to. The family comes first – I'm afraid everything else will have to take second place.'

'Absolutely. Sorry, I've got a patient coming any minute and have to read their notes before they arrive.'

He watched her lovingly escort poor Violet into the bedroom opposite the one that her children were in. He no longer thought of it as Julia's room.

There was no time to worry about what was happening upstairs. He couldn't do his job efficiently if he didn't concentrate on what was in front of him. By seven o'clock he'd seen his last patient, Jill had written out the invoices and he was ready to venture back into his house. He'd kept the communicating door shut so if there'd been trouble with either of the children or their mother, he wouldn't have heard it.

'Out of the seven patients you saw tonight, Doctor Denny, only two of them will pay you actual money for your services. Over the next few days you'll receive rabbits, poultry, jam and vegetables. You really should be firmer with those people.'

'They give me what they can afford and it means less has to be spent on food. Now I've got three extra in my household, being paid in rations will be ideal.'

She smiled, said good night and, after pulling on her

gloves and pinning on her hat, she left to return to the home where she lived on her own with only three cats for company. Jill had worked for him since he'd bought the house twelve years ago and, if he was honest, she seemed happier now she was a widow than she'd been as a wife. She was about his age and he had to tread carefully where she was concerned as he was pretty sure she had a soft spot for him.

There was an appetising aroma drifting down the hall. However, the house was worryingly silent. Where was everyone?

He walked to the kitchen window and his hands unclenched. There was no sign of Violet but Nancy was in the garden playing with the children and the dog was joining in. Betty could toddle around unaided and was squealing with excitement every time Polly came over and licked her. Not very hygienic but it didn't matter as long as the children were content.

The table was laid for two adults and two children and there was a tray ready to be taken upstairs. A highchair had mysteriously arrived during his absence and this would make things so much easier. He headed outside to join in the fun.

'Doctor Denny, the children have never had any contact with dogs or cats. Polly's kept them entertained for ages.'

'She loves little ones and would never bite them, whatever they did to her.' He gestured with his head at the bedroom window with the drawn curtains.

'She's still asleep. I got her to drink a cup of tea and eat a sandwich. So far she's not said a word, shown no interest in Billy or Betty. I'm really worried about her.'

He checked the children were occupied and couldn't overhear their conversation. 'Most doctors would have her sent straight to an asylum but as long as she's not dangerous I want to keep her here. I don't know a great deal about mental illness but I'll do my best. It certainly won't do her any harm to sleep undisturbed in a warm, comfortable bed for a change.'

'When I got them up I took them in to see that their ma was back. I told them she's not very well and that I'll be looking after them instead. I don't know how we're going to manage this, David, because I can't stay here overnight and you might get an emergency call.'

'I could have asked my receptionist but...'

'But she's after you herself so it wouldn't be a good idea to have her here any more than it would to have me living in.'

He grinned. 'You're very observant and absolutely right. If I get called out tonight can I ring you? Would you be prepared to come over and stay here until I get back? I'll try and sort out something more satisfactory as soon as I can.'

'I remember me brothers had me – had my ma up and down half a dozen times some nights. I reckon these two might get you up. Billy will probably wet the bed and Betty might want something to drink. Who's going to do that?'

'I'll do it until I can find someone else. I'm quite capable of changing a wet sheet and finding a baby something to drink. I'm a medical man – not a nitwit.'

'I don't know any other bloke who'd be prepared to do women's work like that. You're a saint, and no mistake,

David. But you need your sleep and it isn't your job to tend to Violet's children in the night. She's supposed to be looking after them.'

'The only alternative is to get Mrs Arkwright to hand the children over to someone who will put them in an orphanage. Do you want me to do that?'

She didn't like being asked that sort of question. It wasn't any of her business and it wasn't fair of him to put her on the spot like this.

'It's your decision, not mine. I'll do what I can, but unless I'm living in, which we both agree isn't a good idea, I can't see that you can keep Violet or the children here.'

Betty fell flat on her face and screamed and she rushed across to pick her up. 'There, nothing hurt, baby, so no need for all that noise. Shall we go in and have our tea? Are you hungry, Billy?'

He stared at her as if she was talking nonsense. Then he sidled up to her and grabbed her hand. 'We had somethink to eat earlier. Do we get another feed today?'

She blinked back tears. It wasn't fair that these two had had such a hard life. Children shouldn't have to go hungry. 'Whilst you're here, Billy, you get three meals a day. You get breakfast when you get up, lunch in the middle of the day before you have a nap and tea before you get ready for bed.'

'What, Mrs Smith? Every day?'

David overheard him. 'Yes, young man, nobody goes hungry under my roof. Something really delicious is cooking in the kitchen. Shall we go in and see what it is?'

Nancy thought she might have to feed Betty but the toddler crammed the food in with her hands and Billy would have done the same if David hadn't stopped him and showed him how to use the knife and fork.

She'd taken up the tray and woken Violet but the girl had just turned over and gone back to sleep, ignoring the food.

After tea she removed the food stuck all over the children's faces. It was almost dark and she was pretty sure children of this age should already be fast asleep and not eating their tea so late. Hopefully, things would settle down after a few days and they wouldn't sleep for so long in the afternoon.

'It's time for bed now. I'm going to take you upstairs to have a nice wash and clean your teeth. Then I'll tell you a story once you're in bed.'

The children settled down quickly and she crept out to collect the uneaten food from the other bedroom. There was something she needed to ask David about her own situation. He was in the kitchen and had made two mugs of cocoa and used all milk and no water. That was a real luxury and no mistake.

She waited until they were sipping the lovely warm, sweet, chocolatey drink before asking her question.

'Why haven't I been feeling dizzy like I did last week? Does it mean I'm not actually expecting? Shouldn't I be feeling sick and all in the mornings now? It's been almost three weeks since I missed my monthlies.'

'Are your breasts tender? Are you having to urinate more often?'

She choked on her cocoa and the heat rushed from her toes to the top of her head. How could he ask her something so personal when they were just sitting at the kitchen table?

He ignored her coughing and just sat there looking

professional, waiting for her to recover from her embarrassment and be able to answer.

'Yes to both of them questions. A right nuisance having to run to the bog all the time.'

'Then my original diagnosis remains the same. It's quite possible your dizziness was caused by not eating. I'm sorry to tell you that morning sickness doesn't always start in the first weeks and you could still suffer from it.'

'Am I likely to have twins like me ma?'

'It's quite possible, I'm afraid. They do run in families.'

'Blimey, it's going to be hard enough with one, let alone two babies.'

'Let's not worry about it now. I'm beginning to think our arrangement isn't good for you even if it suits me. I think I might have come up with a satisfactory solution but I'd still like you to be my temporary housekeeper, if you don't mind.'

Should she tell him that she was relying on his money? He didn't understand what it was like for ordinary folk – he obviously had plenty if this house is anything to go by.

'I need the work, David, especially as I might be expecting twins.'

'If you're sure you want to continue then I'd be delighted to make the job permanent. When you have your child you can bring it with you – there'll be no need for you to stop work.'

'What's your solution then?'

'A colleague of mine, who works at St Thomas's in London, has found me a couple whose house was destroyed and they're looking for live-in employment. Mrs Brooklyn has worked as a nanny and I thought she could look after the children and their mother, and Mr Brooklyn can take care of the garden. They will be arriving sometime tomorrow.'

'Just the ticket – that means there'll be someone here of a night. I'm happy to cook for everyone but I reckon you'll have to eat separate like, in the dining room. I'll eat at the vicarage and them – those new people – can eat in the kitchen with the children.'

'You don't have to worry about feeding Billy and Betty, or their washing and so on. Mrs Brooklyn is going to be employed to take care of everything to do with Mrs O'Brien and her progeny.'

'Doesn't make sense to have two cooks in the kitchen. She can make their breakfast and tea and I'll do their hot meal at lunchtime.'

'As you wish. We need to make this official, Nancy. Your wages will be the same as I gave Sally. Did I hear you say that you're a seamstress?'

'I am. Part of me duties – my duties will be to take care of your mending.'

'Good God, I didn't ask because of that. People have been donating all sorts of things for the children and Violet but none of them are the right size.'

'Don't worry about that, I'll soon alter them to fit. Mrs Stanton has got a lovely treadle machine and I'm going to use that to make my own clothes. I'll do what's needed for the children and Violet first.'

'Another thing, as the Brooklyns will be living in then we can continue your lessons here in future.'

'Righty ho. I'll be off now. I'll take those clothes and get on with that tonight.'

★

David had only told her half the story. His friend, Toby Sotheby, the doctor who was sending him the Brooklyns, had also suggested that Dr James Rankin could take over the Chalfont Major practice. Rankin, a bachelor, was in his sixties and finding working in the casualty department too much for him. David was going to London to discuss this possible exchange of duties once things were sorted out here.

Working in a big teaching hospital where injured servicemen and civilians were being treated was the perfect compromise. No one could say he was shirking his duty as he would be in constant danger from the bombs being dropped every day with such devastating results.

He'd spent two years in a busy casualty department, had completed half his surgical training, before he'd met and fallen in love with Julia. She hadn't wanted to live in London so he'd bought this practice and whilst she'd been alive, he'd not regretted his decision.

Fortunately, he got no emergency calls that evening and didn't have to ring the vicarage and ask Nancy to come and sit with the children. He worked late sorting out his paperwork, making sure his patients' notes were up to date so Rankin, or someone else, would be able to take over without difficulty.

He jerked awake the next morning, his heart racing, thinking he'd forgotten to do something essential. The children – it was after seven o'clock and he'd not even checked on them. He tumbled out of bed and dashed, still in his pyjamas and bare feet, down the passageway.

The room was empty. He checked on Violet and she was fast asleep. He could hardly go downstairs as he was. Then he smiled. Nancy was here and the children were in the kitchen with her. He'd stop panicking as he could hear them chatting and laughing.

He nicked himself twice when shaving in his rush to get ready. He was downstairs within fifteen minutes of waking up and he thought that might be a record.

'Good morning, Doctor Denny, just in time for tea and toast. The children are having porridge first – would you like some?' Today Nancy wasn't wearing Julia's old frock but something floral. It fitted her perfectly and was much more her style than navy blue with white spots.

'Good morning, Mrs Smith. Good morning, Billy, Betty. I can't believe you didn't wake up in the night.'

Billy answered with his mouth full of porridge. 'I found the po and never wet me bed at all.'

'Well done, I'm very impressed. I'll have tea and toast, please, Mrs Smith. I'm not an aficionado of porridge even with sugar and cream.'

'Are you telling me you don't like it? You use such funny words I don't understand you half the time. Tea and toast coming up.'

He could hardly believe two such traumatised children had settled in so quickly and were apparently content. 'I'll take up something for Mrs O'Brien when I've finished. I want to try and persuade her to eat and take an interest in her surroundings.'

'She got up to use the bathroom. The chain hadn't been pulled when I went to empty the pot.'

'Excellent. Maybe things aren't quite as grim as we feared.'

'I'll not be able to do much housework as I'll be looking after the kiddies. I'll have a quick rush around when they have an afternoon kip. I've got plenty in the pantry for the next couple of days. I found a bag of vegetables and a couple of rabbits on the doorstep when I came in.'

'I'll skin and clean them for you – I don't suppose you want to do that.'

She surprised him by laughing. 'Blimey, I went on a butcher's course. A couple of bunnies are no trouble at all.'

'I get paid in kind a lot of the time round here.'

'Thought as much. You're not doing this job for the money – you couldn't live like this if you were.'

'Live like this? Not sure what you mean.'

'Either you come from a wealthy family or you married money, that's for sure. I don't reckon that anyone else within a hundred miles has got one of them electric washing machines.'

'Both are true. I'm very comfortably situated and consider myself fortunate to be so.'

He was uncomfortable talking about his financial circumstances and she really shouldn't have brought the subject up. Julia had thought money was vulgar and they'd never discussed it.

Violet was sitting up in bed, which was an improvement. She didn't look exactly animated, but her eyes were focusing better.

'Good morning, I hope you slept well. Billy and Betty are

eating breakfast in the kitchen and I've brought yours up for you.'

She looked at him blankly as if she didn't understand what he was saying. However, when he put the tray across her lap she picked up the tea and drank it immediately.

'Violet, do you know where you are?' She ignored him, drained the mug and then started on the toast. He tried again. 'I'm Doctor Denny. You were brought here because your house was bombed and you had nowhere else to go. This is going to be home for you and your children until the war's over.'

She continued to eat. Finished both slices and then pushed the tray aside and slid back under the covers. Only his fast reaction saved it from crashing to the floor. Yesterday she hadn't eaten anything apart from half a sandwich so maybe once she was in better physical shape her mind would begin to recover too.

She didn't look depressed, more disinterested in the world around her. When he went up to London tomorrow he'd find a consultant who knew more than he did about this sort of thing. He wasn't going to rush into anything – if this Rankin chap wasn't suitable for a country practice, he'd take this particular offer no further.

He was determined to find himself a position in a hospital with a casualty department in the thick of things and find a locum to take over from him here for the duration. The General Medical Council should have a list of retired general practitioners and there was bound to be somebody who would jump at the chance of doing something useful again.

12

The Brooklyns soon settled in and Nancy was impressed with the way Mary – they were on first-name terms almost immediately – got on with the children. She was firm but loving and they responded to her care and were almost unrecognisable as the poor little scraps that had arrived from London covered in nits and filth.

Since she'd now missed her third monthly there was no doubt she was expecting. Like David had warned her she was now feeling sick on and off all day. At least she wasn't fainting all over the shop nowadays.

He'd been to London a couple of times but hadn't told her why and it wasn't her business to ask. It was getting dark earlier and the weather was wet and windy; she reckoned the trees would be bare before the end of November.

She continued to have reading and writing lessons and now she was as good as she was going to get. Spending this time alone with him had begun to be something she looked forward to. She thought of Tommy most days but she didn't miss him as much as she'd expected to. David had been miserable for months after his wife had died but then they'd spent ten years together. She and Tommy had only known each other a few months and she reckoned they'd not spent more than a week – if that – together.

'I've been to church a couple of times and I've joined the choir now. I can read the prayer books and that, and I know a lot of the tunes and don't need your help any more. From now on Mary and Fred are going to bring the children to church with them as I won't be here of a Sunday morning.'

'I was going to say the same thing, Nancy. You've been an apt pupil and it's been a pleasure to teach you.'

'Ta, David, I've really enjoyed learning with you. I don't miss Tommy as much now and I'm not sure if that's a good thing or not. He's only been gone a few months and I think he deserved to be mourned for longer.'

'Nonsense, there's a war on. Hundreds of people are being killed every night in London in the bombing raids, not to mention the dozens of RAF bods who are constantly shot down. There's no time to dwell on what might have been – like everyone else who's lost a loved one you just have to get on and put it behind you.'

If he believed this why hadn't he followed his own advice? She and David were as different as chalk and cheese, but they got on all right. He was a good man and she no longer thought of him as old.

'Billy and Betty are happy as larks with Mary looking after them. Fred has turned your garden into an allotment and I reckon we'll have enough vegetables and that to feed an army next year.'

He laughed. 'Not to mention the two pigs we've got now. They're a shared project with three other neighbours. They bring their leftovers to feed them and when I have them slaughtered next year, we'll share the meat.'

'I don't mind the pigs; I still can't get on with your chickens, especially now you've got another dozen. I like the eggs well enough, and the meat, but I'm really glad you've got Fred to take care of them. Mrs Stanton doesn't ask me to fetch the eggs for her now that I'm working for you.'

'Everything is going along smoothly here, apart from Violet. Although she's eating and is now going out into the garden occasionally, it bothers me that she hardly speaks and completely ignores the children.'

'I don't reckon she recognises them. Billy's been invited to tea and is ever so excited, bless him. Betty never stops chatting and is running about safe as houses now. Mind you, you can't understand half of what she says.'

At the end of their lesson he always made cocoa for them both and tonight was the same. He seemed restless. Several times he started to say something and then changed his mind. Something was up and no mistake.

'Did I tell you that my friend Charlotte's finally coming for a visit? She's got some important hush-hush job that she can't talk about. Not like me – I didn't get special duties. Mary's happy to take over my work while Charlotte's here.'

'You've not had any time off since you started and you should have every Sunday free in future. I wanted to talk to you about something else. You'll be coming out of your first trimester soon and you're going to have to see the midwife in a couple of months.'

'I'm beginning to show a bit as well. My belly's much bigger, but me bum hasn't changed at all.'

He smiled. 'No one would know that you're pregnant at the moment. I'd like to examine you myself before I go...'

'Go? Where are you going? You've not gone and signed up have you?'

'No, but I'm moving to London to work in the casualty department of the Royal Free Hospital. Doctor Simon Jones will be taking over here. He'll be arriving first thing Monday morning. I'll stay a day or two and introduce him to everyone before I leave myself.'

She didn't know what to say. She was used to seeing him every day, making his meals, doing his laundry and that. He was funny, kind and generous and not like anyone else she'd ever met. She swallowed the lump in her throat.

'Well, better that than being sent to Africa or something I suppose. Is it an old geezer coming to do your job?'

'He's fifty-three but looks younger. He's a widower like me but has three grown-up children scattered around the various services. I'm sure he'll be only too happy to tell you all about them.'

'If you like him then he's all right with me.'

David collected the empty mugs and took them through to the scullery and then waited for her at the door. 'Come through to the surgery; you'll feel more comfortable there.'

She wasn't comfortable about him looking at her at all. What if he wanted to poke about inside her? She'd just die of embarrassment. She wasn't going to do more than pull up her frock and pull down the front of her knickers.

There was a smart green screen pulled around the bed and she scuttled behind it.

'There's no need to undress…'

'I wasn't going to. I'm ready now.'

He was so calm and professional she soon calmed down.

His hands were a bit cold but he knew what he was doing. He took a long time examining her bump.

'What do you think? Is everything all right?'

'Everything's absolutely splendid. I'm certain as I can be that you're carrying only one baby.'

'Thank God for that.'

He left her to climb down from the examination table – it was too hard to be called a bed. She could hear him in the waiting room and hurried out to join him.

'Ta for that, David. I'm going to tell Charlotte when she comes tomorrow. I wrote to Jane the other day and told her. I'm ever so grateful that I can now send letters to my friends because of you.'

'My absolute pleasure, my dear. Do you have your torch?'

She didn't have her gas mark as nobody in the village bothered to carry one. 'From the sound of it I'd be better off with an umbrella. See you in the morning.'

David was going to miss the time he spent with Nancy. She'd metamorphosed from a brash East End girl into a confident young woman. He was somewhat put out that she still regarded him more as a father figure than a contemporary.

Over the past few weeks there'd been the stirring of something close to desire – if she'd shown the slightest interest in him as a man he might have been tempted to act on it. Good God! What was he thinking? Not only was she pregnant, but the father of her child had been dead for not much more than a couple of months.

It would have been taking shameful advantage if he had taken her to bed. It had been more than three years since he'd slept with anyone and he thought he'd never want to after Julia died. He'd always be grateful that Nancy had been the catalyst to his moving on and beginning to live his life again.

He could scarcely remember Julia's face now. He must have loved her but he couldn't remember that emotion any longer. When he thought about her, which was rarely, it was like thinking about someone he scarcely knew. Had he really been as deeply in love with her as he'd always thought?

He wasn't sure he ever wanted to get married again but he was rather hoping he might meet a like-minded, experienced female doctor or senior nurse once he was settled in London.

The Royal Free Hospital had pioneered medical training for women and there were quite a few on the staff and even a handful of female consultants. He hadn't needed to apply for a position there. When he'd turned up, they'd pounced on him with eagerness and gratitude.

He didn't go to church on a regular basis, just attended at Easter and Christmas and so on. However, tomorrow he would go as he rather liked seeing Nancy looking angelic in her choir robes. Already her ability as a seamstress was bringing a stream of customers to the vicarage hoping she would alter, mend or make some item of clothing or other.

Mary and Fred attended church every Sunday and formerly the children had remained with Nancy. He hoped they behaved themselves in this new situation. He'd told his employees of his intention to depart in the middle of next week and they'd been remarkably supportive.

This morning he walked with them and the children up the road to the church.

'What if I want a wee, Auntie Mary?'

Billy had started to call his nanny this of his own volition and Mary had seemed happy to let it continue.

'You will just have to wait, young man, like all the other children who will be sitting quietly on their best behaviour in the congregation.'

'What if Betty…'

'Enough of the silly questions. You only have to remain with the grown-ups for a little while and then you and the other children go out to Sunday school. Remember I explained that you will draw pictures and listen to stories.'

'Betty can't draw anything.'

'Betty will remain with Auntie Mary,' Nancy said. 'She's too young to go with you. You're a big boy so you are allowed to go but she has to sit on someone's lap and be very quiet.' David was holding the child's hand as Mary was carrying Betty. Fred, although pleasant enough, avoided contact with the children if he could.

As always, the church was full. Apart from the occasional Saturday night social at the village hall there was little opportunity to dress up and go out. It wasn't called *Sunday best* for nothing.

They were fortunate at St Mary's to have a decent organ and still someone to play it. The congregation stood up to sing the first verse of the first hymn whilst the vicar led the choir down the central aisle.

He heard Nancy before he saw her. She was the most beautiful contralto and was singing with confidence. He wanted to turn round and look, as many others were, but managed to restrain himself.

As she walked past Billy piped up. 'Cor, that's our Mrs

Smith. I never knew she could sing so good.' His comment came just as people were drawing breath to begin the final verse and so was heard by half the congregation.

David ruffled the child's hair and smiled and the little boy beamed back. He was about to say something else but Mary put her finger to her lips and he nodded and kept silent.

Betty dozed throughout the service and only woke up when her brother came back at the end. The sermon, thankfully, didn't go on for the entire hour. They all trooped out in under two hours, which was still too long in his estimation, but considerably better than it could have been.

They waited in the churchyard until Nancy joined them. 'I do enjoy being in the choir. I'm so glad I was able to join.'

'You sing beautifully and I'm sure the choirmaster is already planning to give you solos at Christmas.'

'Blimey, it isn't even the middle of November yet. I don't want to think about Christmas.'

'Auntie Mary, I liked Sunday school. Can I go tomorrow?'

'It's called Sunday school for a reason, Billy. It only happens on Sunday, which is today when we go to church. If you tell me what you did then I'm sure we can do something similar ourselves during the week.'

'Smashing. Look over there – there's a lady soldier in a blue uniform waving at us.'

Nancy waved back. 'Excuse me, that's my mate, Charlotte. She's staying here until tomorrow. Don't know how she got here on a Sunday as there's no buses.'

'Then go and ask her. Please bring her round after lunch as I'd love to meet any friend of yours.'

'I'll do that, Doctor Denny. TTFN.'

She ran across and the two girls embraced. Charlotte

was a head taller than her, with dark hair and could be considered attractive. However, she lacked the vibrancy and sparkle that Nancy had. He knew quite a lot about Jane – the Stantons' daughter-in-law – but nothing at all about this other WAAF.

He was looking forward to meeting her and perhaps discovering more about Nancy's life before she came to the village. She was reluctant to talk about her past as it reminded her of Tommy. She'd done remarkably well to be able to function normally just three months after the event.

The three years he'd spent moping about were wasted time as far as he was concerned. If he'd got a grip, pulled himself together like she had, heaven knows what might have happened. His life would certainly have been better.

He owed her such a lot. If she hadn't literally fallen at his feet he'd still be dwelling on the past. Now, he was about to embark on a new career as a senior registrar at the Royal Free Hospital. If he hadn't fallen in love with Julia then he would have completed his surgical qualifications and would certainly be a consultant by now.

Maybe it wasn't too late to pursue his original intention of becoming a surgeon. Once he was established then he'd make enquiries. This hospital produced exceptional women doctors; they obviously had a much more broad-minded view of medicine than most of the big teaching hospitals he'd originally planned to work for. Therefore, they were more likely to accept someone in his thirties into their training programme than one of the other places.

'Nancy, it's months since we were together. I can't believe

how well you look considering everything,' Charlotte said as she hugged her.

'I'm doing all right; people here are ever so kind. As long as I ignore what's going on in the sky, I can sort of forget about what happened. It's not that I don't care, it's just easier for me not to think about it.'

'I gather you were the star turn at church this morning. I got a lift from Felixstowe to Ipswich in an army lorry, then a train to Chelmsford. I had to travel in a farmer's lorry the rest of the way.'

'I'm glad that you did. I've got so much to tell you. Shall we sit in the garden? Mrs Stanton insists that I don't need to help today as I've got a guest for lunch.'

'We'll do the washing-up for her and make tea tonight. I wish Jane could get time off. Whatever she's doing it's so crucial she's not getting more than a few hours off a week.'

'You do something hush-hush too so how do you get an overnight pass with these blooming bombers backwards and forwards every day?'

'We're supposed to get a thirty-six hour pass every eight days but at the moment it's every sixteen days – still – better than nothing.'

Nancy told her about the baby due next May, about David, and about the evacuee family living at his house. 'I'm going to miss him when he moves to London. He's taught me to read and write and, I hope you noticed, I'm talking more like you and Jane now.'

'Of course I did. You've changed out of all recognition. No, that's not actually true. You're still the same Nancy but with the rough edges smoothed over. I was expecting to hear that Jane and Oscar are having a baby so it's a bit of a surprise to find that you're going to be the first of us to become a mother.'

'The last letter I had from Jane said she'd not seen Oscar for ages so I don't reckon they've had much opportunity for you know what. Anyway, her job's too important and she's better off where she is. I was only in catering and anyone can do that.'

'We have to take what life throws at us. Am I going to get a chance to meet the chap who's changed your life?'

'I'm taking you over after lunch and we're going to go for a walk with the children and David so Mary can have a couple of hours off.'

Nancy didn't want to talk about herself; she wanted to know what was going on in her friend's life.

'Obviously, I can't tell you what I'm doing as it's top secret. However, I'm enjoying it and I hope you notice that I've been promoted again. The Queen Bee has said that I'm going to be sent to officer training when this flap's over.'

'Blimey, I always knew you and Jane were cut out to be officers. What's your billet like?'

'The WAAF sleep in the old house and the men are in little cottages dotted about the grounds. We only fraternise on a Sunday night when there's a dance of sorts. I don't have to sleep in a dorm but share accommodation with the girl in charge of the other shift. I've only spoken to her a few times as either I'm asleep or she's working.'

'What's the food like?'

'Absolutely dire. We have to fill up on toast and marmalade that we make ourselves – strictly against the rules – in our dorm.'

They spent another half an hour chatting and were then

called in for Sunday lunch. This was always eaten in the dining room and Nancy felt guilty that she hadn't been helping. It was roast chicken and apple pie for afters – all very tasty.

She and Charlotte insisted on clearing and doing the washing-up. The Stantons knew they were going across to David's and would be back in time to make tea. Now it got dark early evensong had been cancelled until the spring, which must be a relief for those involved.

'Make sure you have your torches, girls. It's so grey out there I think it'll be dark before you come back,' Mrs Stanton said.

'We'll only be over there an hour. We were hoping to go for a walk but I doubt we'll do that now. Thanks for the lunch. See you later.'

13

David had already reorganised his house to accommodate Mary and Fred – the little-used front room had been given over to them. Sleeping arrangements were more difficult as there was only one bathroom and lavatory upstairs, and one washroom and WC downstairs, which patients also used.

The doctor taking his place would have to move into his room as there were no other bedrooms available. If Violet was sleeping with her children as had been the intention then Simon could have had the back bedroom. David was going to sleep on the couch in the sitting room for a couple of nights and he wasn't looking forward to it.

Mrs O'Brien had taken to wandering off and he'd no idea where she went or if she met up with anyone on her walks. It wasn't the going out that was the problem; it was the fact that unless someone was there to prevent it, she didn't bother to put on outdoor shoes or a coat. She was a member of the household but an almost invisible one. Just occasionally Violet would stop and appear to be listening to the radio, a conversation, but so far, she'd not said a word.

He'd discussed the matter with Simon and they'd decided that if she didn't improve by the New Year she would be sent to an asylum where there were trained psychiatrists who might be able to help. This was something he'd not mentioned to Nancy as he was certain she'd disapprove.

It was approaching the end of November and it was already cold enough to be the middle of winter. Last year the weather had been arctic with sixteen-foot snowdrifts and was said to be the worst winter on record. He sincerely hoped there wouldn't be a repeat this year.

The only good thing about sub-zero temperatures was that it meant the Germans couldn't continue to bomb Britain. The RAF had won what was now referred to as *The Battle of Britain* and no one was talking about an imminent invasion any more – thank God!

'Doctor Denny, Mrs Smith and her friend have just arrived,' Mary called from the kitchen.

'Thank you, I'm coming.'

He was sorry when the two girls left as they'd been lively and entertaining company. They'd regaled him with stories about their training and he'd loved the one Nancy had told him about some officers sliding down the over-polished linoleum on their backsides after Jane had been overly industrious in her duties.

Everything was in order for the arrival of his replacement. He checked his appointment book and saw that both morning and afternoon surgeries were packed. Simon would sit in with him on these and also accompany him on any house calls he had to make.

His suitcase was packed; all he had to do was put his shaving gear and toiletries in on Wednesday morning. He looked around the waiting room and surgery that had been his workplace for almost ten years. The plan was for him to return at the end of the war but somehow he doubted he'd ever live in this house again.

The real reason he'd brought forward his intended departure by two months was because of his growing attraction to Nancy. She wasn't available, was highly unsuitable and was pregnant with another man's baby to boot. Moving away was the right thing to do.

Nancy brought Charlotte with her the next day and her friend was a welcome addition. Jill, for the first time in years, sent a message that she was unable to work without giving any explanation as to the reason and Charlotte immediately agreed to act as his receptionist for the morning influx.

'She's fed up about you going, David,' Nancy said as she put his toast and tea in front of him. 'I don't blame her really – we're all going to miss you. I'm sure this bloke you've employed will be fine but he won't be you.'

'Maybe when things calm down a bit in Town you could come up and I'll take you to the theatre and for a meal somewhere smart.'

'That's something to look forward to, but I don't reckon it'll be this year. Them blooming bombers just keep coming night after night. I dread to think how many have died in the East End.' She smiled. 'Anyway, I'll be as big as a house by then and you won't want to be seen out with me like that.'

'It's not just London that's being hit. The Jerries are bombing cities all over the country now,' Charlotte said gloomily. 'It just doesn't seem right killing civilians but we're doing it too. War is absolutely beastly.'

'Both governments seem to think that demoralising the civilian population somehow changes the outcome. It doesn't make sense to me either.' He didn't want to talk about anything so depressing when he had so little time to spend with Nancy before he left, possibly forever.

'It was good meeting you, Charlotte. Good luck with whatever you're doing. I'm sure it's vital to the war effort.'

'Being a doctor in the middle of a blitz is just as important, David,' she said with a friendly smile as she offered her hand. 'Goodbye, and don't take any unnecessary risks.'

Just before Charlotte left to catch the bus her friend said something that bothered Nancy.

'I noticed that you and David are getting very chummy, Nancy. I think he's perfect for you and I hope you make a go of it.'

'Blooming hell, Charlotte, he's just a friend. I really like him but there's absolutely nothing going on between us.'

'If you say so, Nancy, then I'll say no more. Don't worry about seeing me to the bus stop – you get off to work and hopefully we'll catch up soon. I'm certainly coming when the baby arrives if I can't get here before then.'

Her and David? What could possibly have made her friend think something as daft as that? Then she realised she'd not thought about Tommy for ages – the only person she dreamt about now was David and there was never going to be anything romantic between them. He wouldn't take advantage of her and she couldn't ever marry someone like him because she was just a girl from the East End and he was a posh doctor from Surrey.

Nancy was quiet the following morning as she bustled about the kitchen. The children, Fred and Mary had their breakfast after him whilst Nancy was tidying upstairs. She no longer took a tray to Violet and the girl usually drifted down sometime during the morning and ate whatever was put in front of her at the kitchen table.

'David, I know it's none of my business and you don't like to talk about money but I've got to ask as it concerns me and my baby.'

He had a good idea what was coming and unlike the last time the subject had come up he was ready to explain how things were. 'Fire away. I'll answer questions on any subject. I consider you a close friend and I'd like you to know everything pertinent.'

'I don't know what that means but it doesn't matter. I overheard you talking to this new bloke – I didn't mean to eavesdrop but you were in the hall and I was in the sitting room doing the dusting.'

She paused, closed her eyes as if marshalling her thoughts. He loved the way she did that – in fact he feared he was falling in love with her altogether, which was another reason he needed to remove himself from temptation as soon as possible.

'You're paying this Simon to work here and from what Jill has said you don't earn enough to pay his wages. The ten bob a week you get for each of the evacuees doesn't go far and certainly doesn't pay for Mary or Fred or me.'

'You don't have to worry about that, Nancy. Julia came from a wealthy family as did I and I can't think of a better way to spend that money than on keeping this household together. The village needs a doctor, the O'Briens and the Brooklyns need a home. I'm in a position to provide for them and it's my pleasure to do so.'

'I've said so before, David, and I'll say it again. You must be the most generous and kindest man in the country to spend your own money on a bunch of strangers. I can see why you did it when you were living and working here yourself but once you're in London your responsibility for this house and all of us should end.'

'I told you that I'm happy to pay the bills. This brings me beautifully onto something I needed to discuss with you. Would you be good enough to take over the household finances? The bills will need paying, wages and so on too.'

'You'd trust me with your money? I'm ever so pleased that you think I can do it. I'm good at numbers – it was just letters I found difficult before. I've never written a cheque though – from where I come from everything's paid for in cash.'

'I've set up a bank account for you and will transfer sufficient funds every month to cover everything. This means you'll have to go into Chelmsford to pay the bills and withdraw cash.'

'I could do that. As we get paid weekly it would be a lot easier for me if you put money into the post office for the wages and such and then I'd only have to go into town once a month and not every week.'

'I should have thought of that myself. I'll make the arrangements before I go. I warn you that Jill might be difficult about you knowing how much I pay her, but she'll have to get used to it.'

'Blimey, I hope I don't have to pay this doctor bloke.'

'Absolutely not – I shall send his salary by cheque every month. You don't have to be involved with that at all.'

The doorbell rang and he swallowed his tea and removed the crumbs from his mouth before jumping up. 'That will be Simon now. You'll meet him at lunchtime.'

The new doctor was a bit of all right – she couldn't believe he was in his fifties. He had reddish hair, lots of it, laughing green eyes and was at least six foot tall. He fitted in a treat and even Jill, who'd been a bit sniffy for a few days, seemed to warm to him.

David had put her wages up by a pound a week because of the extra work involved. The Stantons refused to take any money for her board and lodging as she was doing their mending and had already made a frock and a blouse for Mrs Stanton.

She was that busy she didn't expect to miss David but she did, and every day she wished he hadn't gone. What with the choir and the extra practices because of Christmas coming up, the wages, the commissions she'd got to make and all the mending, she rarely had a minute to herself.

Towards the end of the month the sickness had gone and she'd never felt fitter in her life. The bump was now big enough to warrant wearing a smock. She'd already told everyone in the house that she was expecting and they were happy for her.

Doctor Jones – she'd decided to keep it formal with him – refused to eat in the dining room on his own so had his meals in the kitchen and insisted that she sit with him.

'I enjoy your company, Mrs Smith, and as basically I work for you, I feel I can speak more freely.'

'You work for Doctor Denny – we all do. I just pay the bills here and keep the books straight.'

'You also run the household and make clothes for half the village. I don't suppose I could impose upon you to make something for me?'

'I could run you up a couple of shirts easy enough but finding the material's the problem. I reckon I could do it if you don't mind me using second-hand.'

'Make do and mend – aren't we told that all the time in posters and in the newspapers? By the way, Mrs Smith, I see from your notes that you're approaching your fourth month. I take it that you're having the baby at the vicarage? Have you spoken to the midwife?'

'Blimey, I can't think about that at the moment. It's not due until around the beginning of May and it's only just December.'

'Nevertheless, Mrs Smith, arrangements must be made. You'll feel the baby quicken by the end of next month and I'm prepared to leave it until then – but no longer.'

'Righto, Doctor Jones, but let's get Christmas out of the way first. Mary and me want to make this a bit special for Billy and Betty.'

'I don't suppose they've ever had much in the way of gifts or extras. I know Billy's excited to be in the Nativity play. I believe he's one of the shepherds.'

'He is and he even has a few words of his own to say. Betty's going to be a little angel – fortunately, we've got costumes for most of the children. I've just got to make a couple of angel frocks for the little ones who are joining in for the first time.'

'Your industry and energy are a constant amazement to me, Mrs Smith.'

'I'm fit as a flea, ta; expecting seems to suit me.'

'And why should it not? It's a perfectly natural state for a woman to be in.'

There was a slight sound behind them and Violet slipped past, heading for the front door in her nightgown and slippers.

'Just a minute, love, you need to get dressed before you go out. Come on, I'll help you.' Nancy moved swiftly in front of Violet so she couldn't open the door. Doctor Jones joined her.

'It's damned cold out there, Mrs O'Brien. You'll freeze to death if you wander about like that.'

There was no reaction to what had been said but the woman allowed them to turn her around and gently guide her back to her bedroom. Nancy always put out day clothes as otherwise the patient didn't get dressed. Instead of changing Violet clambered into bed and pulled the blankets over her head.

'She's getting worse, Doctor. I'm a bit concerned that she might do something to hurt herself or someone else.' Nancy had been trying to think of a way to tell him what she'd seen but knew it would push him into sending the poor lady away to an asylum.

'What did she do that alarmed you?'

'Yesterday, when I arrived, she was in the kitchen holding the bread knife and about to take it upstairs with her. She let me have it without a fuss, but...'

'But indeed. Doctor Denny left the matter to me and I think it's time to make that unpalatable decision. I'll set things in motion after surgery today.'

They'd been talking outside the bedroom door as if Violet wasn't there. Well – she wasn't really there, not mentally anyway.

That evening she retreated to her bedroom in order to write letters to Charlotte and Jane. The fact that she could now do this was a constant source of pleasure to her. David had given her a dictionary and a fountain pen as a parting gift and she kept them by her stationery folder and reckoned she didn't make many mistakes nowadays. She'd not heard from him, but she thought Doctor Jones had spoken to him on the telephone. She had his address in London and decided she would write to him as well as her two friends.

Dear David

I hope you're enjoying working in a hospital. It's a bit different from being in the countryside. It would be nice to hear from you if you get a moment to write back.

Dr Jones is going to have Violet committed as she's getting worse. The thought of her being locked up, not able to see anyone she knows, is very upsetting. I don't think the children will even notice as they now think of Mary as their ma.

I've been ever so busy but that's how I like to be. Billy's a shepherd in the Nativity and even Betty is going to be a little angel. You were right and I'm going to be singing a solo at the carol service. I was a bit nervous at first but now I'm enjoying it.

It's not the same without you here. I miss you and pray that you keep safe with all the bombs dropping and that.

Best wishes

After carefully blotting the page she folded the single sheet and put it into the envelope. She'd addressed one the day after he'd left but hadn't had the courage to write to him until now. It had been over three months since her Tommy had died but it could have been three years. She could scarcely remember his voice, or what he looked like even.

Her head was filled constantly with thoughts of David and she didn't understand why this was so. She was beginning to think that maybe what she'd felt for Tommy hadn't been that strong. If she'd truly loved him the way that David had loved his wife then she would still be grieving.

There was a faint fluttering inside and she put her hand protectively across her bump. Her baby was moving, letting her know that he or she was in there. How different her life would have been if she'd not got in the family way. She would still be in the WAAF, probably been promoted again, and would be an independent woman with nothing to worry about but herself.

Her lips curved. She didn't regret anything. Things happened for a reason and she believed she was meant to be here helping in a different way. Going to church every Sunday had made her begin to think that there might be a God after all. If she hadn't come to this village then she wouldn't have met David and he'd become very important to her.

David slotted into his new position without difficulty. It might have been almost a decade since he'd worked in a casualty department but his knowledge and skills had remained. The Royal Free was now only using the ground-floor wards and those only for casualties of which there were a growing number.

Bombs dropping in the vicinity were a regular occurrence and everyone just carried on regardless of what was happening around them. He worked, sometimes for thirty-six hours, without sleep and had learned to catch thirty minutes in whatever corner he could find whenever he had a moment to himself.

He had digs nearby but was rarely there – he just returned to change clothes, wash and shave whenever he got the chance. Things couldn't be more traumatic even on the frontline and he didn't regret for one minute making this decision. Finally, he was doing something useful.

There'd been no time to form a liaison with a suitable young woman even if he'd wanted to. As soon as he'd left Chalfont Major he'd understood he was in love with Nancy – it wasn't lust but love he felt for her. He'd decided that as Nancy wasn't available, he'd remain celibate. The idea of a casual affair no longer appealed to him.

He'd deliberately not written to her although he'd started to write a couple of times before things got too busy. Better that the connection was severed completely as he doubted that he'd have the strength of will not to act on his feelings if he did see her again.

He was well aware that she was about to become an unmarried mother and that she might be tempted to accept his offer of marriage for the sake of her child. He'd be prepared to take her on any terms but it wouldn't be fair. She deserved better than a marriage of convenience.

One morning a few weeks after he'd taken up his post a bomb dropped on the Church of Scotland, near the medical school, where a conference was being held. God knows why the clerics decided to meet there when the area was being bombed every day.

The seriously injured were being stretchered in and soon he was up to his elbows in blood and guts trying to save the lives of the unfortunate clergy who'd been caught in this attack. The consultant paediatrician, Ursula Shelley, had been dragged from her outpatients' clinic with a couple of students in order to help. All medical staff were needed this morning.

There was a clergyman in bloodstained robes, his face plastered with dust, kneeling in the middle of the casualty department, getting in everybody's way and praying like a maniac for God to save them.

Ursula tolerated this for a while and then stepped in. 'Pray to God, man, but for God's sake, pray quietly.'

This did the trick and he subsided into a defeated heap. A porter grabbed his arm and half-walked half-carried him out of the way.

Twelve hours later the last of the injured had been dealt with and the bodies of those who hadn't survived had been taken to the morgue. He'd been working without food or drink for twelve hours. He was knackered – but so was everybody else.

He needed to pee, eat and sleep in that order. The night shift had taken over and he was free for a few hours at least. He stumbled into the canteen and after three mugs of tea and three sandwiches he had just about enough energy to drag himself to his digs.

When he pushed open the door to his room he stepped on an envelope that had been pushed through in his absence. He glanced down and recognised the writing. Nancy had written to him; seeing this letter lifted his spirits in a way nothing else could do. It had been a bloody horrible shift. Dozens had died from their injuries and even more had been killed outright in the blast.

He kicked the door shut and ripped the envelope open. It was a short letter but he was smiling by the end of it. She missed him – that's all he wanted to know. He'd been holding back but now she'd instigated the reconnection he was free to move things forward.

Not bothering to remove even his shoes he flopped down on the bed, the letter still in his hand, and was instantly asleep.

14

Nancy had posted all three letters on her way to work two days ago but didn't expect any replies for a while. Officially she didn't have to be there until seven thirty but was always there before seven. It was dark, the air icy and the puddles crunched under her feet. She'd been lucky to find some sturdy boots, almost as good as new, for the winter when she'd gone into Chelmsford to pay the bills at the end of last month.

She was about to take the path around to the back but noticed the front door was ajar. At first, she was merely puzzled but then her stomach turned. The only person who used the front door and left it open was Violet. She rushed in expecting to find Polly in the kitchen on her bed but she wasn't there.

This confirmed her worst fears. The dog would only be out if she'd followed Violet. Before she panicked unnecessarily, she tore upstairs and into the back bedroom. The blackouts were still drawn so she put on the light.

Her hands clenched. The bed was neatly made as if no one had slept in it but it had been occupied when she'd left work last night. The clothes that she'd left on the chair were gone so at least Violet was dressed.

On opening the wardrobe she discovered this was empty – the suitcase that had been on the shelf was gone. The constriction in her throat eased a little. This wasn't a random wandering into the darkness without thought, but a planned departure.

Whatever it was, she had to wake Dr Jones and tell him the bad news before she went out to search for both Polly and the missing woman. As the door was open it was quite possible the dog had just gone out and the two things weren't connected.

There was no need to wake Mary and Fred; this wasn't their problem. She tapped on the door and heard movement on the other side. 'Doctor Jones, Violet has packed a bag and left. I'll wait downstairs for you,' she whispered.

'I'll be there in a minute.' His reply was equally quiet and she was confident no one would have heard her.

She riddled the range and filled it up with the waiting fuel. Once it was roaring away she opened one of the heavy, iron lids and put the kettle on the hot plate. As she'd only half-filled it, it boiled quickly and the tea was brewing when Dr Jones came in.

He rubbed his chin and grinned. 'Thought it best not to stop and shave – don't look so horrified, Mrs Smith. I'll do it before my first patient arrives.'

'In the circumstances I don't think they'd care what you looked like as long as they were able to see you. I'm going to drink this tea quickly and get off. She's taken Polly's lead so the dog's definitely with her.'

He sat at the table and drank his tea before answering. 'I'm pretty sure she was there when I went up around eleven last night as there was a light under her door.'

'The light was off this morning. What bothers me is that there are no buses until the first one at eight o'clock. Do you think she might have been meeting someone?'

'It's possible. I've a nasty suspicion that her disappearance is because she overheard us talking about having her committed. We've assumed she'd not been following anything as she never spoke but we could have been wrong.'

'That's dreadful – we should never have talked about her like that. She's obviously not as muddled as we thought.'

'That's all very well, Mrs Smith, but don't forget the bread knife. I can only think of one reason she'd be taking it upstairs and that was to self-harm.'

Nancy shuddered. 'I don't want to think about it. Do you think she was intending to commit suicide? That could mean she's gone somewhere else to do it.' She jumped up so suddenly her chair crashed to the flagstones. 'I'm going to check the knives and that…'

'She packed a suitcase, my dear Mrs Smith. I don't believe anyone intending to end their own life would bother to take a change of clothes with them. Whilst you're on your feet why don't you see if her ration book is with the others behind the tea caddy?'

It wasn't and the lump in her throat disappeared. 'She's taken that. Blimey, and the housekeeping money.' That too was gone. 'There was more than twenty pounds in there. I didn't even know she was aware I kept it in the Toby jug.'

'It's not your fault. I think we've all misjudged Mrs O'Brien. I believe she could have been planning this for some time. The blank expressions and the refusal to speak might have been a ploy to deceive and when she overheard us talking about an asylum, she put these plans into action.'

Nancy sat down again. 'I don't understand why she wanted to do that. She wasn't a prisoner here and could have left at any time if she'd wanted to.'

'Good grief, I'm not suggesting she's of sound mind. If she was well then she wouldn't have behaved as she did. What might seem as logical planning on the surface is, I think, part of her mania. If you've finished your tea, let's find our torches and go in search of her.'

'That makes more sense. No one in their right mind would leave in the middle of the night like that.'

'I'm going to leave a note on the table telling Mary where we are. If I'm not back in time for the first patient then at least she can tell Mrs Andrews what's happening.'

Outside the first glimmer of dawn made it possible to see without the torches but he'd said to take them anyway as they might need to look in sheds and outbuildings and these would be dark.

There were lights in the windows of quite a few houses. The village was waking up and soon they could ask others to join in the search but she prayed that wouldn't be necessary.

She called the dog, whistled and stood still to listen for any sounds in the gardens or the fields beyond. 'It doesn't make sense for us to be searching together, Doctor Jones. We'll cover more ground if we separate.'

'That's perfectly correct but – how can I say this without alarming you? – I think you're going to need me when we do find her.'

'You think she's done herself in? I thought you said that no one intending to commit suicide packed a suitcase?'

'I did indeed. However, I fear she might have been out

here for hours and with the temperatures well below zero it's possible she has hypothermia.'

The appalling weather conditions had prevented the nightly arrival of the bombers and David was able to eat a meal in the canteen undisturbed and then return to his digs to actually undress and get into his pyjamas for a decent night's sleep.

He wasn't due to start his shift until ten o'clock the next morning unless, of course, there was an emergency and then everyone was called in.

As he was leaving the next day the telephone rang loudly. Whoever was nearest always picked it up – all those living here were doctors and the calls were always for one of them.

'Doctor Denny speaking.'

'David, thank God. Violet has disappeared. She vanished some time the night before last and we've had the whole village searching but there's no sign of her. Even worse – she's taken Polly with her.'

'Things are quiet here today so I'm coming down. Don't worry, Nancy, we'll sort this out.'

He could hear her crying. 'Sweetheart, it'll be all right. None of this is your fault and my dog will find her way home.'

'I hope so. I really need to see you. It's been horrible these past two days. The children are distraught and I thought they didn't care about their mother any more.'

'We'll talk about it when I get there. I've got to grab a couple of things, ring the hospital, and then I'll be with you later this morning with any luck.'

He was entitled to time off. He wasn't in the services, but like most of the medical staff at the Royal Free they worked whenever they were needed. He explained why he was going to be taking time off for a few days, and didn't allow his boss to refuse permission, but just hung up.

Violet disappearing, even his dog going missing, wasn't as painful as hearing the woman he now accepted that he'd fallen in love with crying. Several times he'd started to reply to her letter but what he wanted to say couldn't be written; it had to be said face to face.

This domestic emergency was the perfect excuse to take a couple of days' leave – God knows he was owed ten times that amount – and return to Chalfont Major. It probably wasn't the best time to begin his courtship but he might not have another opportunity. He'd narrowly missed being killed by falling masonry the other day and this had focused his mind wonderfully.

This bloody war was likely to go on for years and he wasn't going to waste another moment. If people disapproved of him wanting to marry a girl whose supposed husband had only been dead a few months, a girl who was pregnant, then so be it. He'd wasted three years of his life moping about after Julia had died and he had no intention of wasting another minute if he could help it.

He got the underground to Liverpool Street and then was lucky enough to find the Norwich train waiting to steam out. A porter practically pushed him head first into the train as it was moving off and then slammed the door behind him.

'Just made it then, mate. Doubt there'll be another one for an hour or two,' a soldier said as he shuffled his kitbag along the floor to allow him to find himself a space in the corner.

'Thank you – sorry if I stood on your toes.'

'Not on his, but you did on mine.' The speaker was a young officer, ten years his junior, who was staring at him as if he might be something unpleasant that needed scraping off his boot. 'Conscientious objector I presume.' This was said with a sneer and David lost his temper.

'It's none of your bloody business, but I'm a doctor at the Royal Free and am getting a couple of days off for the first time in six weeks. When did you last save someone's life?'

There were half a dozen soldiers crammed into the corridor and they'd all heard the exchange. He heard a murmur of approval. They couldn't speak out openly against an officer but several of them made it clear they supported him.

The man he'd snarled at was opening and closing his mouth like a fish in a bowl. Colour was seeping up his neck. Then he recovered sufficiently to answer. 'I beg your pardon. I think that chaps like you are doing a fine job.'

'What you think is irrelevant. I suggest you mind your own business if you don't want someone to punch you on the nose.' His fists were clenched and the unfortunate officer recoiled. He snatched up his kitbag and shoved his way past the soldiers and vanished down the passageway.

'Good for you, Doc. I wish you'd smacked him one. Jumped-up little prick,' one of them said with a broad grin.

'I've not punched anyone since I was at school. I apologise, gents. I'm not usually so belligerent.'

'Since we got back from Dunkirk there ain't been nothing to do but drill, training and more of the same. He's straight from Sandhurst – no battle experience at all. God help us when we're in action again with stupid bastards like him in charge,' another one said morosely.

'I've nothing but admiration for those of you who survived that evacuation. I'm more use in London as a civilian. At the moment I think I'm more likely to be killed than he is.'

He became quite friendly with the group and learnt a lot about life on an army camp for an enlisted man by the time he disembarked at Chelmsford. They were transferring to Colchester where there was a big barracks.

Again, fortune favoured him and the bus that he wanted pulled in five minutes after he arrived at the bus station. He checked his watch. He'd left his digs at nine o'clock and it was now eleven thirty – two and a half hours wasn't bad considering everything. There were several people in it whom he knew and, although no one mentioned it, he got several sympathetic looks. They all knew why he was returning so precipitously.

He smiled inwardly at the thought. They would be scandalised if they knew that his real reason for racing home was to declare his feelings to someone most people would consider a highly unsuitable candidate for his affections.

There was no escaping from the drama of Violet's disappearance. Nancy couldn't understand why no one at all had seen the woman wandering about with a suitcase and David's dog. That Polly was with her should have made things better but in fact made them worse.

The local bobby had pedalled up and down looking

official but had been of absolutely no bloody use at all. PC Arthur Black was in his fifties and so fat Nancy was surprised the bicycle didn't collapse under his weight.

Billy was distraught and his constant crying and calling for his ma set Betty off as well. Mary was at her wits' end trying to comfort them both. Probably they were both more upset about the missing dog than they were about Violet.

She'd rung David on an impulse and if he hadn't picked up the phone she'd have hung up and that would have been it. Now he was on his way back and she didn't know how to face him. He meant a lot to her – she thought she might be a little bit in love with him despite his being a lot older than her and not a bit like Tommy – and she'd let him down badly.

The dog was David's last link to his wife as Polly had been a gift from Julia the year before she'd died.

He'd left her in charge and she'd made a mess of it. There was also the missing housekeeping money, which she'd not told the bobby about. She didn't want Violet to be arrested when she turned up – if she turned up. David couldn't possibly be here until late afternoon so she'd no need to tell anyone he was coming until after lunch.

Blimey! She'd better sort out the room that Violet had been using or he'd have nowhere to sleep. He'd been on the sofa for the last two nights before he'd left and that wasn't right. The telephone rang several times but was answered by Jill. The receptionist seemed rather taken with Dr Jones and he was definitely interested in her.

There must be something in the air at this house for the four of them to be romantically inclined. Upstairs was spotless, the room ready for David, the soup was simmering on the hob for lunch, so she'd got a couple of hours free. More than enough time to dash back to the vicarage and write to Jane. Her friend probably knew nothing about the disaster unless Mrs Stanton had told her.

Dear Jane,

The most dreadful thing has happened here. Violet has disappeared. She's not well and Dr Jones was going to have her committed. That's why she ran off – although he reckons she'd been planning it for ages.

I rang David just now and he's coming back from London to try and sort things out. It wouldn't be so bad if the dog wasn't gone as well.

I pray for my family not to be killed in the bombing and also for Oscar, you, Charlotte and David to keep safe. Who'd have thought it? Being in the choir and going to church every week has made God seem more real to me somehow.

Charlotte came to see us a few weeks ago and I expect she's written to tell you she's going away to train to be an officer in the New Year. I expect you'll do the same when they can spare you.

I'm keeping tickety-boo as far as the baby's concerned. Little blighter's wriggling and kicking all the time now. I've made myself a couple of nice smocks as I couldn't get into my clothes any more.

I'll let you know what happens.

Love

She carefully blotted the sheet and pushed it into the envelope. She'd run out of stamps but had enough time to nip into the post office on her way back to work.

'Good morning, Mrs Smith. Any news of Mrs O'Brien?' The postmistress, the worst of the village gossips, asked brightly.

'Nothing, but we've not given up hope she'll come back.'

'Her kiddies will be missing her. I don't understand how a mother can abandon her own children like that.'

'Mrs O'Brien wasn't thinking straight. She's not been herself since she was bombed out just after her husband was killed at Dunkirk.'

'How sad. Mind you, Iris Stanhope, from Little Chalfont, said she often walked over there and was friendly with…'

'Why didn't you say this before? For God's sake – if we'd known she had friends somewhere else we could have started there with the search. What were you thinking?' Nancy snatched up her stamps and rushed out knowing she'd offended the postmistress but didn't care. They'd wasted valuable time, perhaps been worried unnecessarily, and Violet might still be there in this friend's house.

She pushed her letter into the post box and as she turned to walk to David's house, she realised she hadn't actually asked the name of the friend or the address. She hesitated. Should she go in and apologise and get this information?

David would be back later and he could go instead of her. She blinked back tears. She was blubbing at the slightest thing nowadays and it was getting on her nerves.

Little Chalfont was about three miles away and Violet could easily have walked that without too much trouble, even though it had been bitterly cold. The woman had been given a decent winter coat and should have been all right.

Mary, Fred and the children ate first as Dr Jones didn't finish surgery until one o'clock on some days. They were sitting at the kitchen table enjoying her soup with freshly baked bread and margarine. She indicated to Mary that she wished to speak to her in private and then walked into the hall to wait for her.

'Doctor Denny's going to be here later this afternoon. He'd got two days free and is going to try and find Mrs O'Brien.'

'Good. A fresh pair of eyes might come up with something we've missed. The children will be pleased to see him. Do you mind if I tell them?'

'Perhaps it might be better to wait until he actually arrives – even though he said he was on his way if there's an emergency before he leaves then he'll have to go to the hospital.'

'There were no bombers over during the night or so far this morning.'

'That's why he can come. The only good thing about this horrible, cold weather is that it stops the bombers of both sides from flying.'

15

David arrived cold and hungry just after one o'clock. If he'd expected to be overwhelmed with greetings then he would have been disappointed as only Nancy was waiting for him in the kitchen. Her smile gave him hope that he hadn't mistaken the matter. It felt wrong to be coming in and not have Polly gambolling about his feet trying to knock him over in her excitement at seeing him again.

'I'm so sorry to call you back like this, but I can't tell you how happy I am that you came. Here, you look ever so thin. You've been working too hard and not eating enough. I'll have something ready by the time you've got yourself sorted. You're in the back bedroom.'

'Right, good idea as I feel decidedly grubby after my journey. It's very quiet. Are the children asleep?'

'No, Mary's taken them for a quick walk. Fred's somewhere out in the garden feeding something or other and Doctor Jones was called out on an emergency about ten minutes ago.'

'You look very well, Nancy, positively blooming. Pregnancy obviously suits you.'

'I feel a lot better now you're here, that's for sure.' She turned away and began fiddling with the saucepan and he knew why she'd done so. Like him, she was nervous about revealing too much before she knew how things were between them.

He dropped his overnight bag in the corner of his temporary accommodation and ran a sink full of hot water. She was right. He looked haggard and had black smuts on his forehead from the train. He didn't give a damn about his appearance as long as he looked okay to Nancy. If her expression was an indication of how she felt to see him he wasn't about to make a total arse of himself.

On his return there was a bowl of vegetable soup on the table, plus two hefty sandwiches and several jam tarts. God knows where Nancy had got the ingredients for the pastry or the jam to make these. He demolished all of it in an embarrassingly short space of time.

'Golly, you were hungry. There's a delicious game pie, and fruit crumble for afters, tonight. I know you like a bit of crumble.'

He smiled and held out his empty mug. 'That was the most delicious meal I've had in a long time. Is there any more tea in the pot? I'm sorry I ate like a pig but I'd not realised just how hungry I was or how much I've missed you and your cooking.'

'That's all right, you'll get plenty of what you like whilst you're here.' She poured two mugs and brought them to the table. 'I'll tell you what I learned this morning.'

He listened and nodded. 'I'll ring the post office now. It bothers me that Violet took the dog deliberately. It doesn't make sense.'

'We think it was for protection just in case she was stopped by anybody.'

'Could be right. I won't be a tick.' The postmistress gave him the information and he returned to the table with it. 'There's only one problem: it's a three-mile walk and it'll be dark before we get there. I don't even have my bicycle as Simon's using it.'

'I was thinking that maybe you could ring the vicarage there. The vicar or his wife would be able to make enquiries for you.'

'My brain's not functioning as it should. I should have thought of that myself. I'll do it now.' This time she followed him and was standing so close it was all he could do not to reach out and take her hand. He breathed in deeply and to his delight she moved a few inches so she was leaning against him. He snatched up the telephone and asked the operator to connect him to the vicarage at Little Chalfont.

'I'm so sorry, Doctor Denny, I do know of whom you speak. I saw Mrs O'Brien a few times in the village, but not recently, and wondered who she was. However, I can categorically say that she's not here now. I wish I could be of more help.'

He stood up slowly. His hands were trembling like a schoolboy's before his first kiss. She didn't move and he turned to face her. She swayed towards him, he opened his arms and she was right where she was meant to be.

For a moment he just held her close, loving the way she fitted so snugly against him. Then her hands were around his neck and his hold tightened. She tilted her face and he kissed her. At first it was a gentle exchange, just lips pressing against each other.

Then their passion ignited and a breathless few minutes later he regained control in the nick of time. He smoothed her hair back from her flushed cheeks. 'That was close. Imagine Mary's expression if she found us making love on the stairs.'

'Making love? I don't think so, Doctor Denny. Whatever gave you that idea?'

For a horrible moment he thought he'd upset her but then she giggled. 'I think you'd better take a quick walk around the garden before anyone sees the state you're in.' She glanced pointedly at his arousal and he shifted uncomfortably.

'Come upstairs with me. I love you, Nancy, and I intend to marry you at the earliest possible opportunity.'

Instead of being happy at his announcement she stepped away from him, eyes wide and her expression anything but excited. 'Marry me? Are you daft? I'm a girl from the East End – not the sort of wife you want.'

'You're exactly the sort of wife I want. If these past weeks have taught me anything it's that no one knows how long they've got on this earth. I loved Julia, but what I feel for you is quite different.'

Their conversation was interrupted by the sound of Billy shouting. They both ran towards the kitchen door and a very muddy, overexcited dog erupted through the door. Polly jumped and, despite her considerable size, landed in his arms. He staggered backwards into the dresser and half a dozen plates cascaded from the shelves and smashed on the tiles.

He hung on to the dog and managed to stagger away from the shards of broken crockery before putting her down. He crouched beside her. 'Good dog; clever girl to find your way home.' Whilst he was fussing her he realised the lead was still attached to her collar.

Nancy was on her knees regardless of the mud spraying from the dog's coat. 'Where's Violet then? Can you take us back to her?'

Mary had picked up Betty and grabbed Billy's hand to stop them crunching through the debris. 'Come into the scullery, children, and we can take off our outdoor garments and put them away. Then you can speak to Doctor Denny and the dog.'

'I'll get her something to eat and drink. She looks as thin as you do.' Nancy bounced to her feet, leaving him sitting with his back against the wall and the dog spreadeagled between his legs. She was whining and wagging her tail but apart from being filthy and a lot thinner she'd no other injuries. Even her pads were undamaged so it was unlikely she'd run home along tarmac.

'Here you are, you brave girl. Some lovely rabbit and veggies and a bowl of water.' Nancy waved both bowls in front of the dog and immediately her attention turned from licking him to scrambling up and almost knocking the bowls from Nancy's hands.

Hastily she put both down. The dog drank most of the water and then turned her attention to the food and that vanished equally fast. Then the animal licked both their hands and flopped down on her waiting blanket and with a sigh of contentment was fast asleep.

Before he could get up both children fell into his lap. He hugged them both and was smothered with wet kisses for a second time.

'Are you stopping home with us now?' Billy said as he

scrambled from his lap and went to stroke the sleeping dog. David wasn't sure if he was referring to himself or Polly.

'My doggy, my doggy back,' Betty said and was about to launch herself onto the blanket but he restrained her.

'No, sweetheart, let the doggy sleep. You can play with her when she wakes up.'

Mary picked the little one up. 'Shall we go into the sitting room, children? We've got a puzzle to finish haven't we?'

They went without protest and he pushed himself to his feet. He'd not been able to spring up as nimbly as Nancy and this bothered him. Was he really too old to think about a second marriage to someone as young and vibrant as her?

'Do you think the dog would be able to lead us to wherever Violet is?'

He shook his head. 'She'll not be able to go anywhere for twenty-four hours and we can't leave it that long. I'm going to ring round and organise a search. Did they look in the barns and sheds between here and Little Chalfont?'

Nancy thought for a moment. 'I'm not sure. Everybody thought she'd gone towards Chelmsford to catch the train back to London. I don't think folk around here thought she was in any danger but had just decided she didn't want to be with her children any more.'

'I feared as much. I'm going to ring the vicar and the post office and hopefully between us we can get up a search party. Then I'll have an ambulance on alert to come as soon as needed.'

She nodded, her expression sad. He didn't need to tell her the likelihood of finding Violet alive was slim to non-existent.

'I'll make up a thermos of tea, put plenty of sugar in

it. Then I'll find some blankets.' Her cheeks were wet but when he made a move towards her, she stepped back. 'You get on with your phone calls, David, and I'll get on with what I've got to do.'

Half an hour after the return of the dog the search party was assembled. He'd got on his rubber boots and had changed into something more suitable for tramping about the countryside in freezing temperatures. He'd not taken his country clothes to London – they'd been put in the attic.

Mary had said the dog had come home across the fields and that's the way he led the men. Walking across a ploughed field would have been even worse if the ground had been wet. He was the youngest in the party – all the young men were already fighting for their country.

Simon was walking beside him. 'I just hope we don't have to administer aid to any of the chaps with us. A couple of them look a bit ancient to be out here in this weather.'

'They'll be fine. They spend their life out of doors and this isn't really bad weather according to them,' David replied.

'Are you expecting to find a cadaver or a patient?'

'I'm trying not to think about it but on balance it's far more likely she's dead.'

'Which brings me to another point – I know you're a philanthropist, that you're happy to fund our happy little household – but what's going to happen to those children if you're right?'

'As far as I'm concerned things will carry on as they are. I suppose I'll have to contact the WVS woman and update her about the changed circumstances.'

'That's all very well, old bean, but who's actually responsible for them if you're not living here? I certainly don't want to be, Mary is their nanny and Mrs Smith is your housekeeper.'

'For God's sake, Simon, I've more important things to think about than that at the moment. Whatever happens the children will be fine – they'll go to an orphanage over my dead body.'

They searched every building and barn they came across and found nothing. It was beginning to get dark when they approached a small, ramshackle, abandoned cottage with half the roof missing and no glass in the windows.

'This will have to be the last place we look,' he told the others. 'I don't want you to be tramping about in the dark.'

One of the old men shook his head. 'If that girl's out here then I ain't going home until she's found dead or alive.'

There was a mutter of agreement around the group. 'If you're quite sure then we'll keep going for another couple of hours. There's not much else between here and Little Chalfont anyway.'

He called out her name, not expecting to get an answer. Simon reached the door first. It was hanging off its hinges and he stepped around it.

'In here, we've found her.'

David shoved open the door with his shoulder and dropped to his knees beside the shape huddled under a few sacks and not moving. Simon was checking for a pulse.

'She's alive, but barely.'

Minutes later Violet was cocooned in several blankets and in his arms. He and Simon had volunteered to carry the girl who was ominously still. The search party walked on either side shining their torches ahead so he could see where he was going. After twenty minutes he handed the limp bundle to Simon and they continued.

The sprightliest of the men had hurried ahead in order to have the ambulance waiting when they arrived. An hour after they'd found her she was in the back of a vehicle. Simon had volunteered to go with her and said he'd ring with any news as soon as there was some.

David shook the hands of each of the men who'd helped and trudged round the back of his house to hook off his boots and remove his coat. He was knackered, but not cold after all the exertions.

Nancy greeted him with a mug of tea and a question in her eyes. The children were eating boiled eggs and soldiers at the table in the kitchen. He nodded towards the hall and she followed him.

'It doesn't look good but I'm surprised she was alive after being so long in the cold. I think it better not to say anything to the children until we know one way or the other. I think this belongs to you.' He handed her the notes and the ration book he'd found in Violet's coat pocket.

'It's the housekeeping. I didn't tell the bobby about it but I should have told you. It's not my money – it's yours, isn't it?'

'Semantics, Nancy. I'm going to change and then I'll come down and spend some time with the children. Is Polly okay? I expected her to come and greet me.'

'She looked up and wagged her tail but is too exhausted to move. The children sat with her and she enjoyed that.'

He couldn't believe how much Billy and Betty had changed

in the time he'd been away. The boy was more articulate, unrecognisable from the child he'd been when he'd arrived from London. Betty was now talking and he found her mispronunciations and babble enchanting. They scrambled all over his lap and he was happy to have them there.

'Come along, Billy, Betty, time to go to bed. Doctor Denny will be here tomorrow when you get up and so will the dog.'

'All right, Auntie Mary, we're coming. Can you tell us the story about Hansel and Gretel again, please? I like the bit about the horrible witch being cooked in the oven.'

Nancy kissed both the children and so did he. They went off chattering and laughing and he dreaded the possibility of having to tell them that their mother, however inadequate she'd been, had died. He hoped that wouldn't be necessary but feared the worst.

'Are you going to eat with me tonight, Nancy? I don't think there's any point in waiting for Simon. In fact, I think it quite likely he won't be back tonight as there'll be no transport.'

'I told Mrs Stanton I wouldn't be back until late.'

He was about to reintroduce the topic that had been interrupted by the arrival of his dog but thought it might be better to put this on hold for the moment.

'Fred doesn't seem a very convivial sort of person. Surely he can't still be outside?'

She laughed. 'He doesn't like children, which is odd considering his wife's a nanny. He's converted the tool shed into his own domain. He's got an oil lamp and a paraffin stove and a battered armchair. He doesn't come in until after I've gone home. I don't think he likes me very much because I'm expecting.'

'Is he doing a good job outside taking care of the animals and so on?'

'You're going to have plenty of bacon when those pigs are slaughtered, that's for sure. There seems to be a constant stream of your neighbours coming in with buckets of slops to feed them.'

'That's all that matters then. That smells wonderful – I'm absolutely starving after all that tramping about the countryside.'

He glanced at the antique carriage clock that had been his wife's, which still stood on the top shelf of the custom-made dresser. It had been three hours at least since the ambulance had left. This had to be good news as if she'd died Simon would have let them know at once.

Jill had rearranged Simon's appointments for the afternoon and he'd offered to take morning surgery himself if necessary.

He was just on his second helping of fruit crumble and custard when the telephone rang shrilly in the hall. Nancy was on her feet but he shook his head. 'I'll go; finish your pudding.'

16

Nancy watched the door, knowing she'd be able to tell from his expression whether it was bad news. Since he'd made that ridiculous suggestion that they marry she'd been in turmoil. There was nothing she'd like better than to be his wife but that was out of the question. Ma had drummed it into her that people like her shouldn't marry above their station. It didn't work out and in the end no one was happy.

She'd never meant to fall in love with him; didn't even know when it had happened. He made her heart skip a beat when he just looked at her. She no longer thought of him as too old. But being in love with him didn't mean she expected him to marry her and take on Tommy's child.

He had more money to spend in a month than most people she knew had to spend in a lifetime. How was someone like her meant to live in his world? He fancied her – that was for sure – but that was because he hadn't done it for three years. Once he'd got it out of his system then he'd realise he didn't really love her; it was just sex he wanted, not a wife.

David came in and shook his head. Her good intentions vanished and she flung herself into his waiting arms. She'd scarcely known Violet so why was she crying? After a few moments she pulled away. 'What are we going to do with the children? Will they be allowed to stay here?'

'Come into the sitting room so Mary and Fred can eat their supper. We have to talk.'

'The fire isn't lit in there. I know you've got radiators, which keep the house lovely and warm, but I do like to see the flames of a night.'

'I'll see to it. Come through – don't tell Mary until we've talked.'

Nancy knocked on the door that Mary and Fred used as their own front room and told them their food was on the table. David was pacing up and down. Whatever he had to say to her it wouldn't be good news.

'Good. Close the door, sweetheart, and come and sit next to me on the sofa.'

As soon as she was comfortable, he turned and took both her hands. She shouldn't let him do that as it would make him think she'd changed her mind. There was no way on God's earth that she was going to ruin his life by marrying him, however much she'd like to.

'Violet was briefly awake before she died. She told Simon that she wanted me to take the children and raise them as my own...'

'Of course she did – any mother would want you to be father to their children. That doesn't mean you have to do it.'

His hands tightened and his eyes gleamed behind his spectacles. 'I know that but I want to respect a dying woman's wish. I can't do it without you, sweetheart. You have to marry me, put aside your ridiculous ideas that you're not good enough, because if you don't the children will be taken away and God knows what will happen to them.'

'You're talking nonsense, David. Think about it. No man in his right mind would want to take on three little bastards and that's what you're suggesting you do. Not only that – you work in London and won't even be here. How's that going to work?'

He was unbothered by her outburst and when she tried to pull her hands away, he just hung on tighter. 'I love you and I'm damn sure that you reciprocate my feelings.' He grinned, making him look years younger, and despite her agitation she returned his smile. 'That means you return my feelings in case you were wondering.'

'Cheeky blighter! I knew what that meant. I'm learning loads of words every night from that dictionary you gave me.'

'Why the hell are we talking about dictionaries? Listen to me, darling Nancy, meeting you was the best thing that's ever happened to me. You've made me see the world in a different way, made me happier than I've ever been. I loved Julia but nothing like the way I feel about you.

'Why should we both be miserable just because people we don't know, and don't care about, might think that us getting married is a mistake?'

She was about to answer but he leaned over and lifted her onto his lap. He closed his arms around her waist, making it impossible for her to wriggle free even if she'd wanted to. He smoothed his hands over her bump and the baby obliged by kicking.

'See, this little one agrees with me. I always wanted a large family. I've no siblings, no cousins, aunts or uncles and have always dreamt of having a house full of noise and laughter and children.'

'But a ready-made family? We'd start off with three and then quite likely have some of our own.'

'I was planning on it. I might be a bit long in the tooth but I think I'll make an excellent father.'

She relaxed against him and he kissed the top of her head. No one had ever made her feel so special; refusing to marry him was going to be harder than she'd thought.

'It wouldn't be right for me to say yes so soon after Tommy died. Ask me again next August and I'll give you my answer then.'

She thought this was a good compromise and that he'd happily accept it, but she was wrong.

'Absolutely not. Why on earth would you suggest such a ridiculous thing? If we're married then this baby will be legally mine – he or she will never be considered illegitimate. By next summer some interfering busybody might well have spirited away Betty and Billy.'

It was hard to think straight when she was sitting in his lap. Her body burned where it touched his and she just wanted to stop talking and make love with him. It hadn't been like this with Tommy. Although she'd enjoyed being in bed with him it wasn't the same.

'Let me go. I don't want to be on your lap. What if someone walked in and saw us? I've got my reputation to think about.'

His arms relaxed and he lifted her to the floor. 'I'm sorry, I'm getting this horribly wrong, aren't I?' He took off his glasses and rubbed his eyes. She couldn't bear to see him look so unhappy.

'Trying to blackmail me into marrying you isn't right. But, you're not wrong about my feelings for you. I love you but I can't be your wife. I really want to go to bed with you but I'm not going to.' She held her bump protectively. 'Wouldn't be right in the circumstances. When the baby's here that will be different.'

He smiled sadly and pushed his spectacles back on his nose. 'Okay, we'll put the question of us marrying to one side for the moment. Do you have any suggestions as to how we can solve the problem of the children being taken away?'

This time she sat on the floral-covered armchair on the other side of the room. 'There must be hundreds of poor little buggers like these two. I reckon the authorities will be only too happy to leave them here and by the end of the war nobody will care where they are as long as they don't have to deal with it. Leave well alone. Better safe than sorry.'

'Are you suggesting we don't even ring the WVS woman?'

'Let sleeping dogs lie.' She didn't usually quote these old sayings and now she'd said three in a row. Maybe she could think of a fourth and make him smile. 'All's well that ends well, David.'

He caught on and grinned. 'Don't poke a stick in a hornets' nest.'

'There's no smoke without fire,' she replied with a giggle and pointed to the dying embers. 'I'll make us a nice mug of cocoa if you put a couple of logs on.'

The kitchen was empty and spotlessly clean. Mary always washed up after herself and Fred. They had their own radio in their sitting room and she could hear *ITMA* blasting out and the two of them laughing.

When she returned with the drinks there was a cosy glow coming from the grate but no sign of David. He must have gone to the downstairs WC. She put his cocoa on the coffee table and returned to the armchair.

Ten minutes later he still wasn't back and she was becoming concerned about his absence. He'd been laughing when she went out and she was certain he hadn't gone off because she'd refused him. She checked the downstairs lav, but it was unoccupied. Had he gone into the surgery for some reason?

She tried the communicating door and it opened. This was always locked after evening surgery so he must be in there. She stepped into the darkness. Why hadn't he put the light on? 'David, your cocoa's getting cold. What are you doing in here?'

The door closed with a snap behind her. She heard the key turn. She couldn't see a blooming thing. Then he was beside her and pulled her close.

'I was waiting for you, sweetheart. I want to make love to you, show you how happy we could be together. Nobody will see us or hear us in here.'

She intended to say no but somehow the words wouldn't come. He could go back to London and be blown up tomorrow. Look what had happened to poor Tommy when they'd both thought he was safe working as ground crew.

'What about the baby?'

He was nibbling her ear, kissing her throat and her skin was on fire everywhere he touched with his lips.

'I promise you, my darling, making love won't harm your baby,' he whispered between kisses as he drew her from the waiting room into the surgery, kicking the door shut behind him. How could he see when it was pitch-dark?

'That blinking examination bed thing's too small,' she managed to say before she was incapable of speech.

'There are blankets on the floor, sweetheart, if you're ready to use them.'

There was no need to answer. Her hands found their own way to his shirt buttons but her fingers were trembling too much to open them. His laugh was deep and sent pulses of heat racing through her.

'Let me take care of things.' He released her for a moment and she heard the buttons popping off as he ripped the shirt apart. He'd already removed his jacket and tie. Then her smock was gone, her elasticated slacks followed and she was in her knickers and bra.

He didn't have to ask her to lie down as her knees gave way. She crumpled to the floor shivering with excitement and anticipation and she heard him kicking off his trousers.

Then he was beside her. His vest and pants had gone and her own underwear followed.

Afterwards David held her in his arms and knew that his life had changed forever. The ten years he'd been married to Julia were a pale imitation to the love he had for this beautiful, intelligent, lively young woman who was now curled contentedly in his arms.

'Our cocoa will be cold,' she murmured against his chest.

'You can warm it up again later.' Why in God's name were they talking about cocoa at a time like this? 'I apologise for ambushing you, sweetheart. I'm only here until tomorrow morning and…'

'Don't say it, don't even think it. Even if we can't be together officially, there'll never be anyone else for me.'

He wasn't going to argue with her. Whatever she thought, eventually they would marry but until then he'd settle for what she was prepared to share with him.

This time he would make love to her more slowly. He wanted to be sure she had as much pleasure from it as he did.

An hour later the cold finally drove them from the floor. They found their clothes by the light of his desk lamp and she laughed when she saw the state of his shirt.

'Pass me my smock, I'm blooming freezing. You should have put the electric fire on first.'

He chuckled. 'Next time I'll do so.'

'Who says there'll be a next time?' This was intended to be a teasing comment but she gulped and turned away.

'Don't cry, my love – nothing's going to happen to me. We've been given a second chance at happiness and the Man upstairs wouldn't be so cruel as to snatch it away.'

'I was told when I was a nipper that God sees everything – I hope He didn't just see what we did.'

Having now got his trousers buttoned he reached out and held her against his naked chest. 'One of the ten Commandments is that we should love each other.'

She giggled as he'd intended. 'I'm sure God wasn't thinking of this when he wrote that on those tablets. I'm ready – get yourself decent and I'll do the cocoa.'

He bundled up the blankets and returned them to the store cupboard and then checked there was nothing out of place in his surgery for the eagle-eyed receptionist to spot tomorrow. He doubted that Simon would notice, but Jill certainly would.

This brief interlude on his own had given him time to question his relationship with his wife. What they had shared in bed was best described as pleasant, but what he'd just experienced with Nancy was genuine passion, real love.

To his amusement she was sitting in the armchair sipping cocoa as if nothing untoward had occurred, as if they hadn't been making passionate love half an hour ago. Her cheeks were still slightly flushed and there was a definite glow about her. He felt ten foot tall and happier than he ever had in his life.

Her smile was blinding. 'Let's hope you don't bump into Mary or Fred looking like that. I can't think why you bothered to put your tie on when you've got no buttons down the front of your shirt.'

He pulled the front down and tucked it firmly into his waistband and then did the same with his tie. 'There, is that better?'

She was openly laughing at him and he wanted to snatch her up and kiss her breathless again. He scowled and dropped into the sofa, knowing that his pretence hadn't fooled her for a moment.

'I don't suppose there's any crumble left? I could do with a snack after all that exercise.'

Her response was to stick her tongue out and roll her eyes. He joined in her laughter. The shared moment of happiness ended when Polly barked and the kitchen door opened.

'Oh God, Simon's back. I don't have time to change my shirt.'

'He's a man – he won't notice. I expect you want to talk to him. I'll make you both a sandwich and then head off to the vicarage. I'm always here by seven and nobody's up then.'

He choked on his cocoa and was still spluttering when Simon walked in.

'Nancy's making me something to eat. I was lucky – an ambulance was needed in the next village and they dropped me off the end of the road. It's bloody freezing outside. Nothing airborne again tonight.'

David had been about to explain why Nancy was still there but decided it was none of Simon's business and would only draw attention to the fact if he mentioned it.

'Take a pew; you must be knackered. Have you got anything new to tell me?'

'Not really. I took the liberty of contacting the local undertakers on your behalf. I thought you wouldn't want the poor girl to have a pauper's funeral.'

'Good show, exactly what I should have done myself. The funeral can be held at the local church and she can be buried in the churchyard.'

'There was a nurse and a doctor present when she said that she wanted you to be guardian to her children. It will stand up in law if you want it to.'

'Nancy thinks it better not to alert the authorities to the change in their circumstances. I don't think it need make any difference to you. Violet ignored them and I doubt she'll be missed.'

Simon sighed. 'Rotten thing to say, but you're right. It

makes no difference to me as, to be frank, I had nothing to do with my own children until they were old enough to have a sensible conversation. Probably the reason they scuttled off to join the army at the earliest possible opportunity.'

Nancy came in with a tray and put it down on the coffee table between him and Simon. David was conscious of his gaping shirt but needn't have worried. His companion wandered across to the radio and switched it on, giving him time to pick up a sandwich and tea and head for the door.

'I've got six weeks' worth of sleep to catch up on so I'll say good night.'

Spending the night in the marital bed for the first time since Julia had died would have been unthinkable a few months ago. It was a little over two weeks until Christmas Day and he felt as though he'd already had the best gift in the world.

Halfway through the night he was woken by the drone of bombers heading for London and his heart sunk. The bastards were back, which meant he must return to his post immediately. The first bus to Chelmsford left at eight o'clock and he'd be on it.

God knows when he'd see Nancy again, but one thing he was very certain of was that she was now irrevocably linked to him. However long it took he would overcome her objections and persuade her to marry him.

17

Nancy dashed home with only the feeble light from her torch to guide her. She shuddered as a wave of Jerry bombers droned overhead on their way to drop death on London. She hadn't contacted her family and friends in Poplar since she'd returned months ago but they must be all right as the police would have contacted her if they weren't.

Violet had died today and yet she was skipping along happy as Larry because David loved her. Instead of slipping in through the back door of the vicarage as she always did, she detoured and went into the church. She'd not been in here in the dark before and it was freezing and unpleasant.

God wouldn't mind if she didn't stay long but she needed to be closer to him and this was the best place. She ducked into a pew and turned off her torch. She didn't need it whilst she was sitting down and batteries were almost impossible to replace.

After a few moments in the cold her thoughts calmed. First, she apologised for being happy when Violet had died, leaving her children as orphans. Then she asked for God's protection for David and for her family. Her final request was for the strength of will to continue to refuse his offer of marriage because if she agreed it would ruin his life.

Her teeth were chattering by the time she'd finished praying and she scuttled out of the building, pulling the door closed behind her. To be honest she still wasn't sure if praying was just talking to herself but it always made her feel better so it couldn't be a bad thing to do.

Only when she was surrounded by the choir, the congregation and listening to the old-fashioned words did her faith seem credible. Sometimes she believed that it was wishful thinking and the life you had was all you got and there was nothing wonderful to come.

Surprisingly she slept well and was up at her usual time of half past six. She always laid up for breakfast, got the range going and cleaned out all the fires and got them ready to be lit. No central heating in this old vicarage and it was perishing first thing everywhere but the kitchen.

The sky was red in the distance and she tried not to think of the damage that had been done to cause this amount of fire. Two weeks to Christmas Day and she reckoned it was going to be a miserable one for most people. Last year the government had told everyone to enjoy themselves but now there was nothing in the shops and very few extras to be found even if you had the money to buy them.

The meat ration had just been cut from two shillings and two pence to one shilling and ten pence. Living in the country meant there was the occasional rabbit and plenty of vegetables available. Fred was going to kill a cockerel for Christmas lunch so they were lucky.

On her last trip into Chelmsford she'd managed to buy a large box of chocolate peppermint creams. This was hidden away and would be shared by everyone on the day itself. She'd made clothes for the children as well as a rag doll for

Betty and a cloth teddy bear for Billy. Mary had a scarf and Fred three initialled handkerchiefs.

Mrs Stanton was getting a pretty blouse with a Peter Pan collar that she'd made from a length of material she'd found in the attic at David's house. The vicar had got handkerchiefs like Fred. She'd bought nothing for David as she didn't know if she was going to be seeing him.

Polly almost upended her when she arrived at the back door. 'Silly dog, what are you doing out here so early?'

The blackout curtain stopped light from escaping into the garden when you opened the door. She almost wet her knickers when David spoke to her from a few feet away.

'We are out here waiting for you, my darling. No regrets about last night?'

'Absolutely none. I don't want to hang about out here – it's even colder than last night.'

Before she could protest she was tugged into his arms and thoroughly kissed. Something so lovely couldn't be wrong, could it?

He'd been busy and the table was laid, her early morning jobs already completed. 'Ta ever so for getting things ready. It's blooming cold at the vicarage and there was ice on the inside of my bedroom window this morning.'

'Move in here, Nancy. Now Violet's no longer with us you can have her room. You spend so much time here it makes sense for you to actually live here.'

'Now you don't live here I can't see that anyone will object.' She smiled and his eyes blazed. 'Don't you get any ideas, Doctor Denny – no more hanky-panky this visit.'

'Then I'll just have to come here more often in future.' His smile made her hot all over. 'I'll sleep on the sofa, naturally.'

'I don't want to let the Stantons down. They've been so kind to me. Another thing, I can't do without her machine either. I get a fair bit of extra money making things for people of an evening.'

'I'm sure you can continue to do that. You also sing in the choir and that won't stop, will it?'

'I'll speak to them when I nip home later after lunch is over. Are you catching the first bus?'

'I'm afraid so. I promise you that if I get even a day off then I'll come down.' He was munching through the toast she'd made and was on his second mug of tea.

'I've not changed my mind about the other thing.'

'I know, which is why I've not mentioned it again. I still think you're wrong but I respect your reasons for refusing.' His expression became serious. 'I've rewritten my will – I'd done it before I came down. Everything I have has been left to you. I want to be sure that you and your baby will be taken care of if anything happens to me.'

She was rarely speechless but for a few moments was incapable of responding. 'You can't do that – what will folk say?'

His laughter filled the room. 'I won't be there to hear them so I don't care. I've got no one else and I've no intention of leaving it to a cats' home or something equally ridiculous. You have no say in the matter, sweetheart, it's a *fait accompli*.' He raised an eyebrow and she threw the tea cosy at him.

'I know what that means. Sometimes I really don't like you, David Denny. You're...' She paused to gather her thoughts and choose exactly the right words. 'You're arrogant, assertive and overbearing.'

He pushed himself slowly to his feet with a gleam in his eye that she didn't trust. She backed away but he continued to approach. 'I'm impressed, Mrs Smith, with your grasp of vocabulary. I'm surprised you didn't add – amorous, adorable and...'

'Asinine,' she said as his bulk blocked her escape. 'I only know the A words really well.'

'I shouldn't tease you, but I love you so much and everything you do, as far as I'm concerned, just makes you more perfect for me.'

Eventually she escaped from his kisses and was able to rush into the scullery so she could thoroughly clean the waiting room and surgery before the receptionist arrived. She'd been worried he would follow her in and expect a repeat of what had happened in here last night but fortunately for her Simon arrived.

Like David he just wanted toast and tea and insisted that he was capable of doing that for himself so she'd no need to go back to the kitchen. Keeping busy was the answer as it stopped her thinking about the time and how little of it there was before David left.

The house was busy, the children rushing about wanting to say their goodbyes as well, which meant she just smiled and nodded as he walked out with his small bag to catch the bus. He'd forgotten to tell the children about their mother and she had no wish to do so herself. Mary would be the best person to break the bad news.

David left to catch the bus feeling ten years younger. He would have been happier if he'd been able to spend more than a few minutes alone with Nancy this morning. He was smiling as he jumped on the bus thinking what a bundle of energy she was – the polar opposite of his first wife.

The bus rattled and bumped its way to Chelmsford where everybody disembarked. The conversation he'd overheard between the housewives sitting in front of him had been about the damage done to the East End again last night.

He kept his stethoscope and white coat in his locker at the hospital so there was no need for him to go to his digs first. Nobody mentioned his absence or his return. He just stepped in as if he'd not been away and dealt with whatever patient needed his expert attention.

He worked straight through until eight o'clock. 'Sister, I'm going to take a break for twenty minutes. I've not eaten since early this morning and won't get through until the end of my shift if I don't.'

'Don't be long, the second wave of ambulances are on their way.'

He grabbed a couple of sandwiches with some sort of anonymous meat filling, a mug of tea and found himself an empty chair at a table already occupied.

'Evening, David, missed you last night. Someone said you'd taken the day off – lucky bugger.' The speaker – Galley – was one of the team of surgeons who worked around the clock sometimes, and was his immediate superior.

'Domestic emergency – all sorted now. Don't look so disapproving. I've been working non-stop since I got here two months ago. I'm supposed to have a minimum of two days a week free so...'

'Point taken. For God's sake, don't vanish without

warning another time. Give us the opportunity to put someone in place.'

David grinned and continued to munch his sandwich. 'Does the word *emergency* not register? Sorry if I left you in the lurch. That said, I'm going to take every opportunity to go home that I can. I almost went for a burton last week and things are going to get hairier here over the next few weeks.'

'How long does it take you to get back to the godforsaken place you call home?'

'I've done it in just under three hours.'

'Then if push came to shove you could get back here quickly?'

'Three hours, yes, but obviously there's no transport in the middle of the night and I no longer have a car.'

'Mr Billings wasn't pleased. He appears to be taking an interest in you, Denny, so don't bugger it up.'

'Thanks for the warning. I'll apologise to him if I see him.' This was unlikely as the chief of surgery was rarely seen in casualty.

Galley nodded and stood up. 'It's easier for those of us who live in London to get home and see the family. You really need Mr Billings' permission to take twenty-four hours when things are quiet, on the understanding that you come back PDQ if necessary.'

'Thank you, I'll speak to him now. I won't bore you with details but things are complicated back there and until decisions have been made, I'll need to be there as often as possible.'

Galley nodded in acknowledgement and strode off. He'd no doubt got many hours of surgery to perform before he could go home. Tonight several new doctors turned up at the hospital and he was able to leave at midnight. He headed for his digs to catch some much-needed sleep.

Strolling through the blackout with only his torch to guide him no longer caused him problems despite his poor night vision. However, tonight he didn't need his torch. The bombers were flying relentlessly overhead, the Bofors guns boomed out and searchlights crisscrossed the sky. Fires made it light enough to see. Fire engines and ambulances clanged their way through the streets. The all clear siren was unlikely to go until the morning. Those who had started to use the underground stations as air raid shelters wouldn't bother to go home even if it did.

There'd been no respite from the devastating attacks since they'd started in September. Only when the weather was so bad that the planes iced up and couldn't fly had there been a break. He was supposed to stop work at midnight and report back at eight o'clock the following morning. All too often when things were grim everyone worked until the patients were dealt with regardless of how long they'd been on their feet.

The next two weeks were relentless and even a letter from Nancy, telling him that the children were fine and excited about Christmas and performing in the Nativity play, failed to raise his spirits. For a second time he had narrowly missed being exterminated by falling masonry on his way to work.

How in God's name did the poor sods in the East End manage to keep cheerful? Nancy's family lived in Poplar – right in the firing line – but she'd not mentioned them having been bombed out or injured so far. He scarcely had time to scribble a quick note in reply saying that he loved her and would come for a visit whenever he could.

He heard two casualty nurses talking about going to the cinema. He couldn't remember the last time he'd gone as Julia thought films were vulgar and had refused to go anywhere apart from the theatre. In the *Sunday Dispatch* there'd been numerous advertisements for what was available in the West End. He certainly wouldn't go and see anything war-related like *Neutral Port*.

If he had the opportunity he'd love to take Nancy to see *The Thief of Bagdad*, on at the Odeon Leicester Square, as this was in what they called the "Magic Technicolor". The chance of being able to do that was non-existent. Even if she'd come, he wouldn't risk taking her anywhere in London with the nightly raids from the blasted Germans.

Tomorrow was Christmas Day and he'd heard that there would be an unofficial truce between the Luftwaffe and the RAF for two days. He went in search of Billings and was fortunate enough to find him.

'I'm going to take tomorrow and Boxing Day off, sir. I've arranged cover with one of the new bods and will leave directly after my shift tonight.'

'Fair enough. How the hell are you going to get there? I don't want you marooned in the back of beyond if I need you in a hurry.'

'I've managed to borrow a motorbike with a full tank. It won't take me more than an hour in either direction with so little traffic on the road.'

'Don't run out of bloody petrol.'

'I didn't ask where my friend found it, but there's a spare

can in one of the side panniers so absolutely no chance of that.'

It was bitterly cold with snow in the air and he was glad Jonathan – one of the junior doctors who'd been kind enough to loan him the bike – had also let him use his thick greatcoat, helmet, goggles and leather gloves. What he really needed were flying boots as the wind, despite the bicycle clips around his trouser legs, was making them flap.

As he hadn't known until this afternoon that he would definitely be able to nip home for thirty-six hours he'd not alerted Nancy. No point in raising her hopes and then having to disappoint her if nothing had come of it.

He'd managed to find an hour to do a bit of shopping. He had sweets for the children, a box of chocolates to share for Fred and Mary and a lovely gold locket that he'd found in a pawnshop for Nancy.

He'd never ridden a motorbike before but Jonathan had assured him if he could drive a car and ride a pushbike then this would be a doddle. One thing it wasn't, was easy. Twice he'd almost catapulted over the handlebars when the bike had skidded on a patch of black ice. By the time he arrived home he was half-frozen and a bag of nerves from the experience.

He switched off the engine and pushed the bike up the drive so he didn't wake anybody. It was a damned noisy beast but certainly efficient, although he was dreading having to make the return journey. He would make sure he travelled in daylight next time.

The back door was never locked as Polly would wake

anyone by barking if a stranger tried to come in. He spoke to her through the window as he walked past and she was waiting at the door, her tail wagging so hard that her entire body was waving from side to side in time with it.

'Hello, old girl. I'm glad to see you too. Merry Christmas. Now, you daft dog, let a fellow get in and get warm.'

He crept around the place like a burglar expecting someone to get up and confront him at any moment but the house remained quiet. After a quick cuppa he was ready to find his way upstairs and into Nancy's room.

They both knew he'd no intention of sleeping on the sofa, whatever he'd said to the contrary. The dog returned to her bed with a sigh of happiness and he knew exactly how she felt. His intention was to oversleep and be discovered sleeping in the same bedroom as Nancy and forcing her hand.

As he was about to go upstairs he reconsidered. This would be grossly unfair to her. Hastily, he collected the blankets from the store cupboard and made himself up a rudimentary bed on the sofa in the sitting room. Julia had always called it the drawing room – but it wasn't grand enough for that title in his opinion.

There was a splendid tree in one corner. His mouth curved as he examined the strange collection of decorations obviously made by the children. He put his gifts with the others under the tree and was delighted to see the children had a stocking each.

He dumped his bag, removed his shoes and socks, jacket and tie and only then went upstairs. He hadn't turned on any lights as doing so might have woken someone. He hesitated outside her door, wondering if he should knock then thought: better not as Mary or Fred or, even worse, the children might hear him.

'Blooming heck, you took your time, David. What were you doing downstairs – cooking the Christmas dinner?'

Nancy's voice coming from the bed startled him and he dropped his torch on his bare foot. 'Bloody hell – that hurt.' His surreptitious approach had obviously failed miserably.

'Shush. You'll wake everybody up. Please don't use bad language, I'm not comfortable with it.'

This was exactly what he'd said to her when he'd first met her and he laughed. The remainder of his clothes were dropped on the floor and he joined her in the bed. There was no necessity to remove her nightgown.

A couple of hours later they lay entangled and sweaty. He was drifting into a satiated sleep when he was poked sharply in the ribs.

'Oh no you don't, love. I'm not having anyone find you in my bed, even if they all know you've been here.'

With a resigned sigh he rolled out and found his discarded clothes. 'I'm going to go downstairs as I am. If I'm seen then it's entirely your fault.'

She giggled but this changed to a squeak of horror when he did exactly what he'd threatened.

18

Nancy sat up in bed holding her breath. Then she heard Billy's voice. 'Are you that Father Christmas bloke Auntie Nancy's telling us about?'

She tumbled out of bed, snatched up her nightie and dragged it over her head. If it wasn't so awful it would be funny.

Quietly she opened the door a crack. It was pitch-dark. Billy wouldn't be able to see.

'I am and if you don't scamper back to bed this minute no stocking for you.' David's voice sounded deeper, unrecognisable, and she stifled a giggle when he continued. 'Ho, Ho, Ho.'

She heard Billy's door snick shut and was finally able to breathe. She poked her head out but David had strolled off, in his birthday suit, and she could hear him laughing quietly as he went downstairs. Heaven knows what Billy would say to Mary tomorrow morning, but it was funny.

She was learning more about him every time they met. She'd never known he had such a wicked sense of humour and this was just another thing to love about him. She found it hard to believe that when she'd first met him she'd thought him old and not very attractive.

Being in bed with him was nothing like it had been with Tommy. Maybe that was because he was older, more experienced – she'd have to ask him. He was a medical man and was bound to know the answer to that sort of question.

Her alarm went off at six thirty as usual and she tumbled out of bed and hurried to the sink to have a strip wash. She spent a little longer on her appearance than she usually did; after all it was Christmas Day and they would all be going to matins. There was no choir at this service so she needed to look her best if she was going to be in the congregation.

David pounced on her when she stepped into the kitchen. 'Merry Christmas, my darling, I can't tell you how happy I am to be here with you.'

'Not half as happy as I am to have you here. What were you thinking last night? I doubt that Mary would have been fobbed off the way that Billy was.'

He grinned and kissed her, preventing further conversation for several wonderful minutes. She pulled away and smiled up at him. 'I hope you haven't mussed my hair. Don't forget we're all going to church at ten o'clock. Don't you have anything tidier to wear?'

'I was working all day in this outfit and didn't have time to go back to my digs and change.'

She wrinkled her nose. 'You do pong a bit, love, a nasty hospital smell. Didn't you put most of your clothes up in the attic? If you nip up there and find something quickly then I've still got time to give it an iron before anyone else's up.'

He kissed the tip of her nose and stepped away. 'That's a very becoming frock, sweetheart. I assume you made it.' She nodded. 'You're a very accomplished woman. You can cook, sew, take care of children and are amazing in bed.'

Her cheeks coloured at his comment. 'You mustn't say things like that out loud. You never know who might be listening.' Then she stretched up and kissed him. 'You're not too shabby yourself. Now, buzz off, and let me get breakfast ready. We're having it all together in the dining room today.'

He vanished and she went to check that the prepared vegetables for Christmas dinner hadn't frozen solid in the pantry. The fat cockerel was already stuffed and waiting for the oven. She'd not been able to get enough dried fruit to make either a Christmas cake or a Christmas pudding. However, she'd managed to buy four Mrs Peek's tinned Christmas puddings. They wouldn't be as good but better than nothing. The fruit she'd managed to get had been turned into mincemeat so at least there would be mince pies for tea.

The children were going to be allowed to have their stockings after breakfast but the gifts under the tree wouldn't be opened until this afternoon. From the banging about she could hear above her Billy and Betty were now up and very excited.

The little boy burst into the kitchen, his eyes shining with excitement. 'I saw him, Auntie Nancy. That Father Christmas bloke was here like what you said he would be.'

'How exciting – have you checked in the sitting room to see if he left you and your sister anything in your stockings?'

When she'd moved in a couple of weeks ago he'd started calling her Auntie Nancy and she actually preferred that to being referred to as Mrs Smith. The folded blanket was ready on the kitchen table and the electric iron was good and hot. All she needed was the shirt and she could do it before she served breakfast.

David handed her three shirts, two pairs of trousers, a tie and jacket. 'I didn't know which one to wear so I brought all these for you to choose from.'

Mary had appeared in the door and overheard his remark. 'It's not for me to say, Doctor Denny, so I'll do all of them. It won't be until after breakfast mind, as the boiled eggs and soldiers won't keep.'

'It's very kind of you to do this for me, Nancy. I'll go and speak to the children. Call me when things are ready.'

Fred was already outside feeding the chickens and the pigs and she doubted he would actually sit at the same table as everybody else whatever Mary wanted him to do. He was a very antisocial old man, but good at his job so she supposed it didn't really matter if he wouldn't talk to anyone.

Doctor Jones eventually appeared and was suitably surprised to see David. 'Didn't know you were coming – good to see you. Did you come on that motorbike?'

'I certainly did and unfortunately I have to return on it. I'm hoping I won't kill myself as I nearly did so more than once on the way down.'

'Let's hope you're not called back in the middle of the night. Hopefully this unofficial truce will hold until after Boxing Day and give us all a break.'

Nancy wasn't sure how Dr Jones was helped by the lack of bombs but didn't comment.

After breakfast the children rushed into the sitting room and the adults, even Fred, followed to watch them empty their stockings. If they'd been given a chest full of gold coins they couldn't have been happier.

Every small item they pulled out was exclaimed over and

held out to be examined. 'Look at this, it's a sugar mouse. I ain't – I've never had one of those before,' Billy said.

'Mousy mousy, yum yum,' Betty chanted and promptly bit off the head and crunched it up.

The little girl was now proudly out of nappies and had very few accidents. She was also talking and sounded more like Mary every day. It was harder for Billy to correct his speech but he was getting there. Nowadays Nancy rarely made a mistake and Charlotte and Jane would be amazed when they saw her next time.

She left the children to play with their bits and pieces. Not only did she have to clear away the breakfast, wash the dishes, but also get the Christmas dinner cooking. On top of that David now wanted her to iron and press his entire wardrobe.

Her eyes filled. It wasn't fair that she was the only one not having Christmas Day free.

'Don't cry, sweetheart, I'll help you. I'm not going to sit about watching you wait on everyone.'

She turned into his arms forgetting that someone was likely to come in and see them embracing. 'I don't know why I keep blubbing, love. The slightest thing sets me off nowadays.'

'It's your condition, darling. It's very common for pregnant women to be more emotional.'

Something small and sticky tugged on the hem of her new frock. She looked down and Betty was standing there holding out a piece of half-chewed sugar mouse. 'For you, Auntie Nancy.'

'Thank you, that's so kind. Can I keep it for later?'

'Yes, later. Need a wee wee now.'

David reacted instantly. 'Come along, little one, I'll take you to the lavatory.' He picked the child up and dashed off to the downstairs cloakroom.

When they left for church Nancy was satisfied everything that needed to be done was done. The children had helped Mary lay the table and put their home-made crackers next to each place. The cock had been in the slow oven for two hours already and would be absolutely perfect when they sat down to eat at one. Mrs Andrews was joining them and they were meeting her at church.

Mr and Mrs Stanton had gone to stay with family and the curate took the service. The carols were sung with gusto, the curate's sermon was brief and the congregation trooped out in just over an hour. There was a watery winter sun giving no warmth but bathing everything in much-needed light.

It took far longer to get away today as they had to wish everybody merry Christmas. David and Dr Jones were particularly popular and from Mrs Andrews' expression she took a dim view of the ladies simpering and smiling at them. Goodness knows what she was going to say when she eventually discovered that she and David were involved.

Christmas had always been a subdued affair and David now realised what he'd been missing all these years. Maybe things would have been different if Julia had had children but somehow, he doubted she'd ever have sat on the carpet playing with them the way that Nancy was.

The telephone rang halfway through the afternoon and as he was nearest he went into the hall and picked it up, fearing it might be from Billings asking him to return immediately.

'Doctor Denny, I didn't know you were returning for the holiday. Merry Christmas to you,' Mrs Stanton said. 'Could I speak to Nancy please?'

'I'll get her for you. Happy Christmas to you and the vicar – I hope to be back again in a few weeks and actually see you in person.'

He turned and Nancy was watching from the doorway. He shook his head and smiled. 'It's Mrs Stanton for you.'

He thought now would be a good time to put the kettle on. The sandwiches were made and resting under a damp tea towel and from the delicious aroma wafting from the oven the mince pies were heating up ready for tea.

'Uncle David,' Billy said from behind him. 'I wasn't lying about Father Christmas. Auntie Mary says I mustn't tell lies but I never did.'

'I believe you and so does Auntie Nancy. Are you enjoying Christmas Day?' It was strange but it was as if Violet had never existed. Like dropping a pebble into a pond, the ripples had spread and disappeared leaving no trace behind.

'It's the best day ever. I never knew Father Christmas gave us things. I reckon he never found us where we lived before. And we got more presents just now.' He waved the patchwork teddy bear, that Nancy had made him, in the air. 'This is my favourite.'

'He's absolutely splendid. Does he have a name yet?'

'I'm calling him Teddy. Betty likes her dolly ever so much. I like it better here now that Auntie Nancy lives with us. Are you going to live with us all the time soon?'

'I hope so, Billy, but I have to be in London to help the

people who get hurt by the bombs. One day I'll be back and we can be a family.' He spoke without thinking and prayed that the little chap wouldn't rush off and announce this to the others.

Unfortunately, Jill decided to help make the tea and take it into the dining room and did overhear.

'Good heavens, David, I didn't know you were intending to keep the children.'

Thank God she hadn't grasped the fact that he was including Nancy in his comment. 'Why wouldn't I? I always wanted children and now I've been blessed with a ready-made family. Violet, on her deathbed, asked that I would become their guardian, but I would have done it anyway.'

'They are quite pleasant as children go, but as I didn't even want any of my own I couldn't possibly consider taking on anyone else's offspring.' She looked around and then pulled the door almost closed behind her. 'I wanted to speak to you about something personal. Has Simon said anything about me?'

'No, he hasn't. However, this is only the second time I've been here since I left so there's hardly been time for confidential conversation of any sort. I noticed the two of you seemed a bit more than casual friends.'

Her smile told him everything he wanted to know. 'Oh, do you think so? I feared the interest was on my side alone. I know Simon's quite a lot older than me but that doesn't matter at all.'

'I think you will make the perfect couple. I think he's the sort of chap who will take his time to make up his mind but from what I've seen he sees you as a potential partner.'

The door swung open with a bang and Betty came in waving her new doll. 'My dolly. See my new dolly, Uncle David.'

He dropped down to her level and solemnly examined it. 'It's absolutely beautiful, sweetheart. Does she have her own name?'

The toddler screwed up her face, closed her eyes and swayed from side to side. She did this when she was thinking and he found it absolutely charming.

'Polly dolly, she's my Polly dolly.'

The dog, hearing her name, bounded over and sent both of them sprawling. Nancy arrived whilst he was still attempting to disentangle himself from the dog and Betty. Jill was making absolutely no effort to help but had wandered off to get the mince pies out of the oven.

'What a palaver! Come on, Betty love, come to Auntie Nancy and let Uncle David get up. Polly, on your bed, silly dog.'

'Thank you, I came in to make the tea and didn't expect to be flattened by my stupid animal. Nancy, take Betty back into the sitting room. Jill and I are getting the tea ready and will call you when it's on the table. You've done enough for today.'

She didn't argue. 'Ta ever so, I could do with a sit-down for half an hour.' She glanced across at Jill. 'Thank you. Everything's ready; you just have to take it through and put out the plates and so on. There's jelly and evaporated milk for the children for afters.'

Jill pulled a face and this annoyed him. 'I hope there'll be enough for me; jelly and evaporated milk is my absolute favourite,' he said firmly.

Betty was wriggling to be put down and rushed off banging the walls with her rag doll as she went and singing *Polly dolly* at the top of her voice. Only by sticking his foot out did he prevent the dog from dashing after her.

'I can see her choice of names is going to be a problem. Maybe you can persuade her to think of something else?'

'I'll do my best. Your dog's going to be very confused if we don't.'

The remainder of the day was equally enjoyable and even the curmudgeonly Fred actually smiled a couple of times before he and his wife retreated to their own domain. The children went to bed with no fuss, Simon offered to walk Jill home and she accepted with alacrity, which left him to spend some time alone with Nancy.

They sat together on the sofa and he dipped into his pocket and handed her the pretty velvet box containing the locket. He'd decided not to put it under the tree as this would draw attention to its value when it was seen by everyone else.

'You shouldn't have got me anything, I don't have anything for you.'

'I don't need you to give me a present. I just need you to love me.'

She raised her eyebrows and giggled. 'None of that saucy talk, David. It's the Lord's birthday and we should be suitably devout, not talking about you know what.'

'Open the box, darling. I do hope you like it.'

Instead of laughing in delight she burst into tears when she saw the gold locket. 'It reminds me of Tommy. He gave me a lovely engagement ring – real gold and a diamond – it belonged to his grandma.'

'Don't cry, sweetheart, I want you to be happy.' He didn't dare put his arms around her as Simon could come back at any moment.

'It's really lovely. Put it on for me please.' She dried her eyes and put her head down so he could reach round and fasten it.

'There, it's absolutely perfect on you. You didn't open it but it has places for you to put photographs.'

'Have to be a blooming small photo to go in there.' She reached up and touched the heart. He saw that she was no longer wearing either of her rings. He wasn't sure if this was a good sign or not. She noticed him looking at her bare finger.

'They were getting a bit tight. I didn't want to have to have them cut off.'

Immediately his professional side took over. Any swelling of fingers or ankles was a bad sign of pregnancy and especially so early on.

'Let me see your hands.'

She understood immediately he was talking as a doctor not a lover, and held them out. 'Nothing to worry about. No discernible puffiness. Can I see your ankles too?'

Before he could lean down and look she lifted both feet and put them in his lap.

'All splendid, my love; sorry to have alarmed you.'

'I reckon I'm fatter all over and not just my belly. I've always been curvy, but not fat. It's because I'm eating better. Even in the WAAFs food wasn't as good as it is here and often I didn't fancy anything after spending all day cooking.'

'You're on your feet all day so I'm certain you've not put on any weight apart from your pregnancy. And anyway, as far as I'm concerned every inch of you is flawless.'

'You're not too bad yourself.'

Then Simon spoke from the door. 'Don't mind me, I'd guessed how things were between you.'

19

Nancy tried to remove her feet from David's lap but he kept his hands on them. This was all her fault and now everyone would know that she was not only having an illegitimate baby but was also David's mistress. She would have to leave. No one would want to know her now.

'We don't want to make it public at the moment, Simon. I'm sure we can count on your discretion.'

'Absolutely; none of my business. I expect you've noticed that I'm quite taken with Jill and discovered tonight that she feels the same way. Who am I to cavil about a bit of romance in the air?'

Whilst David was distracted she'd managed to wriggle free, push her feet back into her slippers, and duck out before he could call her back.

What had she been thinking to get involved with him so soon? They were playing happy families as if everything was how it should be. Jill and Dr Jones was quite a different matter and nobody could possibly object to them getting together.

She was quite certain that even Mrs Stanton and the vicar would disapprove – you shouldn't do it before you were married and she'd now done it with two men.

There'd be no cocoa tonight and she was going to lock her door. Whatever David might think he wasn't coming into her bed again. There was no key and she was sure there had been yesterday. Had he taken it knowing what she would do if their secret was discovered? There was a chair and that would work almost as well. She turned it round, tilted it onto its back legs, and pushed it under the doorknob. She tried to open the door but it remained firmly closed.

She was all of a dither and didn't know what to do for the best. Her instinct had been to run away but she knew that didn't make sense. She was needed here and didn't have anywhere else to go. All she could do was end the relationship with him and that would not only break his heart, it would break hers as well.

Every time she heard a noise outside she expected him to be trying her door but he didn't even come upstairs to use the bathroom. Was he waiting until he was certain Dr Jones was fast asleep?

He didn't come and she wasn't sure if she was glad that he'd understood the situation had changed or sad that he hadn't even tried to persuade her to change her mind.

The next morning he wasn't waiting to speak to her in the kitchen. Was he still asleep in the sitting room on the sofa? Then her heart thudded uncomfortably and there was a lump in her throat. Had he already left without even saying goodbye?

Forgetting her good intentions she burst into the room and he was sitting up smiling, waiting for her. He didn't say anything, just held out his hands, and she couldn't help herself. She collapsed into his arms and he stroked her back and murmured nonsense until she'd recovered.

'You didn't come; you weren't in the kitchen. I thought you'd gone.'

'I know you did. Believe me, my darling, it was the hardest thing I've ever done staying downstairs. What we feel for each other is just too big to be ended the way you wanted to do it last night. Simon won't say anything and I'm going immediately after breakfast.'

'I didn't know this was going to be so hard. I want to do the right thing but here I am back in your arms.' She sat up and moved away so there was a safe distance between them. She couldn't think straight when he was touching her.

'I'm going to try and explain to you why this has to stop. You need to look at it the way everybody else will when they find out – and they will – and see it from their point of view. I'm a girl who not only is carrying an illegitimate baby but has also slept with someone else a few months after her fiancé was killed.'

'There's a war on, Nancy. Nobody cares any more about things like that.'

'They might not in London but they certainly do in Chalfont Major. They'll think that I'm no better than Violet.'

'For God's sake, don't talk such bloody stupid nonsense. You were going to marry Tommy two weeks after you were with him. If he hadn't been killed no one would have been any the wiser.'

'I think people would be all right with that. It's what we've done that will cause the problems. They'll just think you're taking what was on offer. It'll be me and my baby who will suffer. I'll be sent to Coventry. I doubt that even Jane or Charlotte will want to speak to me.'

'I don't know how many times I have to tell you this but I don't care what anyone says. Marry me immediately and then none of it will matter.'

She'd intended to say no but somehow said exactly the opposite. 'I will, but I warn you, you'll regret it. None of your posh friends will want anything to do with you when I'm your wife.'

The look of joy on his face made her words meaningless. Then she was in his arms and his cheeks were as wet as hers. When the war was over they could move away and start again where no one knew anything about their past.

'I'm going over to the vicarage. We'll get married before I leave – I'm pretty sure you don't need to call the banns any more.'

'I think if you don't call the banns then you have to have a licence. You can't get that on Boxing Day.'

'I'm so excited I'm not thinking straight. It might be better to have a civil service. This would avoid the gossip until we're actually married. I'm certain you can get married in the town hall at Chelmsford but we have to give notice. I'm not sure how long that is.'

'Then I'll leave it to you. Before you go I'll write down all my details. You don't even know how old I am, do you?'

'You'll be twenty-one in two weeks' time. I'll be thirty-three in February. Simon's eighteen years older than Jill. Therefore, twelve years is nothing in comparison.'

'I stopped worrying about that a long time ago. It makes sense to leave it until I'm legally of age then we don't have to bother my parents. They still think I was married to Tommy.'

'I'm sure they'll be even happier when they know that you're actually married to me.'

'Pa will be. He'll be touching you up for a handout if he gets half a chance.'

He chuckled. 'I'll get things organised and let you know the day and time. I might well only get a few hours off so a honeymoon and so on will have to be postponed.'

'If you can borrow that motorbike again you should be able to get to Chelmsford easy from the Royal Free. You don't need to bother to get a ring as I can use the one Tommy got for me.'

'You certainly won't. There's a pawn shop where I got your locket that had a tray of rings. If you give me something of yours then I'll make sure I get one that fits.'

'Better to get it a bit bigger just in case. Are you quite sure you want to take on this baby?'

'I've already taken on Billy and Betty and I don't even know who their fathers were. I already think of this baby as mine and I can't tell you how happy you've made me by agreeing to marry me at the earliest possible moment it can be arranged.'

Then she had an awful premonition. Tommy had been all right until they'd set the wedding date and then he'd been killed a few days before the ceremony could take place. Was she putting David in mortal danger by agreeing to marry him?

'You will be careful won't you? Seems like we're tempting fate rushing into it like this.'

'I truly believe that you came here specifically to drag me

out of my miserable existence. You don't know a lot about me so why don't you sit down...'

'No, you come into the kitchen and we can sit at the table and have a cuppa. No one will be up for another hour.'

She looked around this room, hardly able to believe that in a few weeks it would be hers – that she would be Mrs Denny and not the housekeeper.

'That reminds me, love, I'll still carry on running this place; you just won't have to pay me.'

'I never expected you to be a lady of leisure, sweetheart. It's one of the many things I love about you – your boundless energy.'

She poured them both a tea and sat opposite. 'Now, tell me all the things I need to know and then I'll tell you a few things about me and my family.'

'Okay then. I was an only child of elderly parents. I was sent to boarding school from the age of seven and by the time I left to study medicine I was already an orphan and very rich indeed. I met Julia at her come-out ball – I was dragged along by a friend.'

'What's a *come-out ball* when it's at home?'

'Sorry, I should have explained. It's where debutantes go to find themselves a suitable husband.'

'I see. Like a cattle market for rich people.'

He laughed and continued. 'That's about right. I was there looking for a suitable wife. She was beautiful, intelligent and exactly what I was looking for. I asked her out and a few months later we were engaged and her mother was planning a massive country wedding.'

'Blimey, that was quick. You must have really loved her.'

'Of course I did, but looking back I wonder if she

reciprocated my feelings. She did love me in her own way and we were very happy together apart from the fact that we didn't have children. I built this house for her and whatever she wanted me to do, I did it without question.'

'That doesn't sound like the man I know. I can't see you doing that now for anyone.'

'Remember, I was a lonely young man studying to become a doctor. I needed someone to come home to, someone to support me and talk to me. She was more than ready to do that so in return I used the money I'd inherited to give her everything she wanted.'

'Didn't she have money of her own?'

'Not really – doing the circuit took every penny her parents had. Her father was a hardened gambler and the family was heavily in debt. Now I come to think of it, it was like something out of a Jane Austen novel. I agreed to settle his debts and was happy to do so.'

'She might not have loved you as much as you loved her but she was a good wife to you and came from the same background as you.'

This was something that bothered her – had always been a worry – however much they loved each other she wasn't sure it would be enough to overcome the differences between them. She was as good as Julia but she wasn't from the same class.

Nancy listened to the rest of his story and understood him better because of hearing this. 'I'm not sending any of our children away to boarding school so don't think I will.'

'Boarding school was a lot better than some evacuations – are you all right with those?'

'Kiddies were sent away to keep them safe. Sending

children to school's a different matter. Why have children at all if you don't want them living with you?'

'Good question. My parents certainly didn't want me around. As soon as we're married, I'll start legal proceedings to adopt Billy and Betty. Then when our baby comes they'll be his or her big sister and brother.'

The more they talked about this the more complicated everything seemed. 'I suppose you'll want to keep Mary and Fred working here?'

'I don't want you to have to look after two children, a new baby and everything else.'

'Blimey, it's only hard doing that when you haven't got any money. I suppose you need Fred to take care of the garden now you're not here and they've got nowhere else to go, have they?'

'If things go the way I expect then Simon and Jill will get married in a few months, if not sooner, and then he'll move into her house. We can lock this door and keep the surgery separate.'

'That's all right then. I was hoping we could live somewhere else when the war's over. Start afresh where nobody knows anything about us or the children.'

'This bloody thing isn't going to finish in the next year – might go on longer than the last one. I'm going to stay in London as long as I'm needed. As I told you, my intention had been to become a surgeon and if I hadn't married Julia I would have done so.'

'Then that's what you must do. If we lived nearer London when you're doing your training and such you could get home at night sometimes.'

'If I do become the kind of surgeon that I always wanted

to be then I'm going to be working at one of the big hospitals in Town. I'll buy a house in Kensington or Hampstead which is almost as good as living in the country.'

She loved talking to him about what their future life might be. As far as she was concerned she didn't mind where she was as long as he and their family was with her. She reckoned she could pretend to be someone like him and no one would ever know that he'd married so far below him.

There would be posh dinners, cocktail parties and such and she'd be expected to go with him. She wasn't sure she'd be up to that even if she wanted to mix with people who wouldn't like her. David was different to them – if he wasn't then she wouldn't have fallen in love with him.

When he went off on his motorbike the children came out to wave goodbye but she thought it better if she remained inside. Time enough to let people know what's what when they were actually married.

Later that morning Jill remarked on the fact that Nancy was no longer wearing her wedding ring or engagement ring.

'Someone at the post office told me they'd had to have their band cut off as their hands got swollen at the end. I didn't want that to happen to mine.'

'Very sensible. I wonder if you would be kind enough to let me have a closer look at your engagement ring.'

Nancy's stomach lurched. David had taken this with him. To her relief the children interrupted the awkward moment and she hoped that she'd come up with a suitable excuse if the receptionist asked a second time to see it.

He'd suggested that he call her every couple of days but she'd told him not to as this would be suspicious. Instead, they were going to exchange letters frequently. The first one from him would be with the time and date when they were to meet in Chelmsford. As she was always the one to collect the post and sort it out no one would notice.

Two days after Christmas the nightly drone of German aircraft resumed. Jill didn't ask to see the engagement ring again and her relationship with Dr Jones appeared to be progressing fast. It was none of her business and she'd no intention of asking for details.

On the night of the 29th the bombers started to arrive earlier than usual. Wave after wave droned past and she was sick with worry about David and her family in the East End. There'd been no letter with the all-important dates and so on but he wouldn't have had time to arrange things so soon.

She was standing at the kitchen window around eight o'clock watching the searchlights over London when Mary joined her. Even from this distance these were quite clear in the night sky. There was the constant chatter of the big ack-ack guns as they tried to shoot down the invaders. The RAF fighters were up there doing their best to stop the bombers reaching their destination.

'It's a bad night tonight. There'll be thousands of people homeless in the morning and probably hundreds dead. The blackout's no help on a clear night like this as they just follow the Thames,' Mary said.

'Doesn't bear thinking about. I'm going outside to have a better look.'

The sky was already bright with fire. They must be dropping thousands of incendiaries. It seemed as if the whole of the city was ablaze. If it looked so terrifying thirty miles away God knows what it was like to be living through this.

Something cold and wet nudged her hand. 'Polly, you shouldn't be out here.' The dog whined and pressed against her legs. The animal was trembling. 'Let's go back in, silly girl. I'm freezing as I didn't even put on my coat.'

In Chalfont Major folk just carried on as if there wasn't a war waging around them. Nobody talked about the bombing last night. Nancy didn't like to sit with Simon and listen to the news on the wireless as she was just the housekeeper and therefore had no right to be in there with him. The fact that he knew she was more than that didn't make any difference.

This was why most nights she went over to the vicarage to get on with her sewing and mending and also spend time with the Stantons. They never had anything but music playing so she didn't catch up on the news there either.

The telephone rang at seven o'clock in the morning on New Year's Eve. She snatched it up and to her immense relief it was David.

'I've been so worried about you. I'm ever so glad you've rung me.'

'I'm knackered, but unhurt. The Luftwaffe timed their attack perfectly. The Thames was at low tide and the water mains were blown up in the first wave. I heard there were more than 10,000 firebombs dropped.'

'I've not heard anything from Poplar. Do you know if it was badly damaged by the fire?'

'Pretty much everywhere had some damage. I'll try and find out for you – I've got a couple of friends in the police force. I can't talk for long – I'm back on duty at eight o'clock. I fixed the date for twelve o'clock on the 20th. It's a Monday. I've booked that day off, but didn't give a reason.'

'That gives me plenty of time to arrange everything here. Jill asked to see my engagement ring the other day but luckily I didn't have to make up any excuse as the children interrupted. Could you post it back to me just in case she asks again?'

'Will do – and there'll be a letter as well. I've already written that and intended to post it on my way to work this morning. I love you and can't wait to marry you.'

'I love you too. Take care of yourself, love, and I'll see you on the 20th.'

The letter arrived two days later and she put it upstairs on the dressing table to read when she took her break that afternoon. Simon had asked if he could have a small party that evening and she'd been touched that he'd thought he needed her permission.

'Obviously there'll be you, Mary and Fred, Jill and myself and I also invited the vicar and his wife. Is there any chance you can rustle up a few snacks? I've got the drinks side covered.'

'There's plenty of spuds – I'll do something with those.' She smiled at his expression. 'It won't be a pile of mash. Don't worry. Which reminds me, Fred was saying the pigs will be slaughtered at the end of the month. The children have become friends with both of them. I don't reckon they'll be very happy.'

'They'll stop complaining when they've got bacon and roast pork to eat.' He thanked her politely for his breakfast, as he did for every meal, and then wandered off to the surgery.

She'd intended to write to Ma, Jane and Charlotte today and had already half written a letter to David. When she'd read his she'd finish hers and then take all four to the post office. Mary took the dog out with the children for their morning walk, rain or shine, and she did the same in the afternoon. In the evening Polly made do with the garden, which was more than good enough.

The morning dragged as she was desperate to read his letter but eventually lunch was over and she could escape upstairs. She wasn't going to mention that she was getting married in just over three weeks in any of the letters. Time enough to tell them when the knot was tied.

20

David was lucky to get a few hours' sleep each night and on several occasions he'd just flaked out at the hospital on the nearest chair, too tired to walk the short distance to his digs. The letters he received from Nancy were the only glimmer of light in the human misery he was wading through every day.

He managed to grab a few words with Billings about restarting his surgical training. His boss was delighted to discover he had a potential surgeon in his team already.

'You completed the first year and now you're dealing with emergency surgery every day in casualty with bloody good results. Scrub in with me this afternoon and we'll see how much you know.'

'That's good of you, sir. I thought you might think I was too old to continue my training.'

'Bugger that – your general practice experience and the work you've been doing in casualty these past months will just make you a better surgeon. We surgeons tend to treat each operation as if the patient was anonymous. You have a different focus, which might well be useful.'

'Thank you for the opportunity. I'll accompany the next patient who needs your attention.'

His life changed dramatically from that moment. The hospital was desperately short of surgeons, even those with as little experience as himself. Billings was a great believer in learning on the job and was an excellent teacher.

Initially David spent half the time in the operating theatre and the rest in casualty setting bones, sewing wounds and just generally patching up the walking wounded. Three weeks after he'd been given the opportunity to assist Billings things changed again.

'Good work, Denny. You're wasted in casualty. From now on you join my team. You can take the simple cases from my hands.'

'Are you quite sure?'

'I wouldn't have asked you if I wasn't. There's a war on – in case you haven't noticed – the fact that you're not fully qualified doesn't matter. You worked alongside me for dozens of operations and I've seen for myself how good you are.'

'In which case, thank you. I won't let you down.'

'You bloody well better not. I'm staking my reputation on you. By the way, I've spoken to the board and they've agreed to allow you to take the necessary exams in a couple of months but as far as they're concerned, you're qualified. The exams will be a piece of cake for you. Then you'll have the necessary paperwork – no need to do any more book work, just learn on the job.'

David was stunned that a short conversation three weeks ago had been enough to catapult him into a different league of medicine. Surgeons were top dogs in any hospital and the chief surgeon, which Billings was, could do no wrong.

He remembered a joke someone had told him when in medical school. "What's the difference between God and a surgeon?" The answer to this being: "God knows he isn't a surgeon."

He wished Nancy was there to share his excitement. Things were moving faster on his career front than he'd ever dreamt was possible. To add to his joy, he would be marrying the most incredible young woman in three days' time. Five months ago, he'd been wallowing in self-pity, letting life pass him by and then Nancy had literally fallen at his feet. Things had been different from that moment.

There had not been time to answer her last two letters but she would be his wife in a few days and they'd have twenty-four hours together. The fact that he'd booked into the Saracens hotel in Chelmsford for the night he'd kept to himself.

Nancy thought they wouldn't have even one night's honeymoon so this was his surprise. Until he'd made love to her he'd not been bothered about sex. Being totally in love with a person made all the difference.

This time his marriage was his choice. He was marrying someone from a different stratum of society, someone Billings would disapprove of. She would soon adapt to their different circumstances although he wouldn't be moving her to London until this bloody war was over. However hard it was for both of them to be apart, he wasn't going to risk her safety.

The day before his wedding – the Sunday – he was just about to leave for the day after spending several hours in the theatre patching up a variety of injured civilians – when Billings pounced on him.

'There you are. I need you. Come with me.'

You didn't argue with Mr Billings even if you had been on your feet for twelve hours. David thought they were going back to theatre but instead they headed outside. There was an ambulance and a large Daimler waiting both with engines running.

'Very important patient with what sounds like a blocked bowel. We're going to him. Got the nurses and everything we need in the bus.'

A uniformed chauffeur doffed his cap and held open the car door. Billings got in. David knew the drill and waited at the other passenger door for the man to come round and do the same for him.

How the hell did this man have petrol to run such a big car? His Riley was on blocks in the garage for the duration. He'd neglected to ask exactly where this patient lived. Hopefully he'd get half an hour's kip before they arrived.

The whole thing was quite unnecessary in his opinion, as whoever it was would have been better served coming to the hospital and not having the hospital come to him. In which case why was the ambulance with them?

He supposed he should be flattered at being asked to accompany Billings on such a prestigious job. It was a damned nuisance as right about now he should be getting some sleep so he'd be tickety-boo for his wedding tomorrow.

Although the king and queen had remained at Buckingham Palace most of the rich people had moved to their country estates to avoid the bombing. Surrey or Hertfordshire was probably their destination as that's where a lot of the top people lived.

Billings was already asleep so he might as well do the

same. He jerked awake later and to his horror saw they'd been driving for three hours. God knows where they were but it certainly wasn't close to London. How the hell was he going to get to Chelmsford for midday?

Nancy caught the early bus as she wanted to be sure she'd be there on time. Whenever she went into the nearby market town to visit the bank and so on, she put on her Sunday best. This meant no one thought it odd that she'd done so today.

She was hoping to find a few bits and pieces to add to her sewing box as the wonderful collection Mrs Stanton had given her was already half gone. These items weren't yet rationed but the difficulty was finding the things you wanted.

This morning she'd been too excited to eat breakfast and the baby had been turning somersaults all night so she was already tired. When she got married the registrar would think David was marrying her because she was carrying his baby. If he didn't mind people thinking he'd got her into trouble then why should she care?

She discovered a small haberdasher's in a backstreet with exactly the items she was looking for. The fact that the embroidery thread was a bit faded, the reels of cotton grubby, didn't bother her at all. To her delight the young woman behind the counter also had some bolts of material – equally old and faded – and was more than happy to sell her whatever she wanted.

'My mum ran this shop and her mum before her. She passed just before Christmas and now I've got to try and sell the stock so I can get back to my job in the munitions factory.'

'I'm sorry for your loss. I only found your shop by accident. Why don't you box all this up and sell it on the market? I'm sure it would be snapped up.'

The young woman looked around the dusty, uncared for shelves and shook her head. 'I can't see why anyone would want to buy stuff like this – it's years old.'

'The factories that used to turn out sewing materials for home use are now manufacturing what's needed to make uniforms. What you've got in here is now in desperately short supply.'

'I've never been interested in dressmaking or sewing. I was going to join one of the services or become a land girl but the money's so much better in the factory even if the hours are long and the work's horrible and dangerous.'

'I'm surprised they've given you the time off to be in here.'

'They haven't. I had to hand in my notice. The foreman said he'd take me back otherwise I wouldn't have bothered. My fiancé's in the Merchant Navy and we're getting married next time he's home on leave. We want the shop cleared so we can live here.'

Nancy was about to blurt out that she was getting married in a couple of hours but just stopped herself in time. 'My husband's a doctor in London. His eyesight's too poor for him to be conscripted.' It didn't really matter if she lied to a complete stranger and just calling David her husband made her feel wonderful.

'When's the baby due?'

'The beginning of May.' Again, she had to stop herself

from telling this friendly young woman that she already had two other children at home.

Half an hour later she left the little shop laden with exciting brown paper parcels. With what she'd managed to buy she'd be able to finish the layette for the baby, make some new clothes for Billy and Betty, as well as having several lengths of cotton to add to her stock.

The price she'd paid had been a bit less than it would have been for undamaged things and she was really pleased with what she'd found. Some folk bought things on the black market. She'd not had any dealings with anyone who could be called a black marketeer as they sold luxury items – things the posh people were prepared to pay over the odds for.

The government had just issued a law that stopped shopkeepers from putting up the prices of the things that were available. Rich, unscrupulous people would always get what they wanted; it was the poor folk who went without.

The clock on the town hall told her she had another hour to wait. She didn't want to hang about on the steps outside so went into a small café to get out of the biting wind and sleet that had started falling. From here she would be able to see him arrive and hurry out to join him. It was too cold to be outside any longer than necessary.

After two mugs of tea and a sticky bun her stomach stopped grumbling and the baby went to sleep. It was hard to credit that she had a real live human being growing inside her. Now she could read properly and had been given her very own Bible by the vicar, she was slowly working her way through the New Testament. Being unmarried and pregnant herself had made Mary's plight seem more real somehow.

It was now fifteen minutes to twelve and there was no sign of David. Belatedly it occurred to her that he might already be waiting inside having arrived early as she had. Hastily she pulled on her coat, collected her parcels, and made away across the road.

She realised there'd been no need for her to wait on the steps as there was a grand foyer and there were several couples waiting to be called through when it was their turn. All the men were in uniform and one of the girls was in the distinctive blue of the WAAF. David wasn't there.

Her winter coat was loose-fitting but her pregnancy was sufficiently advanced for the bump to be noticeable. She was aware that she got sympathetic looks from a couple of the girls but two of them looked down their noses and turned their backs on her.

It was none of their blinking business. As far as everyone at Chalfont Major was concerned she was a war widow, but even so to be marrying David so soon after supposedly losing her beloved husband was definitely going to cause a stir and a lot of gossip. That horrible Ava would really go to town when she got the news.

Where was he? Their names would be called in a few minutes and there obviously wouldn't be another slot today judging by the number of people here. A happy couple emerged from the door hand in hand and rushed to the exit.

'Doctor David Denny?'

Where there'd been disapproval or sympathy, she now saw pity. Nancy turned and ran blindly from the town hall and straight for the bus station. He'd changed his mind.

That's why he hadn't answered any of her last letters. She'd thought better of him – how could he let her down so publicly? All he'd had to do was write and tell her he no longer wanted to marry her.

With her collar turned up, her scarf around her face, no one could see how distraught she was. She just looked like someone protecting herself from the cold. She was numb all over. Breathing was difficult but she wasn't going to make a scene in public.

She hugged her parcels to her chest as if somehow they could protect her from the pain that was waiting to engulf her if she allowed it to. Thank God she hadn't told anyone the real reason for going into Chelmsford today.

She'd get through this, carry on as if nothing untoward had happened. As if the man she loved hadn't just broken her heart and humiliated her in the most heartless way. The bus arrived and she scrambled on, praying no one sat next to her who wanted to talk.

Her eyes were dry, her throat so tight swallowing was difficult and there was something that felt like an iron band gripping her around her chest. She still had a roof over her head, somewhere safe to bring up her child, therefore nothing had changed as far as anyone else was concerned.

As long as he stayed away then she'd be able to put on a brave face and pretend that losing him wasn't even worse than losing Tommy.

David slammed back the dividing glass barrier. 'Pull over. Do it now,' he snarled.

The terrified man screeched to a halt and the noise woke Billings.

'Where the hell are we? I'm supposed to be getting married at midday today in Chelmsford – I'd booked a day off three weeks ago. You selfish bastard, you...'

'Good God, man, why didn't you say so?'

'Because you didn't give me the chance.' He was so angry he no longer cared if he offended his superior and lost the chance of becoming a surgeon. 'It didn't occur to me we'd be going any further than an hour from Town. If I hadn't bloody well fallen asleep then I'd have stopped the car sooner. You didn't answer my question, Billings; where are we exactly?'

'I've no idea. No point shouting at me, Denny, ask the driver.'

'We're about five miles from Northampton, sir.'

'Take me to the station. I just pray there's a train I can catch and by some miracle get there in time. If I'd known you were dragging me hundreds of miles I'd not have got in the car.'

'Hill, you'll do no such thing. Drive on – it's only another ten miles.'

David was tempted to jump out of the car but it was the middle of the night, in the middle of nowhere and he'd be worse off if he did so. It wasn't the bloody driver's fault; it was the man sitting next to him.

'Look here, Denny, you can patch things up with your fiancée but my patient might die if we don't operate on him as soon as we arrive. Hill will take you wherever you want to go when it's over. Your young lady will be upset but

I'm certain she'll understand when you explain that it was literally a matter of life and death.'

His hands slowly unclenched. Punching Billings would not have been a good idea. He was too angry to talk and leaned against the seat imagining how Nancy would feel when he failed to show. It was all very well for Billings to talk blithely about life and death, about her understanding when she knew why he'd jilted her, but he didn't know their particular circumstances.

Why hadn't he taken the time to answer her letters? To ring her before he'd got in the car regardless of the time? She was already convinced he was marrying beneath him and would now take a lot of persuading to forgive him.

He was in control of his temper. 'I want more than the car; I want a week off. Otherwise you can do the bloody operation on your own and I don't care who dies.' Hardly conciliatory but he really didn't care what the arrogant man sitting beside him thought.

'Take as long as you need to marry the girl and then come back and introduce her to me. She must be someone very special for you to risk your career over.' This was a veiled reference to David's appalling rudeness and he knew in that moment his job was safe.

'I apologise for...'

'No, old man, no apologies needed. You are quite rightly incensed at my thoughtlessness. I'm going to enjoy working with you. It will make a refreshing change having someone who is prepared to speak frankly when necessary and not pussyfoot around me.'

'What an absolute shambles! Being so bloody tired all the time, not having time to think, doesn't help.'

'All the staff at the Royal Free do a splendid job and they're all on their knees. If the Germans carry on bombing cities every night for much longer the war will be lost.'

'Are you suggesting that we'll have jackboots marching down Whitehall this time next year? I disagree. As long as we've got the RAF, we might not be winning but we certainly won't lose. What we need is for the Yanks to come on board. Letting us have weapons without having to pay first is a godsend but it's not the same as having them actually fighting alongside us like they did in the last war.' David truly believed this and Billings didn't argue.

The car slowed and turned into an impressive driveway. He still didn't know who the patient was and Billings obviously had no intention of telling him. He wondered if he would recognise the man. Probably not as he took no interest in the upper classes. He might be rich – through no effort of his own – but he was upper middle class at best. Julia had had an Earl of Somewhere in her recent ancestry so had definitely been a toff.

Despite his disquiet about having to leave Nancy standing in the town hall believing that he'd jilted her, his mouth curved. How strange fate was – with his first marriage one could say that he'd married above him and with his second that he'd be going in the opposite direction. This class thing was nonsense as far as he was concerned; he was definitely going to vote for the Labour Party next time there was a general election.

The patient, nobody he knew, but he was pretty sure he was a lord at least, had a blocked bowel, which hadn't improved by being left for so long. Why the hell the man hadn't gone to the nearest hospital hours ago he'd no idea.

It took the considerable skill of his mentor as well as himself to save the man's life and the whole procedure took far longer than it should have done. The butler escorted him to a room set aside especially for the telephone and David asked the operator to connect him to Chelmsford town hall.

He quickly explained the reason that he'd been unable to make it to the town hall today and the registrar was very sympathetic.

'I don't think that Miss Evans turned up either, Doctor Denny. She wasn't there when I went out to look for both of you but I suppose she could already have left.'

'When is your next available time?'

'I have a cancellation on Wednesday at three o'clock. Shall I pencil you both in for then?'

'Yes, please do that.' He replaced the receiver and then spoke to the manager at the Saracens and rebooked for two nights this time. He doubted that Nancy would be prepared to stay away from home for longer than that as she took her duties as housekeeper very seriously.

Speaking to her on the telephone wasn't an option. His grovelling apology had to be made in person. The fact that he'd got a stunning engagement ring as well as a wedding band would hopefully prove to her that he'd never intended to let her down so badly. He'd also got good news from his solicitors about Betty and Billy and he couldn't wait to share it with her.

He was dead on his feet and slept the entire distance from wherever they were, back to London. The car waited whilst he dashed in to wash and change his clothes and grab what he needed.

'Hill,' he asked the chauffeur when he returned, 'are

you sure you'll have enough petrol to take me to Chalfont Major?'

'I've a full tank now, sir, and am ready to go.'

Something was niggling at the back of his mind. Something the registrar had said. He remembered and his stomach turned over. Nancy possibly hadn't turned up either.

21

Nancy was calm by the time the bus chugged into the village. She wasn't expected at the house until this evening so headed for the vicarage. Mrs Stanton saw her walk past the kitchen window and opened the back door for her.

'I can see your trip to Chelmsford was particularly successful today. Come in and show me what you managed to buy. You don't look yourself. Are you feeling unwell?'

'I'm cold and hungry and think I overdid it lumping this lot around. If there's a cup of tea going spare then I'd really appreciate it.'

Mrs Stanton exclaimed over each purchase. 'The damage is superficial, a careful rinse in warm sudsy water will remove the dust and dirt.' She held out a length of heavy, dark green cotton. 'I don't suppose I could persuade you to make me a blouse in this? It would go perfectly with my best suit.'

'I'd love to. I've got the whole day off so I can wash everything this afternoon and then it should be dry by tomorrow. I'll start cutting your blouse out when it is. Do you want me to use the pattern I made last time or were you thinking of something different?'

Talking about sewing and laundering kept her busy and gave her time to decide how she was going to deal with what had happened. As she hadn't approached the lady at the desk in order to give in her name, had left the town hall without speaking to anyone, it was possible they would think that neither of them had turned up.

The four couples who'd seen her didn't count. The more she thought about it the more it made sense to pretend that she'd changed her mind as he had.

The only flaw in this explanation was that if he'd been the one to be jilted then he would be here now trying to persuade her to change her mind. There was stationery in the room that she'd once occupied and she was sure the Stantons wouldn't mind if she used some.

Dear David

I am most sincerely sorry to have changed my mind and not come for our wedding. I went in with the intention of marrying you but the more I thought about it the more I realised it was the wrong thing to do. I am a most unsuitable wife for someone as important as a surgeon, and I think it best if we stop seeing each other altogether.

I am writing this at five o'clock and understand that you too have decided that we shouldn't be married, which makes things so much easier. I wish we'd both had the courage to tell the other and save us from embarrassment and heartache.

I do love you but not enough to marry you and then be obliged to pretend to be something that I'm not. It wouldn't be fair to me or to you. You need to find

someone from your own class who will make you a
much better wife than I would.

Take care of yourself and I don't regret a moment of
what happened and neither should you.

Best wishes.

Nancy Smith

She read it through a couple of times and was pleased
with what she'd written. There'd been no blots or smudges
from her tears, no spelling mistakes as far as she knew, and
this way her dignity was intact and if he came to see her then
she'd be able to talk to him without being overwhelmed by
her disappointment and his callousness.

The envelope was neatly addressed, the letter folded up
and put inside. All she required now was a stamp so she
could post it and she had several in her room in the house
where she worked. The grandfather clock that stood in
the entrance hall of the vicarage had just struck seven. She
was proud of herself – she'd got through the day without
breaking down and was pretty sure she'd be able to carry on
without him and nobody would know that for the second
time she'd lost a potential husband.

Then she heard heavy footsteps thundering up the stairs
and heading in her direction. It could only be one person and
she wasn't ready to face him yet. Why was he here? He
was the one who'd failed to turn up for their wedding. If
he'd come to apologise, she wasn't prepared to listen. There
was no excuse good enough to explain what he'd put her
through.

The door flew open. She didn't look at his face, just held
out the letter. 'I'm sorry things had to end like this. We both

changed our minds which is a good thing. I explained why I didn't come in this letter. Goodbye, David.'

He took it from her. 'I haven't changed my mind. I love you, Nancy, and thought I'd left you waiting on your own today.'

He sounded so wretched that she didn't dare look at him. Whatever the reasons he'd had for not answering her letters, or letting her know he wouldn't be there, she didn't want to hear them. The man she'd fallen in love with wouldn't have behaved so thoughtlessly. Her David didn't exist – the reality stood in front of her. A man who couldn't make up his mind and didn't care that his behaviour had broken her heart.

'Excuse me, I have to get home.' She walked past him and he didn't try and stop her.

Only the dog was pleased to see her. The children were in bed asleep and Mary and Fred were in their own sitting room with the door firmly shut. The sitting room was dark and quiet so Dr Jones must be with Jill at her house.

She retreated upstairs, fell into bed and cried herself to sleep.

David opened the letter and was devastated, but unsurprised, at the contents. He collapsed onto the bed unable to grasp the fact that in the space of a few hours his world had fallen apart. If he'd rung her last night, if he'd turned up at the town hall, things would have been so different.

At least she'd gone into Chelmsford intending to marry him but had got cold feet. If he'd been there then he could have found her, calmed her down and they would have got married as planned. She quite naturally assumed he'd got cold feet and then regretted it. If he'd actually been in Chelmsford at midday then he would have arrived at Chalfont Major hours ago.

He sat with his head in his hands, the letter dropped on the floor, and fatigue and misery overwhelmed him. His shoulders shook and his cheeks were wet. He'd been upset when Julia had died but more because he felt he'd let her down than from real grief at her loss. This was different – without Nancy his life no longer had meaning.

'My dear boy, I've never seen you so distraught. What you need is a stiff drink and I've got half a bottle of whiskey with your name on it.' The vicar pushed a clean handkerchief into one hand and grabbed David's other arm, leaving no option but to go with him.

A large drink and a cup of tea later he'd recovered sufficiently to be able to speak. 'I apologise. I barged in here without your permission and...'

'My wife and I realised there was something going on between you and Nancy weeks ago. She's been horribly subdued today. Do you want to tell me what this is all about?'

David was about to refuse but found himself pouring out the story. 'I expect you disapprove, that you think Nancy was right to change her mind.'

'I think nothing of the sort. She loves you and you love her. That's all that matters. This disaster could have been avoided, but it happened. What we have to work out now is how to put things right and I fear it's going to take a lot of fence mending to win her back.'

'How do I convince her that she won't be ruining my life by marrying me?'

'Write her a very persuasive letter. Point out how much she's changed since she's been here.'

'You're right – she's almost unrecognisable as the girl from the East End that I first met. Billings expects me to introduce Nancy to him as soon as we're married – if we ever are – and she's just not up to that sort of scrutiny.'

As soon as he'd spoken he realised the significance of his words. For all his talk, subconsciously he must consider that Nancy was somehow inferior to him.

'I see.' Stanton's expression said more than his words. 'I think it might be better if you stayed here tonight, young man; let the dust settle before you go over. If you go at all.' He paused, his expression sad. 'I rather think that you agree with Nancy that she's not a suitable wife for you. I retract what I said before. Your marriage will be a disaster if you enter into it thinking she's got to change in order to fit in with your friends and colleagues.'

'I swear that until this moment I honestly believed the differences between us were unimportant. I love her, I'm very sure of that. Now, what I'm uncertain about is whether that will be enough to make it work.'

'Exactly so. If you would care to write her a letter then I'll see that it's delivered tomorrow after you leave. You'll find pen and paper in the guest room where you found Nancy earlier.'

The vicar walked out making it blindingly obvious David wasn't welcome to join them in the sitting room but should retreat to the bedroom and remain there until he could catch the eight o'clock bus.

This was going to be a very difficult letter to write. He wasn't even sure if he should tell her that he'd intended to be there and that circumstances had conspired against him. He'd sleep on it and write it when he woke up.

He heard someone walking past his door the next morning and was shocked that he'd slept so soundly. When Julia had died he'd paced the room for days unable to sleep at all. Things had been turned on their head yet again.

If he was prepared to give up Nancy so easily was it possible what he felt for her was lust, not genuine love? Was his desire to have a family, and the fact that there was a war on, making him push ahead with something that under normal circumstances he wouldn't have considered?

He was bitterly ashamed of his behaviour. He should never have slept with her; she was a vulnerable young woman and he'd taken shameful advantage of her. If only Billings hadn't dragged him away they would now be married and these uncertainties would never have surfaced. He frowned. Even if he'd turned up on time they still mightn't be married as she'd changed her mind.

Two days ago he'd been happier than he'd ever been in his life and now he could only see an empty, lonely life ahead of him. He would make provision for Billy and Betty, become their legal guardian, but they'd never be his children as he'd planned. Neither would the unborn baby that Nancy was carrying.

His eyes were dry and gritty, his limbs leaden as if he was going down with influenza. He had a letter to write and only half an hour to do it before he had to be outside waiting for the bus. Hopefully, they could both move on with their lives with no regrets. He had the career he'd always dreamt of and she was now part of a close-knit community and had a home into which to bring her child.

From where he was sitting he could just see the roof of his house. No – he would sign it over to her as he'd never visit Chalfont Major again. He'd told her that he was leaving her his money and had no intention of changing his will, but he would add a codicil to include Billy and Betty.

When Simon married Jill he'd offer to sell the practice to him and cut another tie to this place. In future he'd concentrate on his career, become the best surgeon he could be and forget about finding himself a wife or ever having children of his own. That's if he survived the war at all.

One thing he did know was that he'd be a widower for the remainder of his life.

Dear Nancy,

I came here intending to persuade you to change your mind but have decided to accept your decision. I would have been at Chelmsford yesterday but had to accompany my boss to Northampton to perform an emergency bowel resection.

I hadn't changed my mind and am deeply saddened that you have. I'll not contact you again, which will be easier for both of us.

I shall become guardian to Billy and Betty but hope you will continue to act as their surrogate mother. I'll certainly not be involved with them personally although will make sure that they're financially secure.

I also intend to sign over ownership of the house to you and settle a sufficient sum in a trust fund to cover your expenses and that of the household for the foreseeable future. When Simon marries Jill, he will move out and then you can decide if you wish to keep Mary and Fred on in your employ.

I wish you all the best and will always love you and don't regret a moment of the time we spent together.

He signed it with a flourish. He pushed it into the envelope and scrawled her name across the front. He'd not bothered to shave, had slept in his clothes and looked like a tramp. He didn't care. There was nobody he wanted to impress.

He ran down the stairs, his suitcase swinging in his hand, and dropped the letter on the hall table. The bus was approaching and he had to run in order to catch it. It wasn't so much that he was miserable – that didn't describe the way he felt at all. He was crushed and doubted he'd ever be happy again.

Nancy was relieved that she'd had no unwelcome visitor the previous evening. She was busy dusting the sitting room when Mrs Stanton came in.

'Do you have a moment to talk, my dear?'

'I'll make a pot of tea. I always take one in to Doctor Jones and Mrs Andrews about now.'

Her heart was thudding uncomfortably knowing that the only reason the vicar's wife was here was to talk about what had happened yesterday. As long as she didn't think about it then she could carry on without crying.

How much had he told her? She'd no intention of discussing her business with anyone but wasn't prepared to lie if asked directly.

'Doctor Denny told me you were getting married yesterday but he failed to turn up. He also believes that you changed your mind. Is that true?'

The constriction in her throat made it impossible for Nancy to speak. She shook her head and Mrs Stanton nodded sympathetically. 'I thought so. I've got a letter for you. I'll wait whilst you read it.'

Nancy's fingers were shaking so much she could scarcely take the paper out. Her cheeks were wet by the time she'd finished reading. She found her handkerchief, wiped her eyes and then blew her nose noisily. This gave her a few extra moments to pull herself together.

'Why didn't he come over and tell me this himself?'

'After you left he was distraught and told my husband everything. He also revealed that he actually agrees that the differences between you are insurmountable.'

This was news to her as all along he'd been the one to insist that the difference in their backgrounds, education and ages made no difference. That they were meant to be together as they made each other so happy.

'I'm unsuitable? Is that what you mean? Do you think that too?'

'I don't think so but I can definitely see why he might think you'd struggle in the world he would be bringing you into. How would you feel if you were sneered at and patronised when you attended functions as his wife? How do you think he would feel if that happened?'

'I was living in a fairy tale, Mrs Stanton. Deep down I knew it, but carried on as if I really thought we'd get married and live happily ever after. Girls like me don't marry men like him.' Then the band around her chest vanished and it was as if a weight had lifted from her shoulders.

'I really love him, I'll never marry anyone else, but we've done the right thing by breaking it off. I wouldn't have been able to be the wife he needs. We would both have been unhappy in the end.'

'You're a very sensible and level-headed young lady. That's exactly what he said. Continue to be the tragic but respectable Mrs Smith and you and your little one will become part of our community. Then Doctor Denny can become a top surgeon and fulfil his potential.'

'He's going to become the children's legal guardian and will provide for their education and everything else. He's asked me to look after them for him as he doesn't intend to come here again. As far as I'm concerned Billy and Betty will be an older brother and sister to my baby and the three of them will grow up together.

'I've got a wonderful home, good friends, and will never have to worry about making ends meet ever again. Some things are just not meant to be.'

'Nobody will ever know what almost happened, Nancy. It will remain a secret between us. My only regret is that we'll not have Doctor Denny in the parish. I know there will be many others who will regret the fact that he's no longer going to be part of village life.'

The conversation gave Nancy much to think about. Thank goodness both of them had realised in time that they were about to make a dreadful mistake. If this Mr Billings hadn't dragged him away then she would now be Mrs Denny and instead of starting a happy life it would probably have been the beginning of something quite different for both of them.

She wasn't going to make any decisions about Mary and Fred at the moment. Living in such a large house on her own with only the children for company would be a bit daunting after spending her life in a two-up two-down terrace in Poplar.

From now on she would concentrate on being the best mother she could be to the children, a good homemaker, and she'd look forward to the birth of her own baby in three months' time.

22

David immersed himself in his work and if he did get a few hours free he spent it with his nose in a textbook preparing for the two exams Billings had arranged for him to take. He half-hoped that Nancy would continue to write to him but she didn't.

The weeks ground past and the days merged one into the other. He didn't listen to the news, read the newspapers or discuss the progress of the war with anybody. He became taciturn and unapproachable, which meant the invitations to go for a drink or the cinema were no longer given.

He remained professional and fair at all times at work and none of his team had anything to complain about. The fact that he'd returned a week earlier than expected had been sufficient to tell Billings that things hadn't gone well.

He no longer blamed his superior for his part in the debacle and was always civil when in his company. Two days before his exam, the middle of March, he received a letter from his solicitors. Billy and Betty were now legally his wards and he decided that he had no option but to take the documents down to Nancy, but there was no rush. Just the thought of seeing her again made him ill.

Then something changed his mind. The junior doctor who owned the motorbike went for a burton in an air raid. To David's surprise the bike appeared outside his digs two days afterwards. It was delivered by a scruffy-looking individual in a flat cap and rubber boots.

'This is yours, mate. Young Percy asked me to bring it to you if he bought it. Ain't got no family what would want it.'

'Thank you.' He could think of nothing else to say as, as far as he was concerned, he'd been given a pile of junk on wheels. No civilian, apart from Billings and people like him who no doubt got it on the black market somehow, had any petrol so he couldn't use it even if he wanted to.

He handed the man a pound note and he seemed satisfied with the exchange. 'The tank's full and so's the can. You'll get a few hundred miles from that. Young Percy had a mate what drove an ambulance and helped him out like with the fuel. I reckon you could do the same being in the same line of work.'

Referring to the deceased doctor as "young Percy" made him sound like something out of a Shakespearean play. He'd get his exams out of the way and then he'd take the legal documents about the children, and also the title deed for the house and the necessary bank details for Nancy to access the trust fund. This was not only for her use but also to pay any necessary expenses for Billy and Betty.

The exams were a doddle but he rather thought that even if he'd written total nonsense Billings would still have made sure he passed with distinction. He finished the last paper at two o'clock and didn't have to be on duty until midnight. Ample time to get to Chalfont Major and back.

The gift of the bike had come with the necessary clothing

to make riding it more comfortable and safer. He scrambled into the overalls, pushed his feet into the boots, put on the helmet, goggles and gloves and was ready to kick the bike into life.

He roared into the village an hour later. This meant he had a couple of hours before it started to get dark. He didn't want to drive at night in the blackout if he could avoid it. He parked the bike on its stand close to the hedge – no point in taking it in as he wasn't going to be there long.

There was a slight noise and Polly sailed over the hedge almost flattening him when she landed. He staggered about trying to keep his balance and failed miserably. He ended up half in the hedge. The dog was so excited to see him she was yelping and jumping up at him. Each time her front paws landed on his chest he was more firmly embedded in the greenery.

Then Fred peered over the hedge. 'I wondered why the blooming animal had vanished so fast. Hang on, sir, I'll be around to pull you out in no time.'

It took the combined efforts of the passing postman and Fred to extricate him. The noise and fuss had alerted the occupants of the house. This wasn't the way he'd intended to arrive but at least it broke the ice.

'Doctor Denny, what a surprise,' Nancy said, trying hard not to laugh. She was even more beautiful than he'd remembered and to his surprise and concern she didn't really seem a lot bigger than she had when he'd left. She was in her third trimester – around thirty-three weeks and looked much less than that.

'I've got some documents for you and thought I'd bring

them down myself. Rather than standing around laughing at me, Mrs Smith, why don't you go inside and put the kettle on. After being stuck in a hedge I'll need tea to revive me.'

'The children will be delighted that you're here. They talk constantly of you and wonder why you don't come and see them or even write to them.'

She grabbed the dog by her collar and led her away. Her gentle reprimand was well deserved. What had happened between Nancy and himself was nothing to do with the little ones. However difficult it was in future he would keep in touch with them.

'Good thing you're wearing them overalls, sir. You'd have some nasty scratches otherwise,' Fred said as they walked around to the kitchen door together.

'Very true. The garden's looking splendid.' He listened and couldn't hear the happy snorting of the pigs. 'Plenty of pork to eat now I suppose?'

'There is. You won't believe a little thing like Mrs Smith, and her in the family way too, could butcher a carcass so neatly. The neighbours were that impressed. We'll have another couple of piglets coming in the spring.'

The gardener stomped off, leaving David to enter the house without support. He needn't have worried about his reception. The children threw themselves at him as soon as he stepped into the kitchen.

'Uncle David, why were you stuck in the hedge? Auntie Nancy says Polly did it,' Billy said as he grinned up at him. The boy was almost unrecognisable. He'd grown and filled out and even his East End accent had almost gone.

'Uncle David, me's a big girl now. Do you like my new frock? Auntie Nancy made it.'

Betty was no longer a toddler but a little girl – and a very pretty one at that. Her hair was neatly plaited and tied with pink ribbons that exactly matched the colour of her dress.

'Your frock's beautiful, sweetheart. Now, please may I stand up and take off my overalls?'

Whilst Nancy was apparently watching the interaction between David and the children she was actually studying him. He'd lost weight, but it suited him. He certainly looked leaner and fitter but he also looked harder – less approachable.

It had been two months since she'd seen him and she was confident even the Stantons weren't aware how unhappy she'd been. There were posters everywhere telling people to keep calm and carry on – that's exactly what she was doing.

Dr Jones was out on visits and Jill, as always, had gone home until she was needed for evening surgery. Mary was laid up in bed with a feverish cold and Nancy was enjoying having the house and the children to herself.

'Run along to the sitting room, children. I need to talk to Uncle David in peace. I'll call you in a little while for your milk and biscuits.'

They ran off laughing and chatting – they were no trouble at all. She already loved them as if they were actually her own and from the way David's face had lit up, as it used to do when he'd looked at her, he felt the same way about them.

He'd gone back into the boot room in order to remove his overalls, which gave her a few minutes to compose herself and be ready to talk to him as if she'd really moved on with her life and no longer cried most nights at losing him.

'Nancy, are you seeing the midwife?' His abrupt question wasn't what she was expecting.

'I saw her a few weeks ago.'

'I need to examine you. Don't argue – this is a professional matter. It needs to be in the surgery.'

He looked so grave she didn't argue. She'd been concerned herself that she'd not really got much bigger than she'd been when she was six months gone.

'The baby's kicking so I know it's all right.' He was probably concerned the baby had died and that's why she wasn't any bigger.

She hopped up onto the examination bed and he politely turned his back as she pulled up her maternity dress and pushed down her knickers.

'I just want to check on the size of the baby. I expected you to be much bigger by now as you've only got seven weeks to go to your delivery date.'

'What with one thing and another I've lost a bit of weight all over. I do try and eat enough to keep us both healthy but sometimes it's hard.'

Having him lean over her naked belly, having him run his hands across the distended skin, even though he was being totally professional, was agony for her. She wanted to reach up and smooth back his hair. There were flecks of grey in it that hadn't been there two months ago.

He listened to the heartbeat after he'd finished prodding and poking and measuring and then stepped back and turned away. 'Come next door and we can talk as soon as you're ready.'

She walked in and he was smiling. The weight in her chest lifted. 'Is everything all right?'

'Everything is exactly as it should be. The baby's a good size and the heartbeat's strong and regular. I've seen this happen occasionally with expectant mothers. Nothing to worry about.'

'Then why isn't my front any bigger if the baby's the right size?'

'Because you've accommodated the pregnancy by expanding width wise. There's no more room for the baby to develop that way so I'm certain your front will become much larger over the next few weeks.'

'I mustn't stay in here any longer because I can't hear the children if they need me. Mary's not well.'

'Then we'll continue our conversation in the kitchen with that cup of tea you promised me. I don't suppose you've got anything to eat – I've been taking exams since early this morning and haven't eaten since last night.'

'I'm not surprised you've lost weight if you don't eat for twenty-four hours. You work too hard. Don't tell me there's a war on – I blooming well know that.'

Soon he was munching his way through the remainder of last night's rabbit stew and draining his third mug of tea. She took the children's mid-afternoon snack in to them.

'You can eat this in here if you promise not to make a mess. I know Auntie Mary doesn't like you having food or drink in the sitting room but just this once I'm sure she won't mind.'

Once she was seated again he pushed over some official-looking brown envelopes. 'These are the legal papers you need in order to look after Billy and Betty properly. If there was an accident of some sort you might not be able to contact me quickly so I've arranged it that you can make decisions for them in my stead.'

She didn't open the documents, as she could do that when he'd gone. She didn't want to waste a minute of this visit on something as boring as paperwork.

'Thank you for taking the trouble to bring them in person. Doctor Jones and Jill are now engaged and intend to get married in June. She's got a lovely big house so there's plenty of room for the both of them.'

'Have you made any decision about Mary and Fred?'

'I have. I've spoken to them about it and they're keen to have their own home again. An old gentleman just up the road died last week and the cottage belongs to the church. The vicar's agreed to let them rent it from him.'

'That sounds like a good idea. You need Fred in the garden but I can see that you don't really need Mary.'

'She's found herself another job looking after an old lady in the big house at the end of the village. It's not a live-in appointment and she won't be needed every day either as the daughter-in-law lives on the premises as well.'

'I don't want you to do everything here. It's a large house. You're going to need some help with the housework at least.'

'I can manage just fine without anyone else. I don't like being waited on. You promised to spend a bit more time with the children before you leave so why don't you join them whilst I tidy up in here?'

'Keep Mary on until after you're delivered. You'll need the extra help until then.'

'All right I'll ask her when she's better. They'll be moving as soon as the cottage has been sorted out but her new job needn't start before I have the baby.' She pointed at the sitting room from which the sound of the children playing could be heard.

'I'm going; I don't need telling again.'

David did as she asked, knowing she was finding the conversation as difficult as he was. He stayed for another hour and then left, not sure if he could bear to come again when just being close to her and not being able to touch her almost destroyed him.

He made vague promises to the children that he would visit again. The dog, having greeted him so enthusiastically, was now curled up on her bed refusing to look at him. He bent down and stroked her silky head. 'Good girl. I know you miss me but you've got Nancy and the children now.'

His eyes were damp. Bloody stupid crying over a dog but he supposed it was better than doing so over the woman he loved but could never be with. One could only hope that the pain of being separated from Nancy would eventually lessen as the months passed.

His workload increased after he officially qualified. About once or twice a week he scrubbed in with Billings in order to learn the correct techniques and procedures for something more complex. He didn't like the man but he was an excellent mentor.

The Blitz continued and he had nothing but admiration for the women of the East End who somehow kept their families together. Last week, on the 16th April, hundreds of planes dropped around a hundred thousand bombs in an all-night attack and it was declared the heaviest of the war so far.

It took three days to clear casualty and so much death and injury – often the women and children – was the worst part of it. In order to lighten his mood he decided to write to the children and include a bag of sweets he'd managed to buy with his rations. Before he posted the parcel he rang the vicarage.

Mrs Stanton answered. 'Doctor Denny, I'm so glad that you called. I know that you're not keeping in touch with Nancy but I thought you'd like to know there are complications. Doctor Jones is most concerned.'

'I'll ring him now.' He hung up without saying goodbye. He was connected quickly and asked Jill to put Simon on the phone.

'I just heard Nancy has problems with the pregnancy. What's wrong?'

'The baby's breech. I doubt she'll be able to deliver vaginally. It will have to be a C-section.'

'Have you tried to turn it?'

'Good God, of course not. I shouldn't be discussing this with you, old man, confidentiality and all that.'

'Has Nancy agreed to have a caesarean?'

'Like a sensible girl she'll do whatever I advise. I've a string of patients waiting so forgive me if I get on with it.' The line went dead – Simon wasn't happy that his medical judgement had been called into question.

Nancy only had just over three weeks to her due date and could go into labour at any time. He couldn't stand by and do nothing even though, as Simon had reminded him, she was nothing to do with him now.

He went in search of Billings. He explained the situation. It was immediately assumed that he was actually the father of this child and he didn't disabuse his boss.

'Why the devil didn't you marry her when you had the opportunity?'

'I would have done if you hadn't dragged me to Northampton. This gave her time to reconsider and she decided she wouldn't fit into my world. She's beautiful, intelligent and compassionate and makes me laugh; however, she has little formal education and I taught her to read and write properly myself.'

Billings was looking at him with disgust. 'You fathered a child with her. A gentleman would have done the right thing. I don't know you – you're not the man I thought you were.' He stared down his aristocratic nose and then strode away, disapproval apparent in every step.

God this was an absolute disaster on all fronts. If he told the true story then, instead of being thought an absolute bastard for abandoning the mother of his unborn child, he would be considered unhinged.

They hadn't got as far as discussing time off but he was going anyway. A junior houseman ambled past and he grabbed his arm. 'Let the theatre sister know I'm going to be out for a few days. Family emergency. Ask her to tell Mr Billings.'

'Yes, Mr Denny, I'll do it immediately.'

David still thought it odd that he was no longer called

Dr Denny but the convention was that surgeons were always Mr Something, not Dr Something. His brain was fixing on trivial things in order to avoid thinking about the reality. Was it possible that, for the second time, he could lose the woman he loved because of a pregnancy?

23

Nancy shook her head. 'I've still got three weeks to go and I'm not having the baby cut out of me on your say-so, Doctor Jones. The midwife isn't worried and she knows a lot more about babies than you do.'

He wasn't used to his patients arguing with him and he looked as if he was sucking a lemon. 'My dear girl, Nurse Reynolds is not a doctor. I have years of experience and I insist that...'

'You can't tell me what to do. It's my baby, my body, my decision.' This was the last straw as the wretched man had been pressurising her for the past week to consent to this operation and go immediately into hospital.

'I think it would be better for both of us if you moved out. I expect you to be gone by the end of the day. I'm sure you'll find suitable lodging somewhere in the village. I'll lock the communicating door and there will be no to-ing and fro-ing into my house in future.'

His mouth dropped open and for a moment he was unable to respond. Then he glared at her. 'You are in no position to tell me to leave. Doctor Denny...'

'I'll stop you right there. I own this house and have done for the past few weeks. I'll remind you that I also own the premises where you practise so I suggest you show me more respect if you want to continue working there.' This was a silly thing to say, as if she turfed him out of the surgery as well, not only would the villagers suffer, but it would also inconvenience David.

'Then I wash my hands of you, Mrs Smith. If you and the baby die it will be entirely your fault. I can assure you that I'll be gone by this evening.'

He marched off, rigid with anger, and she regretted her outburst. Until he'd started trying to boss her about over her delivery, she'd quite liked him. Nurse Reynolds had said the baby hadn't dropped and the head wasn't engaged so she wasn't likely to have the baby in the next week or so.

Mary had overheard the exchange in the hall and came out. 'Well done, Nancy, you've done the right thing. He'd have to leave when Fred and I did anyway as it wouldn't be right to have him living under the same roof as you.'

'Jill will be upset with me and I won't be able to take them in their mid-morning tea any more.'

'You shouldn't be waiting on them. I'm sure they can both manage without a hot drink for the few hours that they're there.'

'I shouldn't have told him about the house like that. It'll be all over the village by teatime and people will wonder why the house now belongs to me.'

'It's none of their business. I don't wish to interfere but why don't you arrange to see a consultant at the hospital in Chelmsford? That way you'll be sure that you're making the right decision.'

'The midwife says there's room for the baby to turn itself

and she's given me some exercises to do, which should help with that.'

'It's a mystery to me why Doctor Jones is so adamant you can't deliver normally. It might be because you're only five foot tall. Sometimes small women do have problems.'

'My ma is the same size as me and she had twins without any difficulty. She told me it's something to do with foot size.' She waved her own in the air. 'See, I don't have small feet so I reckon I'm just fine as long as the baby turns in time. Mind you, Nurse Reynolds said she's delivered several breech babies and, granted it's a bit trickier and needs two there at the birth, but she's not lost one yet. I'm going with her experience.'

'Your ankles aren't at all swollen and I notice that you've put your rings back on. That's a very good sign. I might not have had any children of my own but I've been around babies and expectant mothers for years.'

Nancy made herself scarce that afternoon to allow Dr Jones to depart without an audience. Whilst she lay comfortably on her bed reading the *News Chronicle* she could hear him banging about at the other end of the house. He didn't have to leave keys behind as he'd never been given any. The house was rarely locked and Jill had the key to the surgery.

She waited until she heard the front door slam and then scrambled from the bed and went into his bedroom. She stripped the sheets, collected the towels and dumped them outside the door. It didn't take long to remake the bed, give the room a good clean and polish, and then she stood back and admired her work.

This was David's room and all it wanted was for his clothes

to come down from the attic and hang in his wardrobe and it would be as if he still lived there. The stairs were narrow but perfectly safe even for her. After three journeys all his spare garments were back where they should be. She found a box of bits and pieces, books and so on, that he'd stored upstairs and these were also brought down and restored to their original places.

By the time she'd finished the children were on their way to bed. They heard her and rushed in to see what was going on.

'Is Uncle David coming back?' Billy was a clever little boy and had taken one look at the changes and drawn the right conclusion.

'Not right now, sweetheart, but when he does get time off he'll be able to have his own room and not have to sleep on the sofa.' When Mary and Fred moved out she was going to explain to them that she was now their ma and that David was their pa.

The house seemed happier without the doctor and she stretched out on the sofa listening to *ITMA* and drinking her nightly cocoa. The advertisement she'd seen in the paper today said that cocoa was rich in nerve food. She certainly needed plenty of that at the moment.

ITMA stood for *It's That Man Again*; it had been Jane who told her this and she hadn't even listened to the radio when she was growing up.

She'd received a letter from both her friends that morning and had saved them until now to read. She'd told them that she now owned the house and had sole charge of the children as well as loads of money to make sure they all had what they needed.

They didn't know that she'd had an affair with David or that they'd almost got married and she thought it better that they never did. Mind you, Charlotte had mentioned that she'd noticed there had been something between the two of them. Both her friends knew the true circumstances about Tommy but always addressed their letters to Mrs Smith. They didn't think she was a slut, and thought no less of her because of the baby.

She opened Charlotte's first.

Dear Nancy,

You've not got long to go – you must be so excited. I've done extra shifts for a couple of friends and they'll reciprocate. This means that I'll be able to take the time off when the baby arrives and can come and visit.

I'm not surprised that Dr Denny has made these arrangements. I really liked him when I met him and I thought that you and he might make a go of it somehow. How things have changed for all of us.

We couldn't have imagined how different our lives would be when we met at training two years ago. Jane has recovered from her abusive childhood and married her lovely Oscar. She's now doing a hush-hush job like me and loving every minute of it. It must be very difficult for her having Oscar in the thick of it like this.

You have metamorphosed from an East End girl with no prospects into a prosperous house owner and – even more amazing – a member of the church choir. The fact that you're about to have a baby is spiffing.

I'm booked to go somewhere for officers' training in June and I gather I won't be coming back here afterwards.

I'm the only one of the three of us who hasn't fallen in
love. I'm quite happy on my own and don't mind at all
that I haven't got a beau.

Write again soon as your letters cheer me up with
your funny anecdotes about the children and the others
in the village.

Love

Nancy was about to open the letter from Jane when the
unmistakable sound of a motorbike pulling up outside had
her on her feet and moving towards the kitchen before the
sound died away in the darkness. Over the past weeks she'd
forgiven David for his part in the break-up and accepted
that she'd always love him even though they could never
be together.

David was halfway around the house when Polly erupted
from the kitchen and landed on his chest. He was braced for
such an eventuality but still lost his balance and ended up
on his arse.

'Sorry about that, David. I tried to grab her as I opened
the door but she scooted through my legs.'

Just hearing her voice made him happy. 'I've no dignity
left whatsoever. My last visit I ended up embedded in the
hedge and this time sitting on my backside with a large
dog in my lap.' He tipped the animal off, and recovered
his overnight and medical bag, which had flown from his
hands, and stepped into the kitchen.

It might have been odd coming back now he no longer
owned the house but as far as he was concerned it was

just bricks and mortar. Who lived in a house was what mattered.

Whilst he was getting out of his gear in the boot room, he heard her locking the door behind them. Doors weren't locked in the village so what had happened to change things here? She was busy filling the kettle with her back to him and this gave him time to look at her without making a complete ass of himself.

'What are you doing here in the middle of the night, David?'

'It's nine thirty so I hardly think it qualifies as that. Why did you lock the door?'

She gestured towards one of the chairs at the central, scrubbed wooden table. 'I evicted Doctor Jones today and I don't want him creeping back – not that I think he would, but I can't be sure. He wasn't too pleased about being given his marching orders.'

'For God's sake, Nancy, what did he do?'

He sounded so fierce, so protective, her eyes filled. 'Nothing like that. He was bullying me to have the baby by caesarean section but I refused. The midwife's happy to deliver me as I am.' She turned and her smile lit the room. 'You still haven't told me what you're doing here.'

'Mrs Stanton told me what was going on and I needed to see for myself how things were. I still blame myself for what happened to Julia.'

She was about to say that her health and the health of her baby was none of his concern but they both knew that wasn't true. They couldn't get married but it didn't stop them loving each other and caring what happened.

'The baby's feet down, not folded in half with his

feet up by his head. She says she's delivered dozens of babies in this sort of position and doesn't anticipate any problems with mine. Doctor Jones just wouldn't listen – thinks he knows better because he's a doctor and she's a nurse.'

'I'm afraid that's usually the way. I know I'm not your doctor but would you allow me to examine you?'

'Of course I will as I trust your opinion and will do whatever you suggest. We can't go into the surgery because I've locked it up from this side and don't intend to go in there again.'

'It would be more comfortable for you on a bed rather than the sofa.'

'Then we'll go upstairs. Your room's ready so you don't have to sleep down here.'

He cleared his mind of personal feelings and followed her to her bedroom where not so very long ago they'd spent a passionate, wonderful, amazing night together. Doctors shouldn't treat family members but he thought he was in the clear on this one as they weren't actually related – although he sincerely wished they were.

He examined her externally and was relieved he didn't have to do an internal. 'Your baby's certainly feet down but he's lying diagonally at the moment. Was he like this last time the midwife had a look?'

'Is that good or bad? I'm certain the top of his head was under my bosom and his feet straight down.'

'Then I think it's possible he's going to turn of his own volition.' He grinned down at her. 'Have you got to V in your dictionary yet?'

Her laughter made his heart somersault. 'Cheeky perisher.

I've never heard the word but I can guess what it means – under his own steam?'

He was still sitting beside her on the bed and knew if he didn't move immediately she would be in his arms where she belonged. Her eyes widened. She'd seen desire in his expression. He surged to his feet, mumbling an apology but she reached up and caught his hand and pulled.

He closed his fingers over hers. 'This is just going to make it harder when I leave. Are you quite sure, my love?'

'We can't make love but I want you to hold me in your arms. I just wish I didn't love you as much as I do.'

He dropped down beside her and pulled her close. He inhaled her unique scent, lavender and something vaguely medicinal he couldn't quite recognise. They lay entwined for half an hour. He didn't kiss her – just holding her was enough for now.

'I love you. Why are we prevaricating? It's been over two months and what I feel has grown stronger, not lessened. Marry me, darling. I don't care what anyone says.'

Gently she pushed him away. Her eyes were brimming. She shook her head when he tried to comfort her. 'Love isn't always enough. I wouldn't fit into your world and we both know that. I won't marry you and ruin your life.'

'I want to be involved with the children. Would you consider allowing me to visit you all? Consider me in the same way that you would if we were divorced?'

'I think it might be harder seeing you and not being able to be with you.' She brushed her eyes and then said something that shook him to the core. 'We could sleep together sometimes; it would make being apart a bit easier for both of us.'

He was going to refuse categorically to accept her offer but something stopped him. Eventually she would be pregnant with his child and then he could insist that they married and she wouldn't be able to refuse. Not ideal – not what he wanted – but it was better than the misery they had both been enduring these past few weeks.

'It's not what either of us want but better than the alternative. I'll come down as often as I can and this means I can be more involved in Billy and Betty's lives. Billings, head of surgery and the most important man at the Royal Free, thinks you're having my baby and is disgusted with me for not having married you.'

'Didn't you tell him the truth?' She was now on her feet and even heavily pregnant, as far as he was concerned, was the most beautiful woman in the world.

'I think it better that he thinks me an unprincipled bastard than that I'd fallen in love with a recently widowed young woman who's expecting her husband's child.'

'It does sound daft doesn't it? I expect you're hungry. I baked this morning so I'll make you a sarnie with a lovely bit of roast pork and apple sauce in it.'

He dumped his overnight bag in his bedroom but carried the medical bag downstairs. This was fortunate as both Mary and Fred chose exactly that moment to emerge from their private sitting room.

'Doctor Denny, from your expression things aren't as grim as Doctor Jones insisted,' Mary said.

'They certainly aren't. Mother and baby are doing well and I don't anticipate any problems with the delivery.'

They didn't pass on the stairs, not because there wasn't room but because superstition said it was bad luck to do so. The older couple said good night and left them on their own.

She insisted that he sit in the sitting room and listen to the wireless while she rushed about in the kitchen preparing his food. He was tired. He'd done another sixteen-hour shift and it must be thirty-six hours since he'd slept.

'Here you are; don't go to sleep until you've eaten.'

'Don't worry, I'm too hungry. I'm going up immediately afterwards if you don't mind.'

'Good thing the bed's ready for you.' She smoothed her voluminous frock over her belly. 'You were right. I'm a lot bigger than I was. I can't see my toes now.'

'I was thinking that you look better than you did last time despite all the worry and the work.'

'I've been ever so miserable but then you gave me this house plus all the money to live on. Not having to worry about paying the bills for the rest of my life made things a little better.' She rubbed her stomach lovingly. 'This little chap's very lucky. He'll have the best education that money can buy, has an older brother and sister to play with and he'll lack for nothing.'

He finished the last mouthful, drained his mug and somehow managed to push himself to his feet. 'We're both referring to your bump as a boy. Is that what you think it's going to be?'

'I'm convinced that it is. I'm going to call him David Thomas after the two nicest men I know.'

'You do realise he'll have to have your name – he'll be David Thomas Evans. Don't you think that might cause problems for him when he goes to school?'

'It'll be on his birth certificate but nobody else will see that. I'll explain it to him when he's old enough to understand.'

He wasn't going to press the point. He was hoping to persuade her to put his name on the birth certificate, which would mean when eventually they did get married he could legitimise the child. After all, people who didn't know the whole story would just assume the baby was his anyway.

24

Nancy pottered about downstairs after David had gone up, pretending to be a real housewife with her man and children asleep upstairs where they should be. The baby heaved and wriggled and she laughed. 'There you go, Davie, you're as happy as I am, aren't you?'

His full name would be David but they couldn't have two in the family so he'd be called Davie to save confusion. She let the dog out for a last run round whilst she filled up the range and the boiler that provided the hot water and kept the radiators warm in the winter.

She looked around her domain, satisfied everything was where it should be. She was halfway up the stairs when the telephone jangled loudly, almost making her miss her step. This was one aspect of Dr Jones leaving she'd not taken into account. Those who had telephones still thought he was living here and would naturally ring in an emergency.

'Mrs Smith speaking. How can I help you?'

A deep plummy voice answered and she guessed at once who it was. 'Mr Billings here. I need to speak to Mr Denny.'

'I'm afraid that won't be possible. He's asleep and I've no intention of waking him up whatever your emergency might be. He told me he'd not slept for thirty-six hours and if you think I'm going to let him ride his motorbike back to London half-asleep you've got another think coming. I suggest that you telephone in the morning.' She didn't give him a chance to reply but put the receiver down firmly.

Thank goodness it wasn't an emergency in the village. Whatever crisis that Billings bloke had, he wasn't going to be dragging David away to deal with it. It couldn't be that important as there was no way on God's earth that he could be back in London in less than an hour and a half.

She hesitated at the bottom of the stairs waiting to see if the man would ring back. He didn't. She no longer cared about appearances. If the village biddies found out and decided she was a loose woman, no longer acceptable at the WI or WVS, then so be it.

Maybe if that happened then she'd sell the house – it must be worth a fortune – and move somewhere nearer London where nobody knew the truth, and it would be easier for David to visit. Romford would be ideal but there was a risk someone would recognise her as she'd been based at Hornchurch for a while. She drifted off to sleep still considering her options and didn't wake up until the alarm rang at six thirty.

Getting up so early meant she had the bathroom to herself. She would take David a cup of tea as soon as the kettle boiled and she supposed she'd better tell him about his boss ringing up and that she'd given him short shrift.

The dog was chasing pigeons in the garden and would be happy enough out there until she returned to the kitchen. She knocked quietly on David's door and heard a grunted reply.

'Good morning, love. I've got a nice cup of tea here.'

He sat up in bed, his chest naked, his hair tousled, and the hot tea slopped over her knuckles. He was handsome whatever he was wearing but knowing he was naked beneath the covers just made him even more attractive.

His smile sent heat racing around her body. 'You'd better give it to me, darling, before you drop it on the floor.'

'Here you are. I'll open the curtains and let a bit of light in. Do you want me to open the window as well?' Her voice ended in a squeak as he embraced her from behind.

'I want to make love to you. Stop talking about the bloody curtains and come to bed.'

She didn't argue. He picked her up as if she wasn't a fat lump and carried her to the bed. He'd already shut the door and turned the key whilst her back had been turned.

Making conversation was impossible; thinking straight was difficult. He'd removed her clothes in seconds – including her underwear. He kissed her tenderly and then ran his hand over her huge bosoms and distended belly.

'I can't live without you, my darling, and as you refuse to marry me, I'll settle for this.'

An hour later she lay in his arms and didn't regret her decision at all. 'I didn't know you could make love when you were as big as I am.'

'It can't possibly hurt the baby and as long as the mother is happy and comfortable during the process...'

'Process? Don't call what we just did a process. That makes it sound so clinical.'

'I think I heard movement from the children's room, sweetheart. You'd better skedaddle if you want to keep this relationship a secret from them.'

She had never dressed so fast in her life and he remained,

stretched out on the bed, laughing at her and making her fingers even clumsier. She was tempted to tip his cold tea over his head but that would just make her more work changing the sheets.

When Mary came down with the children Nancy was cutting bread and stirring porridge as she always did. Porridge, so Mary insisted, was good for the children. When she had sole charge, when Mary left, there'd never be porridge made in her kitchen again.

'Where's Uncle David? Is he still here?' Billy asked between mouthfuls.

'I certainly am, young man, I just had a lie-in. I'm not a fan of porridge so I hope there's something different for me.'

'Eggs and bacon – the children are having that too, after they've eaten their porridge. I'll bring it through to the dining room when it's done.'

'There's no need for you to wait on me, Nancy. I only agree to sit in there if you eat with me.'

She nodded and he picked up his full mug of tea and wandered off. Once she'd served Mary, Fred and the children she dished up a similar plate for herself and David. There was already a rack of freshly made toast on the tray. The marge and jam she'd taken in and put on the table when she'd laid up earlier.

They were halfway through their breakfast when the telephone rang noisily. He was on his feet before her and disappeared into the hall to answer it. She'd quite forgotten to tell him about the late call from his boss and she had a nasty feeling it would be him on the other end of the line.

*

'Denny speaking.'

'Thank God – I rang you last night, Denny, but a Mrs Smith refused to fetch you and told me to ring this morning.'

David smiled. Good for Nancy. Whatever the emergency he wasn't going back for a couple of days and was going to spend it here with those he loved.

'I was incapable of making the journey without sleep. What do you want?' His response was terse but he no longer cared what this man thought of him.

'I need you back here to take my list today. I've got an important meeting that I can't possibly miss.'

The fact that Billings thought him good enough to take his list meant David had achieved his ambition and in a fraction of the time he'd expected. It made no difference to his answer.

'No, I'm owed time off and I'm taking it. Find someone else.'

There was an ominous pause. 'Remember to whom you speak, Denny. It was my influence that made you and I can just as easily break you.'

'Go ahead. If I'm not wanted at the Royal Free then I'll go elsewhere. I'm now fully qualified and experienced and I'm certain any of the big hospitals will be only too happy to have me.'

'I'll ruin you. I can assure you that nobody will touch you once they hear of your appalling behaviour towards the young woman carrying your child.'

'Do your worst. I'll take my chances.' He hung up saddened that he'd not be returning to his colleagues at the Royal Free, whom he'd come to appreciate since he'd worked there.

Billings' last remark had been shouted at him and he was aware that Nancy had been standing behind him anxiously listening to the one-sided conversation. With any luck she'd heard the remark and this might persuade her to change her mind.

'Did you hear that? I've just lost my job.'

'I didn't hear what that man said but I did hear you say you would have no difficulty finding another position. This doesn't change how things are between us at the moment.' She smiled but it was a poor attempt. 'We need to talk. Come into the sitting room – we can be private there.'

There was something going on and he wasn't sure if it was good or bad as far as he was concerned. As soon as the door was closed, she explained.

'I don't want the children to suffer because of me not being married to anyone. I want to know if I can sell this house or is it only mine if I live in it?'

'The house is yours to do what you want with. I have no say in the matter.'

'In which case I'm definitely going to move. I want to live somewhere nobody knows our business. I'm going to find something in a town where people don't poke their noses in like they do here.'

'Have you anywhere in mind?'

'I thought at first I'd go to Romford but someone might recognise me and that won't do. I'm not going any closer to London than that because of the bombs. I don't know much about geography. Can you suggest somewhere that will be easier for you to come to us, but will be safe?'

'St Albans or Guildford would both be ideal. St Albans is in Hertfordshire and Guildford in Surrey. It would be feasible for me to get back on my days off to either of them.'

'Then after the baby's here I'll put the house on the market and start looking.'

'Why don't you let me do it? I'm a free agent at the moment and I really don't want you traipsing about the country with a small baby in tow.'

'I don't know much about buying or selling houses so if you don't mind, then I'd much prefer that you did it for us.'

'I'm going to speak to Simon when he turns up, see if he wants to buy the house and the practice.'

'I told him that I owned the house.'

'Then he'll understand how things are between us. It makes perfect sense for him to buy it. Then Jill can sell her house and move in here when they're married.'

She bit her lip. 'I suppose it doesn't make any difference now what you tell him as we'll be moving away in a few weeks.'

'After I've spoken to him I'll go to Guildford and see what's available. What do you want me to look for?'

'Not nearly as big as this house, but indoor plumbing, a decent-sized garden and not too far from the shops.'

It was a shock to think that Nancy still thought indoor plumbing a luxury. She'd lived in a small terrace in Poplar, surrounded by a loving family and friends, until she'd joined the WAAF. Their upbringings couldn't have been more different. He had every advantage that money could buy but there was no love in his house. He was always seen as an unwanted mistake by his parents.

'I also want it to be within walking distance of the station so I can get to work – that's if I can find another job.'

'Why do you have to work in London now? They must need surgeons at all hospitals and there's bound to be one in Guildford or St Albans, isn't there?'

'I'm young and fit and should be doing my bit for the war. I have to be where I'm most needed and that's where the bombs are dropping.'

He shouldn't have to explain this to her – he thought she understood his motivation. Was the difference in their ages and outlooks the reason she'd asked the question? The reason she didn't fully understand who he was?

'I know that. I'm not stupid. I meant that there must be injured pilots and so on that need your assistance and they have to go somewhere, don't they?'

'I'm sorry, I shouldn't have snapped at you. I just saw Simon walk past. Excuse me, I'll go and speak to him before Jill gets here.'

She was clearing the plates with more clatter than usual and knew he'd upset her. Why was she being so stubborn about things? She should just marry him and stop this nonsense as it would make things so much easier.

'Nancy, don't you see? Everything's changed now I've left the Royal Free. Your objections are no longer valid. Marry me. How can you possibly ruin my career if I haven't got one?'

She paused and stared at him. 'Can I think about it for a bit? You've pulled the rug out from under my feet and no mistake. Do you still have a valid licence?'

'I certainly do. I just have to persuade the registrar to find us a slot in the next couple of days.'

'You speak to Doctor Jones and I'll let you know my answer when you come back.'

Nancy carried the dirty cutlery and plates into the kitchen and put them in the sink. The children were out in the garden with the dog and the house was quiet. Was David right? Could she marry him now without damaging his prospects? He didn't need to work, as he had plenty of money in the bank, but he wasn't the sort of man to sit about twiddling his thumbs.

He was now a surgeon, top of his profession, and would be mixing with people like him. Their wives would be top drawer too, would speak with a plum in their mouths and would have been educated at boarding schools. They would have tinkling laughs, dress like something out of a magazine and would look down on her, that's for sure.

Maybe her reluctance to marry him was as much on her account as on his. She didn't want to pretend to be posh, mind her Ps and Qs all the time, not be able to mention her family. If he was prepared to be a family doctor again then it wouldn't matter as she reckoned she sounded posh enough now, but whilst he was determined to become a top surgeon, she just wouldn't fit in.

However much he loved her, eventually he'd stop taking her to social events, leave her at home to look after the house and the children; they would drift apart. If they didn't marry she wouldn't have to go anywhere with him and neither of them would be humiliated or embarrassed.

There was always a possibility he would one day meet someone like Julia and marry her. Would she be able to deal with that if it happened? The relationship would be over the moment he made that decision as she didn't approve of women who slept with married men.

She gazed out of the window across the garden lost in thought. What if she had another illegitimate baby? She'd caught on the first time with Tommy so more children were definitely going to come along.

He came into the kitchen but she didn't look round as she wasn't sure what she was going to say to him.

'Simon's going to buy the house and practice, darling, so I'm going into Chelmsford to get things started. I need to take the deeds of the house with me. You'll have to sign some sort of paperwork but that can wait.'

She was going to stop him but realised selling the house and practice to Simon would suit her perfectly whatever the outcome between her and David. She wanted to move away and intended to do so even if it was just her and the children.

'Will you be back for lunch do you think?'

'I thought I might as well go to St Albans and Guildford whilst I'm out and see what's available. I'll be home before it gets dark. I want your decision about marriage when I return.'

'I promise I'll tell you then. Whatever I decide, it makes no difference to how I feel about you – you do know that don't you?'

'I do, and I love you. I just hope it's enough.' He'd already shrugged into his overalls and put on his boots and so on. He said nothing else; didn't kiss her even though they had the house to themselves, and strode off.

This gave her the remainder of the day to dwell on what

had been said. His last comment worried her. If he had doubts now, what would he be like in a few months when she had a new baby as well as two children and a house to take care of?

During the afternoon she put her feet up and the children joined her in the sitting room whilst Mary and Fred went off to do some cleaning in what was soon to be their new home. The telephone rang and she lumbered to her feet and went to pick it up as there was no one else to do so.

'Mrs Smith speaking. How can I help?'

'Mrs Smith, it's Mr Billings here. I'd like to speak to Mr Denny please.'

'I'm afraid he's out, Mr Billings. I could take a message if you like.'

'Very well. Would you ask him to ring me as soon as he returns?'

'I'll certainly pass on your message but I can't promise that he'll do what you ask.' As soon as she spoke, she realised she'd made an error of judgement and revealed that she wasn't an employee but something more.

There was a noticeable pause before he responded. 'I do apologise, Mrs Smith. I should have realised that you're not a member of his staff when I conversed with you the other night. Therefore, I assume that you know there was a heated exchange between us, which I bitterly regret.'

It was too late to deny that she wasn't more than just his housekeeper. 'You threatened to ruin his career and he no longer works at the Royal Free.' If she'd stopped then things might have been all right but something made her reveal the truth – or at least part of it. 'I'm a widow carrying my husband's baby. David wants me to marry him so he can take care of us. He's also adopted two orphan evacuees and believes that I will make an ideal mother to these other two.'

'That explains it. He's a good man. I jumped to an erroneous conclusion. Why did you change your mind about the marriage?'

'I'm from Poplar. We're like chalk and cheese, and I believe I'll hold him back and that one day he'll meet someone more suitable. I'll look after his wards as I doubt that any future wife would wish to take them on.'

'I don't believe there are many young women in your situation, Mrs Smith, who would turn down such an opportunity. You're absolutely correct. Better to remain friends as I'm certain that you would both come to regret such a catastrophic misalliance.'

It was as if she'd been punched in the chest. She couldn't answer and just put the telephone down and somehow found her way to her bedroom. Mr Billings had spoken the truth, however hard it was to swallow.

Her decision was made – she was going to set him free. He was obviously going to be offered his old job back and now that his boss knew the true state of affairs they couldn't even live together. She had to come up with a way of convincing him that they'd be better off getting on with their own lives and not hanging on to something that wouldn't do either of them any good.

25

David had a successful visit to his solicitors who told him that it wouldn't take more than a couple of weeks to complete the legal matters involved with the sale of the house and the practice.

'I can't complete on the sales until I've found somewhere else for Mrs Smith and the children to live. I'm going to see what's available in both Guildford and St Albans today.'

'Doctor Denny, I assume that the proceeds from the sale of the house transfer directly into err... Mrs Smith's account.'

The solicitor knew that Nancy was in fact Miss Evans but had the good sense to always refer to her by her courtesy title.

'Obviously, as the house belongs to her. If I find anything suitable today then I'll set things in motion and you can complete both sales and purchase simultaneously.'

If his personal affairs raised a few eyebrows it was none of their business and he didn't care anyway. The roads being empty made the journey to St Albans relatively stress-free. He was lucky and found the perfect house immediately.

The owner had recently died and left the property to the Catholic Church who were eager to get a sale as soon as possible. The house was a little old-fashioned in decor but had all the necessary requirements as it had been recently modernised. The garden was large but not unmanageable, with a substantial vegetable plot and room for half a dozen chickens.

He made an offer to the solicitor and it was accepted immediately. As Nancy and the children were going to be living there, he supposed he really should have spoken to her first. Fortunately, the sellers had provided some decent snaps and he was able to take those with him.

Was he mad to be setting up house with her, plus three children that weren't his own? He doubted he would be doing so if Billings hadn't terminated his employment. Less than nine months ago he'd been a country doctor, his life had been calm and ordered, and then Nancy had burst into his well-ordered existence and turned everything upside down.

Sometimes he wished things were as they used to be, dull and predictable definitely, but easier than being in the constant turmoil that his life now was. Being headlong in love didn't suit him at all. Love was like an infectious disease, once it took hold there was very little you could do to stop it.

The children were waiting for him when he got back and he spent a happy hour playing with them before they were taken up to bed. He'd not had time to talk to Nancy but she seemed subdued, nervous almost, as if she too had been reconsidering her options.

Eventually the children were gone, Mary and Fred had retreated to their own space, thus giving him the opportunity to tell Nancy what had happened during the day. Before he had the opportunity to show her the photos she got something out of her pocket.

Her smile was somewhat brittle as she handed him a letter. Surely she hadn't written her response to his marriage proposal?

'What's this?' He flipped it over and saw it was addressed to her. Why did she think a letter from a friend of hers would be of interest to him?

'This came whilst you were out. I think you'd better read it, as it's made me think about things.'

Dear Nancy,

    I'm glad that you're financially secure and in a position to look after yourself and your new baby. I can't get away at the moment as I'm too busy, but I can have a week's leave on rotation as soon as things calm down there.

    I intend to come and see you when that happens. Oscar remains safe but I've not seen him for several weeks and doubt that I will at the moment.

    From reading between the lines I've decided that you and Dr Denny are involved. I'm not surprised you've fallen for him but what does surprise me is that he's interested in someone who is having another man's baby. I doubt that any other man in his position would be prepared to do that.

    Do be careful what you decide, Nancy. If you married him you would be bound to have his children and then your baby could well feel pushed out, not part of the family at all.

    I don't know Dr Denny well enough to hazard a guess as to how he would react in those circumstances.

*I do know what happened to me at my father's hands
because I survived and my brother didn't.*

*Have to go now as I'm on duty in ten minutes. I
look forward to hearing from you as soon as your baby
arrives.*

Much love

He carefully folded the letter and pushed it back into
the envelope. He could think of only one reason why she
wanted him to read it, and that was because she thought
there was actually a danger he would favour his natural
children over the baby she was carrying.

She didn't know him at all if that's what she believed and
he was saddened by her opinion. 'Did you tell Jane that I've
more or less adopted Billy and Betty?'

'No, I don't tell either of my friends things that aren't
directly to do with me. When I'm settled wherever I'm going
in the summer, that will be the time to explain the ins and
outs of everything.'

'I'm going to take Polly for a walk; it's been months since
I did that. I need to think.'

'You can't go out now. We've got things to talk about. I
want to know what happened with the solicitor and so on.'

'I'll talk to you when I get back.'

'I'm really sorry you lost your job because of me. I've
been nothing but trouble to you since we met and I don't
deserve to have you in my life. You'd be better off staying
well away from me and finding yourself a nice young lady
like your first wife.'

He raised his hands in surrender. 'All right, I finally
believe that you genuinely think you're not good enough.

I'm not going to argue. Much as I love you and the children, you're just making it too difficult for both of us.'

The dog enjoyed the long walk. It was dark under the canopy of leaves, as the sun had set. He could smell the bluebells but couldn't see them. The blackbirds were singing their night-time serenade. None of this registered.

He came to the unpleasant conclusion that if Nancy considered he was the sort of man who might brutalise a child then it would be best to do as she suggested and make this the final time they met. She would have the money from the house and be able to move wherever she wanted, make the fresh start she kept talking about.

Having his life in constant uproar wasn't something he enjoyed. Nancy had blown hot and cold these past few months. She'd agreed to marry him, changed her mind about that, thought maybe she would be his mistress and live with him, and had now changed her mind about that as well.

She was right to say that being with her didn't make his life easy. He would also make a fresh start. He would enlist, join the medics who set up camp hospitals and treated soldiers as they were injured in battle. Billings might well be wrong about the other hospitals not wanting to employ him but he wasn't prepared to find out.

Nancy was an independent young woman; she'd forge a life for herself and the children without any help from him. This bloody war was going to go on for several years. This meant that by the time he returned to Blighty they'd both have moved on and it would be safe to start involving himself in the lives of his wards without rekindling his relationship with her.

He'd have tomorrow morning with Billy and Betty, but he wouldn't stay a third night. Neither would he tell her of his decision to become an army medic.

Nancy slumped onto a chair knowing that giving him the letter as if she actually believed Jane's nonsense had done the trick. He'd gone off with a face like a wet flannel and when he got back he was going to tell her it was over.

How was it possible that you could love someone as much as she loved David and he loved her and still all they did was make each other miserable?

He was gone for ages and she was desperate to get it over with. She hadn't told him about the conversation with that stuck-up Mr Billings of his. That was the first thing she'd do when he eventually returned from his walk.

The door banged and she braced herself. He looked as defeated as she felt. She smiled sadly and he joined her on the sofa.

'This is the hardest thing I've ever done in my life. Harder even than losing Julia and the baby. I think we've both realised we can't make this work, however much we'd like to. It's bollocks that love conquers all.'

'You thought you'd never get over your wife dying, but you did. We'll both get over this eventually. I should have told you that Mr Billings rang and asked me to tell you to ring him. He wants to apologise and offer you your job back.'

'I'm not sure that I want it, but I might as well speak to him.'

He closed the door behind him so she couldn't overhear

his conversation. He was talking for some time and then instead of coming back to the sitting room he went upstairs.

Five minutes later he appeared in the doorway with both his bags. Her heart sunk. He'd obviously decided to leave immediately. She wouldn't break down in front of him; she had too much pride for that.

'You're leaving then?'

He stood in front of her, his expression closed, like a stranger, not like the man she loved.

'Obviously. I've always been the sort of man who likes a quiet, calm existence and I'm sorry, Nancy, I just can't deal with the constant turmoil you drag me into. For both our sakes we have to let go of this, accept it was never meant to be and put it aside.'

'You sound like a broken record, David. We've had this conversation at least twice before and yet here you are. I haven't been chasing after you; it's you who keeps coming to me.'

'This time it's definitely over. I'll speak to the Stantons and make sure they understand that I don't wish to be contacted under any circumstances.'

'Well, that couldn't be any plainer. You're the children's legal guardian yet, because things haven't gone smoothly between us, you're going to toss them aside. I thought better of you. I can assure you that we'll manage very well without your help.'

'The house sale will go through in the next couple of weeks. The money will be deposited into your account. You don't have to move out until after you've had the baby.'

'That's all right then. I won't see you out. Take care of yourself, David, and I hope you'll find happiness one day with someone your friends will think more acceptable than me.'

'Goodbye, Nancy.'

He stepped around her and vanished into the boot room where she could hear him banging about putting on his overalls and collecting his motorbike gear. She retreated to her bedroom wondering how yet again something wonderful had turned into exactly the opposite.

She slept little that night and was up and making plans an hour before her usual time. Whatever he said she knew that if he heard she was in trouble he'd come and they'd be back to square one. The only way to prevent this was to move away immediately and leave no forwarding address.

The children were disappointed that Uncle David had left without saying goodbye and wanted to know why she was going into Chelmsford so early.

'I've got things to do. I'll tell you all about it when I get back.'

By lunchtime she'd found a house set in a lane off Springfield Road. It had a large garden, very neglected, and this was bordered by the River Chelmer. It had been built a while ago, when Queen Victoria had been alive, but would suit her and her children perfectly.

Even better, the house was furnished and she arranged to buy the contents as well. The solicitors were happy for her to rent the property until the sale was completed so she could move in immediately. It had been built for someone rich so had indoor plumbing and everything. The old lady who'd lived there until her death a few weeks ago had neglected the garden but the interior was clean and tidy.

The furniture was old-fashioned, but that didn't bother

her. All she had to do now was find a carter to transport her belongings and those of the children. She was now the client of a different solicitor so there was no danger of David discovering her whereabouts from the ones who dealt with his legal matters.

Mr Smithson – the similarity of this solicitor's name to her own was why she'd chosen him to act for her – was only too happy to arrange all the details of her move. She liked him on sight as he was elderly, had a mop of white hair and twinkling blue eyes. If he'd had a beard, he'd look just like Father Christmas.

'Forgive me for asking, Mrs Smith, but is your happy event likely to take place quite soon?'

'In three weeks. I've decided it'll be easier moving with him inside than waiting until he comes.'

'My daughter recently presented us with our fourth grandson. The same woman delivered all four and Nora thinks very highly of her. Would you like me to ask Nurse Middleton to call on you as soon as you're settled?'

'That's ever so kind of you. I'd be really grateful.'

'I'll ask when I see her this evening. I think I can help you out with the services of a gardener as the grounds are somewhat of a wilderness at the moment.'

'I'd appreciate your help, thank you, Mr Smithson.'

She returned to Chalfont Major, with the keys to Springfield Villa in her handbag, after the children were in bed. Now came the difficult task of explaining to Mary that her employment would end in the morning. She wasn't sure if Dr Jones wanted to keep Fred on, but she couldn't see why he wouldn't. Billy and Betty wouldn't be told anything until they were in Chelmsford. The carter would call for the suitcases, crib, bits of furniture, as well as all the toys and boxes, that afternoon and deliver them before tea. Unfortunately, the cot had been returned now that Betty was sleeping in a bed.

'I'm moving to Romford to be nearer my family. I've found a lovely house there – that's where I've been all day. I'm not happy living somewhere so quiet. All three of us come from the East End and although we can't go back there at the moment, Romford's almost as good.'

'This is all very sudden, Nancy. I don't understand why you've decided to move before your baby is born.'

'I reckon it's going to be a lot easier doing it now than trying to move with a new baby. I've been thinking about it for ages and all this fuss with Doctor Jones just made me do it now. I've made up your wages until the end of the month in lieu of notice.

'The house and practice have been sold to Doctor Jones so he'll be moving in, in a couple of weeks. Thank you for your help over these past few months.'

There wasn't much else to say. She and Mary hadn't been close but they had jogged along happily enough together.

'I've enjoyed working here and having two weeks free before I take up my next position is ideal. It will give Fred and I time to get organised in our new cottage. You're going to be missed in the village, especially by the vicar and his wife.'

'It can't be helped. I expect I'll join a choir somewhere else eventually. I'll get the children dressed and ready tomorrow morning. I'd be ever so grateful if you'd bring down the cases, boxes and so on and make sure they go on the cart when the man comes to collect them.'

'I'll do that willingly. I expect you're going across to speak to Mrs Stanton now.'

'I haven't got time at the moment as I've got to pack. I found some tea chests in the attic and intend to take as much as I can with me. David doesn't want it and I don't want the doctor to have it.'

'Fred and I can help you. What about Doctor Denny's things?'

'We'll pack those up and leave them ready for him to collect. I'm sure Doctor Jones will contact him when he moves in. Another thing, I'm taking Polly as Doctor Jones doesn't like dogs. The carter will bring her when he brings the rest of the things.'

Between the three of them they got everything done. The few pieces of furniture she wanted to take had been moved into the sitting room. All the children's toys were there as well as her own clothes and bits and pieces. There were also tea chests full of books, cutlery and crockery and other kitchen utensils. The two wirelesses were coming with her as well as all the bed linen and towels as these had become impossible to find since the beginning of the war.

'I need Fred to put all the garden tools that he doesn't use on the cart when it comes. I'll be having a gardener where I'm going so will need them.'

The next morning she walked out as if she hadn't a care in the world. 'Auntie Nancy, where are we going?' Billy asked as he trotted beside her to the bus stop.

'We're going to Romford. We're catching the bus and then we'll get the train from Chelmsford.'

'A bus and train? Betty, it's going to be a lovely day out. Can we have chips for lunch?'

'I don't know, but we'll certainly have something delicious. Listen, I can hear the bus coming.'

The children chatted loudly about going to Romford and the other passengers smiled and nodded and would hopefully remember if David ever came looking for her later.

She hadn't spoken to the vicar or Mrs Stanton because she didn't want to lie to them. She'd written a letter and had already posted it. As far as everyone was concerned, she and the children were moving to Romford to be near her family. She was cutting all ties to the village.

When she was settled she would have to write to her friends and explain what she'd done. She could rely on them keeping her secret and didn't want to lose touch. She'd also sent a quick note to her mother saying she was moving away and would be in touch later when she knew where she'd be living. The only way she could get on with her life without all the upset was to make sure David didn't find her.

26

Nancy would have to lead the children down Duke Street, through Tindal Square, along the High Street and then turn left into Springfield Road. They were so interested in everything they saw that they didn't think to ask where they were going or why they were in Chelmsford.

Probably both of them thought they were actually in Romford and she wasn't going to confuse them with the truth until they were happy in their new home. She decided to stop at the fish and chip shop and buy the requested chips.

They found a wall to sit on in the sunshine. Betty nearly lost her portion when she held it up to look at the picture on the newspaper that was wrapped around it. As they were licking their lips and crunching up the last of the scraps she decided to tell them the first of the changes to their lives.

'From now on I'm going to be your mum. You're my little boy and girl and this baby in my tummy is going to be your brother or your sister when it comes.'

Billy beamed. 'We'll call you Mum and when Uncle David comes to visit then we'll call him Dad, won't we Betty?'

'Mum, Mum,' she said obediently.

'We're not going back to the village. From now on we're

going to live here in a lovely house. It'll be just the three of us until the baby comes.'

'What about Auntie Mary?'

'She has a new job looking after a nice old lady and she and Fred are moving into a cottage near the church. Doctor Jones will live in our old house now and Mrs Andrews will join him when they get married.'

Betty had lost interest and was studying the grease-stained and ink-smudged photograph of the Prime Minister that had attracted her attention earlier.

'That's all right then. Where's this house that's going to be our home, Mum?'

'It's not far, no more than five minutes from here.' She carefully folded the newspaper and pushed it into her handbag, knowing it would come in handy for lighting fires. There was no central heating in this house but it did have a boiler for hot water and a decent range in the kitchen.

'See that lane down there, children? That's where we're going. Nearly there.'

She let them run ahead as the lane was free from traffic and the worst that could happen was they'd both get scraped knees from the gravel underfoot if they fell. Springfield Villa was the smallest of the three detached houses in this lane but it was quite big enough for her.

The front garden was as wild as the back was, but the children couldn't see this until she unlocked the wooden gate in the six-foot brick wall. The path that led to the front door was also brick. At least this was clear of the worst of the weeds and easy to walk up.

She left the gate unlocked as their belongings would be arriving shortly and the carter would have to use this gate.

She supposed it might be possible to have things delivered by boat but she'd just taken Mr Smithson's word for it that there was a river somewhere as you certainly couldn't see it.

Betty clutched her hand but Billy stood with his hands on his hips scowling at the house. 'I don't like this house. It's not as nice as the other one. I don't want to live here. I want to go home.'

'This is your home, young man, and you blooming well better get used to it and stop moaning.' She hadn't meant to snap at him but it did the trick. He stopped looking so belligerent and ran to the front door.

'Here, Billy, see if you can open the door for us. Can you reach the keyhole or do you need me to lift you up?'

Having opened the door herself yesterday she knew he could do it if he stood on tiptoes. The key turned easily enough and he'd have no trouble opening it once the lock was undone.

It took him a few minutes but he was proud as punch when the door swung open. There was a generous entrance hall floored with pretty coloured tiles. The children must have been expecting something as dismal as the garden and were delighted with what they saw.

'Pretty floor, Mummy, I like the floor. Polly Dolly likes the floor too.' Betty ran from side to side swinging her rag doll about and laughing.

'What about you, Billy? Have you changed your mind about living here now you've seen inside?'

'It's grand, Mum. Where do Betty and me sleep?'

'I'll show you. I can't make up your beds until our things arrive later.'

It took almost an hour for the children to explore every

inch of the house and by the end of it they were all ready for a drink and a sit-down. They had to settle for water until the carter arrived.

There was a long sofa sort of thing in the sitting room. It wasn't as wide as a normal one and had a padded roll at one end and nothing at the other. It was a cross between a bed and a sofa. It looked old and was probably an antique. When she wasn't so tired she'd go around and look at all the furniture. She'd dismissed it as old-fashioned but now thought it might be a bit special.

'This will be perfect for us, children. I can put my feet up and you can snuggle up with me and have a nap as well.'

As she was drifting off she realised there wasn't a telephone here and she'd got used to the convenience of having one in the house. She wasn't even sure where the nearest telephone kiosk was if she needed to ring the midwife in a hurry.

They were woken by Polly barking outside a couple of hours later. The little ones tumbled off the bed and raced to the front door, which had been left ajar. The dog bounded in and the children rolled about laughing and crying in excitement.

Nancy left them to it and went out to tell the bloke and his assistant where she wanted things put. In her condition she didn't want to be carrying boxes about if she could help it. Everything was soon in; she paid the man and he left with a generous tip and a promise not to reveal where she was living if anyone happened to ask.

The baby had been heaving about again today and every time an elbow, foot or hand stuck out she winced. The sooner this baby arrived the happier she'd be, but not for another couple of weeks as she wouldn't be ready for him before then. She was certain he'd turned round and was now the right way up. From the pressure between her legs she thought his head had dropped and was engaged.

They had boiled eggs and soldiers for tea and then she made up their beds – she'd intended them to sleep in separate rooms but they insisted they wanted to be together. Tomorrow she had to go to the nearest shops and register so she could spend her points.

David was in no hurry to speak to Billings. Once he did so he would have to make a decision about whether he returned to work at the Royal Free or looked for something else at one of the other hospitals. If he wasn't going to be blacklisted then there was no need for him to become an army medic, which was a relief as he didn't think he'd be good under fire. Falling masonry, which was just as dangerous, was somehow impersonal, whereas gunfire was the opposite.

One thing he could do was move into a hotel or guesthouse. What was the point of having money if you didn't spend it to make your life more comfortable? He no longer felt guilty about being wealthy as he'd given half of it to Nancy and the children.

Now he had a motorbike he didn't have to be within walking distance of the hospital and could afford to live somewhere more salubrious than his present digs. He wanted his own bathroom, a laundry service and to be able to get meals and hot drinks when he wanted them. He found exactly what he was looking for in Guilford Street, which was still within walking distance if necessary.

A grand Georgian house had been divided into what were best described as suites, each with their own facilities but fully serviced. The concierge showed him around.

'We have our own air raid shelter in the basement but so far nothing has fallen near enough to do more than shake the building a little. There is a dining room and a small bar and food and drink are available at any time of the day or night.' The man nodded and half-bowed as if talking to royalty. 'There is also a public telephone for our guests' convenience in the vestibule downstairs.'

'That's exactly what I want. I'll take it. I'll go back to my digs and collect my belongings and return with them later.'

Jensen, that was the concierge's name, handed him the key and left him to familiarise himself with what was going to be his home for the next few months at least. He had a bedroom, small but adequate, a shower, WC and basin as well as a decent-sized sitting room. There were empty bookshelves and he regretted having left his own library behind. He could hardly go down there now but if he rang Jill maybe she would be kind enough to pack them up so he could collect them when Nancy and the children moved away in a few weeks.

When he arrived at his digs he met Billings coming out of the front door. 'You haven't got in touch with me, Mr Denny, so I've just left you a note in the hope you'd find it when you did eventually return. I'm going to my club for a bite. Would you care to join me?'

'I'm in the process of moving to Primrose House in Guilford Street.'

'About time. A consultant surgeon, even a junior one,

shouldn't live in this dismal place.' Billings raised an eyebrow, waiting for him to react to his new status.

There'd been no mention of this promotion when they'd spoken the other night. He'd made it clear he hadn't decided on his next career move. 'If I'm going to continue to work with you and not go elsewhere then I need to set clear parameters.'

'Of course, my dear boy, goes without saying. My car's waiting to drive us. We can talk over lunch.'

Eventually, he completed the move and unpacked his meagre belongings. Now David had joined the elite club, that of consultants, Billings had made it clear he was expected to attend dinners, cocktail parties and other functions. In order to do this he would need his dinner jacket and the remainder of his clothes.

Evening surgery would be in full swing so there was no danger of Nancy picking up the telephone. Jill answered in her bright efficient way. He was staggered to discover that Nancy had moved out two days after he'd left.

'Simon was obliged to move back as otherwise the telephone would have been unanswered if there was an emergency during the night.'

'Do you know where she's living now?'

'Romford, but nobody has any idea of her exact address. Mrs Stanton was very upset that she didn't bother to say goodbye.'

'I'm sure she was. I need all my clothes and quite a few other things from the house. I've got the use of a car and am coming down now and should be there within the hour. Tell Simon I'll get my solicitor to finalise the sale as there's now no need to wait.'

'Before you go, David, Nancy took all your books, both wirelesses and most of the utensils...'

'I gave her the house and its contents. She was entitled to take everything. Goodbye, I'll see you later.'

It was none of Jill's business and her complaint must have been because Simon had expected to have these things even though they weren't included in the purchase.

The chauffeur was happy to help with the transfer of the carefully packed suitcases and boxes stacked up in his old bedroom. David walked around the house one last time with mixed feelings. There'd been a lot of happiness here over the past decade but also a lot of sadness too.

He would miss his dog but was glad Nancy had taken her wherever she'd gone. He was obliged to sit in the front next to the chauffeur on the return journey as the back of the car was crammed full with his things. He discovered that Jim was deaf in one ear and had flat feet so hadn't been conscripted.

'I like driving and as long as I keep my mouth shut about anything I see then Mr Billings and I get on just fine. He said if you give me your spare petrol can I'm to make sure it's filled up whenever you need it.'

'That would be a great help. I like to get out of the city when I get a few hours free.'

This time it took him a lot longer to unpack. By the time he'd finished his two rooms looked like home. He didn't need any more room than this. He'd cancelled the purchase of the house in St Albans much to the annoyance of the lawyer, but there was no point in buying it now Nancy had vanished.

His intention had been to offer her and the children this

place on a rent-free basis. Probably for the best that this hadn't worked out and that they could both begin their new lives unencumbered by the past.

The baby was due in less than ten days and he was sorry he wouldn't know whether she had the boy she was hoping for or a girl. When this bloody war was over, he'd find them, but until then he must remain in ignorance of the outcome.

He wandered downstairs and bumped into a consultant from the hospital. Hardly a surprise as this was the nearest respectable place to live, in walking distance of the Royal Free.

'Look here, old boy, there's a desperate shortage of unattached gentlemen in Town at present. I receive half a dozen invitations a week to attend various prestigious social events. I shall get your name added and you'll be much in demand.'

'I doubt I'll be able to accept many invitations. I rarely get a night off.'

'Things will be different now you're a consultant. You can delegate.'

David bit back a sharp rejoinder. He wasn't in London to socialise but to save lives. The man was an ass.

Within a week of moving into Springfield Villa Nancy had everything organised the way she wanted. The midwife had confirmed that the baby was the right way up and could come any day. Two old geezers turned up, sent along by Mr Smithson, and were only too happy to clear the garden in return for being able to keep a couple of pigs and a dozen chickens on a patch of land by the river when they'd finished.

The best thing that had happened was the arrival of the midwife's niece, Jenny, a fourteen-year-old who wanted a live-in job until she was old enough to work at Marconi's. The girl was happy to do whatever was wanted, including laundry and heavy cleaning.

As Jenny did all the running about, collected the shopping, went to market and so on this meant that Nancy was able to remain at home. There was absolutely no danger of anyone from Chalfont Major accidentally discovering her whereabouts.

She didn't intend to write to either Jane or Charlotte until the baby arrived. Then she could tell them her new address at the same time. It would certainly be easier for both of them to visit now she was living in Chelmsford.

On the night of the 10th of May she was unable to sleep because of the constant drone of bombers heading for London. The sky was alight with incendiaries and the constant sound of the anti-aircraft guns firing at the Germans added to the racket.

Jenny joined her in the garden; both were in their nightgowns, to watch in horror. 'London's really copping it tonight, Mrs Smith. The moonlight makes it easy for them to see where they're going.'

'It also makes it easier for the fighters. There must be hundreds of Hurricanes, Spitfires and Typhoons up there trying to shoot them down. I've never seen so many German bombers come over at the same time.'

She'd had a dull backache all day and was suddenly gripped by a pain that made her double up. 'The baby's coming, Mrs Smith. I'll get dressed and run round and fetch my auntie.'

A few exhausting and unpleasant hours later Nancy was handed a squalling, red-faced bundle. 'You've got a lovely daughter, Mrs Smith. A healthy pair of lungs on her, that's for sure.'

'I was convinced I was having a boy and don't have a name for a girl. It wasn't quite as bad as I'd expected but I wouldn't want to go through it again any time soon.'

The midwife laughed. 'That's what all my mothers say. I promise you that within a few weeks you will have forgotten all about the discomfort.'

'As I haven't got a husband another baby is one thing I don't have to worry about. I'm sure you've realised Billy and Betty aren't mine. My husband was a lot older than me and they are his children. I think he married me to be a ma to them.'

'I guessed as much. He didn't waste much time finding himself another wife, but I don't blame him. Bringing up kiddies isn't a man's job. He certainly left you well provided for.'

'Not only that, I've now got a lovely little girl to add to the family.'

'Jenny said you were both up because of the raid last night. The papers are full of it this morning. Over five hundred bombers dropped thousands and thousands of incendiaries and bombs all over London. Westminster Abbey and St Paul's were hit.'

'I thought it was bad. My family live in Poplar. I hope they haven't been bombed out.'

'There will be thousands of people homeless, probably

thousands killed and injured. All four railway stations have been damaged too.'

The baby was now sucking noisily and Nancy pretended to be absorbed by this. David could have been killed last night and she'd never know. The thought that he might be dead was unbearable. She could get on with her life all right as long as she knew he was doing the same.

27

David worked five sixteen-hour shifts, which meant he could avoid accepting any unwanted invitations to hopeful hostesses' dinner parties. Then, unfortunately for him, his list finished mid-afternoon and he was free until the following morning at exactly the same time as Billings pounced on him.

'Excellent, excellent, the board and consultants are meeting at the Ritz for drinks at seven tonight. You need to attend as so far none of them have actually met you face to face.'

This was an invitation he couldn't refuse as Billings had a point. 'I'll be there.'

The bike was parked at the back of his accommodation, perfectly safe and easily accessible. It shouldn't take him long if he rode down Gray's Inn Road, turned right into Holborn, along Oxford Street down Regent Street and into Piccadilly. As long as there were no diversions and holes in the road from the previous night's bombing to redirect his journey.

He looked at his reflection, not recognising the man who stared back at him. He was a stone lighter, certainly fitter, and his dinner jacket hung from his shoulders. He rarely looked at himself in the mirror – apart from when he was shaving. There was grey in his hair now that hadn't been there a few months ago.

He smiled wryly. He thought it an old wives' tale that worry could turn someone's hair grey. Was it his present occupation or his tumultuous relationship with Nancy that had done it? It made him look more distinguished and hopefully would convince the board they hadn't made a mistake by backing someone as inexperienced as he.

His overalls had been washed and ironed – thank God they hadn't starched them or they'd be impossible to pull on over his formal attire. He'd allowed himself ample time for the journey as he wanted to be able to park and remove his scruffy outer garments before he went in. It wouldn't be dark for several hours and he didn't intend to be here long if he could help it.

The uniformed doorman was busy hailing a taxi for a waiting mink-clad lady so he walked in unobserved. The spacious vestibule was full of women in glamorous evening wear, dripping with diamonds, and their false laughter set his teeth on edge.

Apart from a couple of army officers all the other men were dressed like him. He'd heard that exiled royalty resided here but he didn't know if that was true. What he did know was that there was a bar downstairs, known as the Pink Bar, where homosexuals mingled freely. As always, if you had enough money you could flout the law with impunity. Ordinary men faced arrest and prison if they were caught. He believed that what people did in the privacy of their bedrooms was their own business.

He should have asked exactly where this reception was

taking place. Then Billings and a woman, presumably his wife, arrived and he strolled across to join them.

'Good evening, I'm Denny. I'm delighted to meet you, Mrs Billings.' He offered his hand but she ignored it. The woman was thin, dressed entirely in black, her grey hair scraped back and only a diamond choker for decoration. The gown was so elegant it needed nothing else. Her smile did nothing to alleviate the impression he'd got that she wasn't pleased to see him. Her smile was fleeting and her words insincere.

'Mr Denny, how delightful to meet you at last.' She glided away leaving him alone with her husband.

Billings frowned and patted David on the shoulder. 'Ignore her, my dear boy, it's what I do and it works for me.'

'I warn you – I don't intend to stay long. If you'd be kind enough to introduce me to the people I need to know, then I'll make my excuses and vanish.'

'It won't just be board members. You've not met many of your fellow consultants and this is your opportunity to do so. We have half a dozen women in that role, which you might be surprised to know I thoroughly approve of.'

'That sounds more promising. Is this just a drinks thing or will there be food as well?'

'Something my dear wife calls *a running buffet* will be set out at eight o'clock. A lot of nonsense if you ask me; I'd rather have fish and chips than devilled eggs and cucumber sandwiches.'

David shook hands with dozens of people and promptly forgot their names. He was cornered several times by middle-aged women determined to discover if he was someone they could invite to make up the numbers at one of their social functions. He was pretty sure when he finally managed to escape that he was now on a variety of lists and would receive a stream of unwanted invitations in the future.

The insincere laughter, the crystal-cut diction, the overdressed guests, just reinforced his opinion that the majority of wealthy people had no idea of the hardship and suffering that the ordinary person was enduring. From their conversation one would have thought that rationing, making do and mending, losing loved ones, possessions and homes, only applied to other people. The people in this room were living as if there was no war.

What bemused him was the fact that a lot of them worked at the Royal Free, saw for themselves on a daily basis the destruction and devastation caused by the bombing, and yet could forget what they'd seen during the day and behave like this in the evening.

Any future invitations of this sort would be politely refused – he'd rather have no friends than mingle with the so-called elite again.

David was on call a few nights later, on the 10th, but didn't wait for the telephone to ring. The sky was clear, it was a full moon and the perfect night for those bastards to come in their droves and drop bombs and incendiaries indiscriminately all over London. The fact that the Thames was at low ebb as it had been in the last massive raid in April would just make things so much harder for the rescue services.

The sirens wailed their warning throughout the city

as he ran towards the hospital. The ARP wardens were blowing their whistles and yelling for everyone to get into a shelter. The fighters were out in force. The boom from the ack-ack guns almost drowned out the noise of the approaching bombers.

The sky was filled with ominous black shapes and as he watched strings of bombs began to tumble towards the buildings. Not only were bombs being dropped but also wave after wave of incendiaries. This was going to be a very long night.

He expected to see his boss turn up and help as he would have been called in too. However, the casualty department was soon overrun with the walking wounded, those on stretchers and a horrific number of patients who were already past his or anyone else's help.

A constant stream of men, women and children were wheeled into his theatre. There was no respite and he lost count of how many patients he'd had to operate on that night.

'We only lost two, sir, quite remarkable in the circumstances,' the theatre sister told him as she helped him to strip off the final gown. God knows how many he'd got through during the night.

'Is Mr Billings now in the other operating theatre?'

'He started ten minutes ago. You need to get something to eat and then go home for some sleep.'

He stepped outside expecting to blink in the sunlight but the air was so thick with smoke he couldn't tell if it was actually out. This was even worse than the air raid a month ago.

It was a miracle the hospital hadn't taken a direct hit

as he was quite sure others might well have done. He staggered home and into the dining room. He collapsed into the nearest chair and Jensen appeared with not a pot of tea, but a large jug of real coffee.

'This is kept for emergencies, Mr Denny. Breakfast is on the way and if you leave your laundry bag outside the door it will be washed and returned to you by this evening.'

After three cups of coffee, a bowl of porridge and half a dozen slices of toast thickly spread with real butter and actual marmalade he was beginning to feel human again.

Jensen was waiting on him personally today, not something that had happened before. 'Sit down, join me – there's at least two more cups in this jug.'

The concierge didn't need asking twice. 'Thank you. I've been hearing the most dreadful things about last night. Paddington and Euston are blocked, King's Cross took a direct hit and most of the railway stations are shut on the south side of the Thames.'

'I'm not surprised. Even with the doors and windows closed you can see the smoke in here and certainly smell it. Was anything around here hit? I'm afraid I didn't notice on the way home.'

'Several fires but they've been put out. One of my other gentlemen came through the West End and said the damage is as bad there as anywhere else. There's an unexploded bomb on Regent Street and the road was blocked by a landmine on the corner of Bond Street. What hasn't been hit by a bomb has gone up in smoke and the roads are covered in broken glass.'

David drained his cup and, with some difficulty, pushed himself to his feet. 'Thank you for your conversation and the coffee. I'm going to have a hot shower and fall into bed and hope nobody wants me for a few hours.'

Nancy could hardly believe that her baby had been born on the actual day she was due. From what she'd heard on the news London had been all but destroyed by the bombing and the fires. There was nothing in the newspaper about the Royal Free being hit so she had to believe David was all right.

The midwife told her she must stay in bed for a week but she'd no intention of doing so. Jenny couldn't manage both children, the cooking and everything else on her own for more than a day even though she was a very capable girl.

Nancy was a bit sore downstairs, had like a heavy monthly, but apart from that was tickety-boo. Her daughter was going to be called Charlotte Jane after her two friends and she decided to write to them immediately and give them the good news. It would take her mind off what might be happening in London.

As well as the letters to her friends she also wrote to her ma telling her that she had a granddaughter. She decided not to put her new address in this letter as she didn't want her family turning up. If they needed to contact her then they could do so at her old address.

As soon as she was up and about she'd go to the nearest telephone box and ring Jill and see if there was any mail for her. It then occurred to her that Mr Smithson would be in contact with David's solicitor so if anything had happened to him the information would eventually filter through to her. There was no need to call anyone and risk giving away her location.

The midwife was unsurprised to find her patient up and about when she came on the Monday. 'Your milk's coming in, little Lottie is thriving and as long as you don't overdo it, I can see no harm in you being up and about so soon. Some mothers need the rest, but you obviously don't.'

'I'm feeding her when she cries – doesn't seem sensible to wake her up to do it.'

'Whatever you're doing, Mrs Smith, if you and the baby are happy then that's all that matters.'

At the end of May Lottie was an established member of the family. The children adored her and Polly now slept by the crib keeping guard on the new arrival. The money from David's house was in the bank and she splashed out and paid a ridiculous amount of money for a lovely new pram. What she'd spent would keep a family of four in food for weeks and she was uncomfortable about having bought it.

'Can I take Lottie out for a walk in the pram, Mrs Smith?'

'I'm not sure – it's market day and it'll be really busy. I don't think a new baby should be in a crowd. If there's an air raid you won't be able to take the pram down and someone will pinch it.'

'It's ten o'clock in the morning and those Germans don't come in the day very often. They've not been coming every night since Lottie was born, have they? Folk are saying that the Blitz is over.'

Nancy smiled. Jenny was right – it would be perfectly safe for her to push the baby around town for half an hour.

'Go on then. Take the ration books and see if you can get any sweets or a small bar of chocolate. We could all do with a treat and Billy and Betty have been ever so good.'

The children were out in the garden with the dog, helping Sid and Danny – the old blokes who were clearing the garden – pull up weeds. She doubted they were actually doing anything useful but they loved being out there and the old men kept a close eye on them.

The front garden was done and she'd been delighted to see there were well established borders with actual flowers growing in them. Now the grass had been cut there was plenty of room for the little ones to play safely as it was surrounded by a high brick wall and had no access to the rear without going through a locked side gate. She was that worried about the back garden, which was huge, and the river, although not that wide, was quite deep enough to drown them if they fell in.

She'd had a brief note from both her friends saying they would come as soon as they got time off. The spare room, which fortunately had twin beds not a double, was ready for when they did arrive. She watched as Jenny wheeled the smart pram out of the front gate. She'd yet to venture into town herself with the pram as she knew it would draw unwanted attention from envious young mothers.

She kept the gate locked as there was a chain with a handle set into the wall by the gate, which rang a bell loudly in the kitchen and the garden so she could hurry out and let any visitors in. The kettle had scarcely boiled when the bell jangled loudly.

That was a very short walk – she hoped nothing untoward had happened to bring Jenny home a few minutes after she'd left. Running was no longer possible as her bosoms bounced around painfully if she did. Therefore, she walked briskly to the gate and unlocked it. She was delighted to see her two friends standing outside. Jane just had her overnight bag but Charlotte had her large kitbag with her. Neither of them were carrying gas masks – nobody bothered nowadays.

'Charlotte, Jane, I can't believe you've arrived together. You must have passed your namesake as Jenny only went out with the pram a few minutes ago.'

'Didn't pass anyone with a pram. You look absolutely splendid, Nancy; motherhood obviously suits you,' Charlotte said as she hugged her.

'This is a lovely house in a perfect position. I can see why you wanted to move.' Jane also hugged her.

'You both look so smart in your uniforms. I can see you've been promoted from the stripes on your arm, Jane. You've got a badge with two animals on it, Charlotte. What does that make you?'

'I'm a warrant officer and am going to Bulstrode Park in Buckinghamshire when I leave here to undergo an officer training course. If you recall I should have gone months ago.'

'Congratulations. I do remember you told me before that they were sending you. What about you, Jane?'

'I'm a sergeant now but I'm hoping to leave for the same reason as you did, Nancy, very soon.'

'Have you missed your monthly?'

'No, but Oscar's broken his arm and will get four weeks' sick leave starting tomorrow when he leaves hospital. As I've not had a day off in months our Queen Bee has given me two weeks' leave. Oscar's coming here to collect me and then we'll spend the time at the vicarage. I'm hoping I'll get pregnant.'

The conversation was interrupted by a frantic barking on the other side of the gate that led to the back garden. 'I've got to let her in and you can meet my oldest two. Billy will be six in November and Betty will be four next February.'

They stared at her as if she was barmy. She grinned. 'David adopted them when their mother died. They were evacuated to Chalfont Major and lived with us. They're my responsibility now and I've the papers to prove it.'

She opened the side gate and the dog and the children rushed in to see who'd arrived. Her friends were lovely with them, as she'd known they would be, and kept their questions to themselves for the moment.

When Jenny returned the baby was fussed over and admired. The day flew past and she didn't have a moment to sit down until the children were asleep. Lottie slept in the crib in the sitting room during the day and in a drawer from the chest in her room at night.

The three of them took their cups of tea out into the garden. Four deckchairs had been found in one of the outbuildings and these had pride of place on the newly scythed lawn. Jenny was listening to the wireless and keeping an eye on the baby so they were free to sit and catch up on each other's news.

Nancy felt the odd one out in her civvies but didn't regret for one moment that her life had changed so dramatically. She told them everything, including how she'd almost married David and why she'd sent him away.

'I can't believe you let him think that you believed him

to be the sort of man who would abuse a child. No wonder he hasn't made a push to find you,' Jane said. 'I wasn't sure about David but have changed my mind.'

'How could the two of you be so stupid that you threw away a lifetime of happiness on so flimsy an excuse?' Charlotte added.

Nancy had expected them to be more sympathetic but they were the reverse. 'You know what I am. Can you see me wandering about in somebody's drawing room making small talk to a crowd of toffs?'

'Then don't do it. For heaven's sake, Nancy, if you don't want to mix with people you don't like and don't fit in with then stay at home and let David go on his own. I can't believe you've both been so foolish. You're two intelligent adults and yet you've behaved like a pair of ninnies.' Jane looked at Charlotte who nodded vigorously.

'From what you said you love each other, you've adopted two stray children together, he's given you a house and a small fortune to live on – why in God's name would you think you didn't deserve to be his wife?'

'People like me don't marry people like him.'

'Poppycock! Believe me, if I'm ever lucky enough to fall in love with a chap I won't care who he is.' Charlotte spoke from the heart and meant every word.

'It's all very well for you to say that David and I should have ignored what people would say and get married anyway. You're forgetting about Lottie, that last August I was about to marry Tommy and as far as everyone else is concerned I did marry him. If it was just a class thing then I'm sure we would have just got married and ignored the gossip.'

'So you chose to run away? How will that help your children? If you'd married him Lottie would be legitimate.'

'Please, Charlotte, don't go on about it. David's gone and I've just got to accept it and get on with my life and do the best I can for my children.'

28

By the end of May David found that his time at the Royal Free was less fraught and his list became more routine operations than emergencies caused by the bombs. It seemed to him that civilians, mainly women and children, were the ones being killed by this bloody war.

Of course, the *Bismarck* had sunk *HMS Hood* somewhere in the Atlantic last week and it was feared that most of her fourteen hundred crew had perished. Since then the Royal Navy had been relentlessly pursuing the battleship and today it too was lying at the bottom of the ocean. Revenge was sweet but not much comfort to the widows and orphans of those poor sailors who'd drowned.

The only drawback with having more regular hours was that it gave him too much time to think. Nancy would have had her baby by now. She certainly had the money from the house, and he wanted to believe that they'd made the right decision. His life was certainly well ordered, no emotional upheavals, and he loved his job and his skills as a surgeon were improving every day. So why wasn't he content?

He was mulling over this at the small bar at Primrose House when he was joined by Digby, a junior consultant in the orthopaedic department, the one he thought was an ass.

'Denny, just the fellow I wanted to see. There's a shindig in Grosvenor Square and I've been asked to bring you along.'

'Not in the mood, sorry.'

'You need to get out a bit more, old boy, meet a few pretty popsies, enjoy yourself. We could all be dead tomorrow so why live like a hermit?'

'I haven't got any petrol in the old bike.'

'I've got a car coming. Someone who works at the war office is going as well and they have their own car and driver. Door-to-door service – what more could you ask for?'

'Very well, you've persuaded me. What time?'

'Seven o'clock and you'll be back by midnight. We've both got a long list tomorrow and it wouldn't do to go in with a hangover and no sleep.'

This was such a ludicrous statement considering what they'd just been through that he laughed thinking Digby was being facetious. He wasn't and looked puzzled by his amusement.

'I've operated after being on my feet for a day and a half but I must admit I've never done so with a hangover.'

'Jolly good show. I heard a rumour that you were engaged – I take it that's not true.'

'Free as a bird, old boy. It's six o'clock now so I'll finish my drink and toddle off and get ready.'

The car dropped them at the front door of a massive house. There were two flunkies at the door checking invitations and he didn't have one. He would be relieved if he was turned away as he doubted that he was going to enjoy himself. This just wasn't his kind of thing.

Digby pulled out a square of gold embossed card, one of the men checked it and waved them through. The party was obviously up the wide staircase as the noise was coming from the first floor. The room was filled with elegant guests – the women in evening dress, the men in dinner jackets like him.

Waitresses were circulating with trays of champagne and he helped himself as one went past. He did his best to be charming, to smile and respond when spoken to, but the longer he was there the more he realised he was as out of place amongst these sorts of people as Nancy would be. He would rather stay at home with his feet up, listening to the wireless, with a good book to read.

Julia came from the same background but she'd never liked occasions like this. With hindsight he understood that she preferred to be the centre of attention, the wealthiest and best dressed woman in the room. This was why she had insisted on moving to a country practice where she'd have no competition.

He was stuck here until midnight unless he was prepared to find his own way home. Walking about the streets of London looking like a penguin wasn't something he was keen to do. He found himself a corner where he could observe without being seen himself.

The conversations he overheard were about the start of the shooting season, hunting, scandals, the lack of staff because so many of them had been conscripted or volunteered – but scarcely a mention of the devastation surrounding them in London, of the fifteen hundred or so people who died in the last night of the Blitz and the thousands and thousands who were now homeless.

The more he heard the less he wanted to be there. Even the constant flow of champagne wasn't enough to keep him where he was for the remainder of the evening. He stepped into the mêlée and looked around for Digby, but he was nowhere in sight.

He dodged the amorous advances of a beautiful young woman who was definitely inebriated and headed for the exit. There was still a trickle of late arrivals, which meant a doorman would be on duty.

'I'm Mr Denny and I have to leave. Mr Digby will be expecting to take me home. Could you make sure he knows that I have already left?' He slipped the man a ten-shilling note and he appeared satisfied with the exchange.

'I'll make sure that Mr Digby gets your message, sir. You might be lucky and find a cab if you walk down to Oxford Street.'

The doorman had been correct and he was able to hail one almost immediately. The journey would probably set him back five shillings including the obligatory tip but he wasn't going to quibble at the cost tonight.

When he hung his dinner jacket in his wardrobe later that night he hoped that he'd never have to wear it again. The only invitations he was going to accept in future would be to places where a smart suit was all that was needed.

A couple of days later he returned to Primrose House after a long day, looking forward to a relaxing evening and then three days to himself.

Jensen was waiting for him in the vestibule. 'A WAAF

is waiting to speak to you, Mr Denny. She is in the dining room.'

'Thanks, did she give a name?'

The concierge had vanished through the staff door and ignored his question. He only knew two girls in the WAAF and both of them were friends with Nancy. Something had happened to her – there could be no other reason why they'd come in search of him.

Charlotte saw him enter and was on her feet and holding out her hand by the time he reached her side. She didn't look devastated so the news couldn't be as bad as he'd feared.

'Charlotte, you're a most unexpected visitor but a pleasure to see you nevertheless.'

'Sit down, David, we need to talk.'

He did as she said, unsettled by her tone. She sounded more like a headmistress about to reprimand a pupil than a friend of Nancy's bringing him news.

'What's going on? I assumed you'd come because of Nancy as I can't think of any other reason why you'd have searched me out.'

'For an intelligent man, a surgeon well respected by his peers, you have been remarkably stupid.'

His eyes narrowed but she didn't take the warning and continued in the same vein.

'Do you love Nancy?'

'It's none of your damn business.'

'That's where you're wrong. She is a very dear friend of mine; in fact one of only two people that I genuinely care for. Therefore, I'm quite prepared to speak my mind if it's going to put things right for her.' Charlotte was a tall girl, striking rather than good-looking, and he decided to let her speak as she obviously had Nancy's best interests at heart.

'I'll answer your question. I do love her but we decided it would be best for both of us if we weren't together.'

'That's exactly what she said. You need your heads knocking together to put some sense in them. By the way, in case you're interested, she had a beautiful daughter on the 11th.'

The constriction in his chest relaxed. He hadn't realised he'd been so tense expecting the worst possible news, despite the fact that she hadn't led with bad news. 'A girl? We both thought she was having a boy.'

'I'm sure you're well aware that Charlotte Jane is illegitimate because you were too cowardly to marry Nancy when you had the opportunity.' She stared at him, daring him to comment but he just nodded and let her carry on. 'Exactly why, David, do you think that a marriage between you is a bad idea?'

He was about to say that Nancy would be unhappy as the wife of an up-and-coming surgeon but instead said what had really made him agree to end the relationship. 'I couldn't marry a woman who thinks so little of me that she believes I would mistreat a child.'

Charlotte banged the table making him jump. 'And there we have it. She doesn't believe that for one moment – she only showed you that letter so you'd leave as she thought that would be best for you.'

'Are you trying to tell me in a roundabout way that Nancy would marry me if I asked her again?'

'I'm not telling you anything you don't already know. She doesn't know I'm here and would be mortified if she did. I want you to tell me why you now think a marriage to her would work.'

'We've both been remarkably dense about this. I've no more wish to mix with the upper crust than she has. We're from very different backgrounds but that's nothing insurmountable. We love each other, we're miserable apart and I'm certain we can have a happy life together.'

Finally, Charlotte smiled, making her look almost beautiful. 'I take it you still have the licence you got a few months ago?' He nodded. 'Then, you buffoon, grab a suit and an overnight bag whilst I book a slot at the town hall.'

'Why has Charlotte disappeared for the day?' Nancy asked Jane. 'Is she meeting a young man that she doesn't want to tell us about?'

'Something like that. Oscar will be here tomorrow. We'll spend the day with you and then catch the mid-afternoon bus to the vicarage.'

'I've got something special planned for lunch. I thought I'd make a nice Victoria sandwich as well as a rhubarb crumble. My gardeners have just uncovered the vegetable plot and there's loads of rhubarb. You get extra points when you've just had a baby so I've managed to get enough marge to do both.'

'Charlotte will be back for supper – will there be any of that delicious bread we had earlier?'

'I really fancy a bit of cheese on toast but I've not seen any cheese for weeks. I could get some on the black market I expect but I don't hold with that. Mind you, I spent a fortune on my pram.'

'It would be silly to do without something you need when you've got the money to buy it. I bet your family would buy as many luxury things as they could if they had the funds to do so.'

'I've arranged for my solicitor to send my ma ten pounds a week. I could afford to give her a lot more than that but my pa would just take it off her and spend it down the pub. It'll make the world of difference to her and knowing they won't be short of a few bob at the end of the week is a great relief.'

Jane encouraged her to make extra sandwiches and like a magician produced a tin of coffee. 'Blimey, where did you get that?'

'I did a favour for a friend who gets a food parcel from America every now and again. I think it's a cousin or something. I thought you'd prefer this to something you'd never use for the baby.'

She frowned. 'What sort of something would I never use?'

'A silver rattle, an engraved silver tankard – the usual sort of thing given as christening presents.'

'Not where I come from. A new mum was lucky to get a bottle of stout. I'm trying to buy a sewing machine but I'm not having any luck so far. I really miss not being able to use the one at the vicarage. It takes so long to do everything by hand.'

Jane was fidgeting, getting up and down and looking out of the window for Charlotte. The front gate had been left unlocked so her friend could get back in.

'Golly, your dog has just streaked across the garden and vanished through the gate. I thought she was in the back garden and couldn't get through.'

Nancy was about to go after Polly but Jane waved her back. 'No, I'll go. You had a baby two weeks ago and shouldn't be rushing around as much as you are.'

'I don't like sitting still. I reckon that's why I've got my figure back so quickly. If it wasn't for my big bosoms I'd be able to wear my normal clothes already.'

'Why don't you put the kettle on? I'm sure Charlotte will want a cup of tea if you're not prepared to share your coffee.'

Jane dashed off, not bothering to put on her uniform jacket or hat; she would be put on a charge if she was seen improperly dressed in public. She couldn't imagine why the silly dog had gone out like that. The gate had been left open before and she'd not made any attempt to escape.

The kitchen faced the back of the house and when the garden was completely cleared Sid had assured her she'd be able to see the river while she did the washing-up. The kettle was singing when she heard voices in the hall.

She dropped the coffee pot and it smashed on the quarry tiles. David was first through the door and she couldn't speak. Was frozen to the spot. He closed the gap between them and she was in his arms. He didn't kiss her, just hugged her so tight she could scarcely breathe.

'My darling girl, this nonsense has gone on long enough. It took Charlotte to bring me to my senses. We're getting married tomorrow but first I want to see my baby daughter.'

Her cheeks were wet. She didn't know what to say, just knew this time he wouldn't take no for an answer. She glanced across at her best friends who'd brought him to her. She'd never be able to repay them for giving her back the man she loved.

David cradled Lottie on his lap whilst he munched through several sandwiches and drank three mugs of coffee. 'I'm so glad you hadn't made the coffee when you dropped the pot, sweetheart – this is just too good to waste.'

Jane and Charlotte had gone up a while ago leaving them to talk in private. She didn't know what to say. Her head was spinning, and she could hardly believe he was actually sitting next to her holding the baby, already as besotted as she was.

He wanted to know all the details of her delivery, complimented her on her recovery but didn't ask why she'd run away. She guessed that Charlotte had told him.

'We're getting married at eleven thirty. Then we can leave it a week and register the baby. I'm not sure how you're going to explain to your neighbours that you're actually Mrs Denny and not Mrs Smith.'

She snuggled into his arms before answering. 'I've told so many lies I can't see that a few more will make any difference. I told the midwife that Betty and Billy were my husband's and that he'd married me to be a mother to them.'

'And now I've mysteriously reappeared.' He chuckled and lifted her hand and kissed her work-roughened knuckles. 'Shall we pretend that I'm an absolute cad and walked out on you for another woman but have now repented and returned? Everyone will just think I'm a bit of a rogue and forgive me.'

'I bet they will. I doubt that anyone where you work will ever hear any of it so it doesn't really matter. Billy's determined to call you dad anyway so nobody will be any the wiser.' She pushed herself up and looked at him earnestly. 'Do we have to tell Lottie when she's older?'

'Absolutely not. Why complicate things if we don't have to?'

'What do we tell the children?'

'We don't need to tell them anything apart from their name will now be Denny like the rest of us. I'll get my solicitor to start adoption proceedings immediately.'

He was quiet and she thought he was thinking but when she looked, he was fast asleep. She slid from the sofa and collected the baby. After putting Lottie in her temporary cot, she dashed back with a pillow and a blanket.

His glasses would be safe on the coffee table and he'd see them as soon as he woke up. She carefully removed his shoes and lifted his head a little to put the pillow under it. He didn't stir. He must be exhausted to sleep so heavily on such an important night.

You weren't supposed to see the bridegroom the night before your wedding so it was better he was downstairs. The midwife had mentioned in passing that you couldn't sleep with your husband for at least six weeks after having a baby.

Getting pregnant again this year, even if it was David's child, wasn't something she wanted to do. He was a doctor; he would know how to avoid her catching on. She'd not expected to sleep but for the first time in months she was gone the moment her head hit the pillow.

Lottie was fed and changed at two o'clock and Nancy didn't stir until the baby cried for her next feed at six.

'Your daddy's home, baby. Today we're going to be a real family.' Lottie continued to suck greedily and she smiled down at her daughter.

'I wish I had a camera, darling. You both look so

beautiful I'd love to capture the moment.' David stood in the doorway looking somewhat dishevelled, unshaven, but ten years younger.

'You shouldn't be in here. It's supposed to be bad luck seeing your bride on the wedding morning.'

'Then you don't want the tea I've brought you?' He padded across in his socks and put it down so she could reach it. 'Good God, surely Lottie isn't sleeping in a drawer?'

'Don't state the blooming obvious. It'll do until she's a bit bigger and I can find a cot. The cribs too heavy to move up and down stairs twice a day.'

'Surely she can sleep in that magnificent perambulator I saw in the hall yesterday?'

'I didn't think of that – anyway, it only arrived two days ago. Will you bring up the crib for me, please?'

He leaned over and kissed her hard on the mouth. 'I'll do anything you want. I love you and I also approve of our new home. I've been exploring and it's perfect. There's a regular train service to London so even when I can't get petrol for my bike I can get to work easily.'

'I'm glad you like it. Why don't you use the bathroom whilst it's quiet? Did you bring a clean shirt or will you be marrying me in that one?'

29

David took the children and the dog for a walk along the riverbank and was aware that he got several curious stares from those he passed. The fact that Billy and Betty were calling him daddy would no doubt be common knowledge by lunchtime.

He hoped that their wedding wouldn't be, as that would somewhat spoil the illusion. He'd been right to think that Nancy could manage without him but that was one of the reasons he loved her so deeply. This was going to be a marriage of equals. His wife would be his closest friend as well as his lover and he couldn't think of anything better.

'Daddy, Daddy, Polly's done a big poo,' Betty said gleefully.

Billy was about to investigate with a stick. 'No, don't do that. Keep your stick for swiping nettles.'

He checked his watch – in two hours' time he'd be getting married for the second time. He could barely recall Julia's face now and Nancy had said the same about Tommy.

Betty stumbled and grazed her knee and howled lustily. 'Up you come, sweetheart. Nothing to worry about. Daddy will carry you home and Mummy can take care of it when we get there.'

Was all this pretence going to come unravelled at some point in the future? Everyone at Chalfont Major knew the true situation, which meant they could never take the children there, which was a damn shame.

Perhaps it would be better not to live in Chelmsford where there was always a chance Nancy would bump into someone who recognised her when she started going out again. He didn't care what anyone thought about his private life, but he cared very much about the potential damage to the happiness of his family.

He handed the children over to Jenny who immediately took them out into the back garden to watch the two old men doing a sterling job clearing the jungle.

Jane, immaculate in her uniform, dashed past him with a smile. 'I'm going to collect Oscar. We'll see you at the town hall.'

Charlotte was equally impressive. The WAAF uniform suited both women but he'd thought Nancy had looked the smartest of the three when she'd worn hers, despite being half a head shorter than the other two.

'Can I use your bedroom to change?'

'Your suit's hanging in the wardrobe. I had the devil of a job nipping it upstairs without Nancy seeing. She'll be impressed – it's a splendid suit.'

'Unfortunately, it no longer fits me as it used to. I just realised why Nancy looked amazing in her uniform. She must have tailored it to fit.'

Charlotte laughed. 'Hardly tactful, Doctor Denny, but you're absolutely right. I know Nancy really misses not having the use of a sewing machine.'

'I've more chance of finding one in London than she has

down here. Is Jenny capable of looking after three children whilst we're away?'

'Nancy's feeding Lottie now and then she'll sleep for at least three hours afterwards. More than enough time to get back.'

He could hear Nancy singing to the baby and he was tempted to join in. It was the kind of day that demanded everybody sang. There was a piano at the far end of the sitting room – probably hideously out of tune – but he'd try it out after lunch.

She was still in the bedroom when he went past. He'd wait for her in the hall. He had the licence and the wedding ring in his pocket. He'd already put the engagement ring he'd bought for her months ago on her finger.

Charlotte joined him. 'You look quite spiffing – nobody would notice the fit's not as good as it might be. Jane's just wheeling the pram round to Jenny.'

'Where does she think we're going dressed up to the nines?'

'I don't think Nancy's told her anything in particular. She's under the impression that you're the missing husband returned to the fold and nobody has contradicted that.'

There was a slight noise on the landing above and he turned. His future wife wasn't wearing a long white dress and veil but she looked as beautiful as any other bride.

Her hair was swept up on top of her head, and a pretty little hat, which exactly matched her frock, was perched on top. She was wearing a hint of lipstick and rouge, which just made her look even more beautiful.

'That's a stunning frock, darling. That colour's perfect on you.'

Her smile was radiant as she ran lightly down the stairs to join him. She reached up and smoothed the lapels of his very expensive suit. 'You don't look too bad yourself, love.' She held out her hands. 'See, I'm even wearing gloves. I feel ever so grand.'

'And you look perfect. Shall we go? We're definitely not going to miss our slot this time.'

They strolled through the town and attracted more attention than he was happy with. She sensed his disquiet.

'Jane says there's a back door we can use so nobody will see us go in and out. Don't want to spoil the pretence, do we?'

Jane and Oscar greeted him warmly and they were whisked straight through and didn't have to hang about in the vestibule at all.

The ceremony was brief, but similar to the one used in church that he'd recited before, just without all the hymns, prayers and homilies. Half an hour later the five of them escaped through the back door and fifteen minutes later he locked the front gate behind them.

He swung his wife from her feet and kissed her thoroughly. 'This is the happiest day of my life and I hope it's yours too. We've wasted almost six months and if it wasn't for your friends this might never have happened.' Her hat was over one eye and he unpinned it and threw it into the flower border.

'You shouldn't have done that; it took me ages to make.'

'Ridiculous thing, you're not a hat kind of woman and I don't want you to wear anything or do anything that you're not comfortable with.'

She tried to look cross but just looked even more adorable. 'What kind of woman am I, then?'

'Exactly the kind of woman I want for my wife, for the mother of my children and to be my closest and dearest friend.'

'Go on with you, you big soft thing. I married you for your money and because I like having sex with you.'

She ran ahead of him laughing, looking more fifteen than twenty-two. He caught up with her and snatched her into the air before she could step over the doorstep. 'It's traditional, Mrs Denny, for the wife to be carried over the threshold by her husband.'

'It's a good thing I'm not a big fat lump any more.'

He was reluctant to let her go but had no option as the children burst out of the sitting room and Lottie began to wail. The women took over and he and Oscar were shooed outside until lunch was ready. Billy and Betty insisted on accompanying them and showing him every nook and cranny they'd discovered in the wild garden.

The two old men busy at the far end stopped what they were doing and leaned on their spades, staring at him with interest. Oscar raised an eyebrow and grinned, obviously amused at the situation and wondering what explanation he was going to give.

Billy rushed up to the more grizzled of the two. 'Sid, this is our daddy and he's come back to live with us again.'

'I'm pleased to meet you both and want to thank you for doing such a splendid job with the garden. Whatever my wife's paying you it's probably not enough.'

'Mrs Smith ain't paying us anything. We're going to keep

a couple of porkers and a dozen chickens in them sheds on the bit of rough ground behind.'

'It's Mrs Denny, not Mrs Smith, by the way. I'd like to make the arrangement official. I don't have time to spend in the garden unfortunately and I'd like there to be sufficient vegetables grown to feed the family. I'd also like there to be sufficient eggs for them as well.'

'Fair enough, sir. As you ain't going to be living here all the time we'll sort out what's what with your missus. You got a lovely family. Pity you weren't here when the baby was born, but better late than never, I reckon.'

They completed the circuit of the half acre and were on the way back to the house when Jenny came out to call the children in to wash their faces and hands before lunch. They scampered off, leaving him to complete the walk with Oscar for company.

'What a complicated life you're living, but it seems to suit all of you. I just hope it doesn't all come unstuck one day when the truth comes out,' Oscar said.

'By the time that happens it really won't matter. I thought I looked knackered but you look as though you haven't slept for a month.'

'Things have been a lot easier since the nightly bombing stopped. We lost so many men and kites during the Blitz.'

'Thousands of civilians have been killed and injured and made homeless. They didn't sign up for this – you Brylcreem boys did.'

'True enough. We've held Hitler off but we're not winning. To tell you the truth, I don't think we will win unless the Yanks get their finger out and become our allies.'

Jane appeared at the French windows that led into the

sitting room. 'Absolutely no gloomy talk today, darling. Lunch is on the table and it smells quite delicious.' She smiled at David as he walked past. 'Nancy might be small but she's an absolute dynamo. She can cook, sew and is also an excellent mother – I might be good at what I do but I doubt I'll ever be able to compete with her on the domestic front.'

He wanted to make a toast to his beautiful bride but obviously couldn't as the children and Jenny were present. Instead he raised his glass and said what was in his heart.

'I love you, Nancy, and I'll not let you down again. I give you my word that you'll never regret being my wife.'

The years ahead were going to be tough, but they'd face whatever fate threw at them together. He looked around the table knowing he was the luckiest man alive. Finally, he'd got the right wife and the family he'd always dreamed of.

Acknowledgements

I wish to thank everyone who has helped this book to be the best it can be. My brilliant editor, Hannah Smith, and copy-editor Helena Newton require a special mention.

Bibliography for Girls in Blue series.
  Hornchurch Scramble, Richard C. Smith
  Chronicle of the Second World War, J & L
  One Woman's War, Eileen Younghusband
  The Stepney Doorstep Society, Kate Thompson
  We All Wore Blue, Muriel Gane Pushman
  The Secret Listeners, Sinclair MKay
  Sand in My Shoes, Joan Rice
  Christmas On the Home Front, Miles Brown
  A to Z Atlas and Guide to London, (1939 edition)
  Oxford Dictionary of Slang, John Ayto
  Wartime Britain, Juliet Gardiner
  How We Lived Then, Norman Longmate
  The Wartime Scrapbook, Robert Opie
  RAF Airfields of World War II, Jonathan Falconer
  The Day of the Typhoon, John Golley

About the Author

FENELLA J. MILLER was born in the Isle of Man. Her father was a Yorkshireman and her mother the daughter of a Rajah. She has worked as a nanny, cleaner, field worker, hotelier, chef, secondary and primary schoolteacher and is now a full-time writer.

She has over seventy Regency romantic adventures published plus four Jane Austen variations, four Victorian sagas and nine WW2 family sagas. She lives in a small village in Essex with her British Shorthair cat. She has two adult children and three grandchildren.

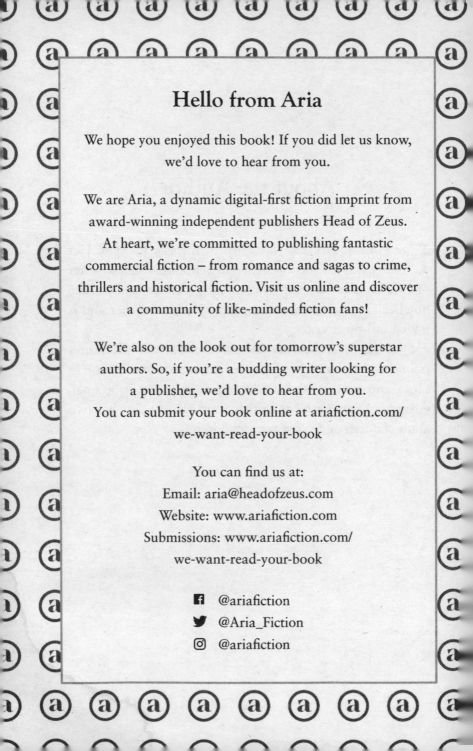

Hello from Aria

We hope you enjoyed this book! If you did let us know, we'd love to hear from you.

We are Aria, a dynamic digital-first fiction imprint from award-winning independent publishers Head of Zeus. At heart, we're committed to publishing fantastic commercial fiction – from romance and sagas to crime, thrillers and historical fiction. Visit us online and discover a community of like-minded fiction fans!

We're also on the look out for tomorrow's superstar authors. So, if you're a budding writer looking for a publisher, we'd love to hear from you. You can submit your book online at ariafiction.com/we-want-read-your-book

You can find us at:
Email: aria@headofzeus.com
Website: www.ariafiction.com
Submissions: www.ariafiction.com/we-want-read-your-book

🅵 @ariafiction
🐦 @Aria_Fiction
📷 @ariafiction